GRACE

PATRICIA DIXON

BOMBSHELL BOOKS

Print ISBN 978-1-912986-50-7

For Brian, Amy, Owen and Harry.
My greatest achievements.
My marriage, my children
and my grandson.
Of these, I am most proud.

'Loneliness and the feeling of being unwanted
is the most terrible poverty.'
- Mother Teresa

ALSO BY PATRICIA DIXON

Rosie & Ruby

Anna

Tilly

Over My Shoulder

They Don't Know

Death's Dark Veil

CHAPTER 1

G race loved the scent of Bonfire Night. The smoking wood
and chemical after-burn from the fireworks that streaked
across the misty sky ignited her senses and always took her back
to childhood. If she closed her eyes, she could conjure the scene
from memory. She'd be standing on the waste ground near her
parents' terraced house with her little sister, Martha, wearing
wellies and a bobble hat, soaked by rain or smoky drizzle. Sometimes, instead of rain they got lucky and it'd be a dry, crisp winter
night. Your toes would freeze while you watched the golden
flames flickering, and the heat warmed pink cheeks and plumes
of smoke stung tired eyes.

Life was so much simpler then and uncluttered by grown-up
hassles and interruptions. It was also, with a certain amount of
wistful resentment that Grace admitted to herself that modern
day Bonfire Nights had become a bit tiresome and something
entirely different from those she remembered.

As with most traditions, like Easter, Christmas and
Halloween, the whole event had become one huge commercial
tidal wave of consumerism. Designed purely to out-do your
neighbours and buy a heap of food and paraphernalia that you

really didn't need – or want. Then, after bowing under the pressure of hard-sell adverts, savvy kids and having it rammed down your throat in every shop you set foot in, the celebration had totally lost sight of its original meaning.

Nowadays, the lovely woody smoke and sparkler smells mingled with whatever à la carte dish the hosts were serving in the kitchen. Not to mention copious amounts of booze, half a ton of cakes, sweets and non-alcoholic cocktails for the kids. Whatever happened to a floppy paper plate swimming with hotpot and then a chunk of treacle toffee?

Returning to the present, Grace chastised herself, 'For God's sake, snap out of it you narky old bag!' Then realising she was talking out loud again, continued to sip her red wine from the plastic (very trendy) black goblet. There was no point in hankering after the good old days because they were long gone so she may as well try to enjoy the evening.

Sighing, Grace scanned the garden which was full of Heidi's friends and neighbours and, somewhere amongst the smoke and bodies, was her son, Seth, and middle child, Amber. She'd already spotted Heidi's husband, Elliot, supervising the barbeque. He was also trying to fend off seven-year-old Skye's persistent requests for more fireworks as he deftly chatted *and* juggled burgers and sausages.

Elliot was a natural with children, not just his own, and put his brains and effervescent personality to good use at the primary school where he taught. He'd been earmarked for promotion and was one of the assistant head teachers, but for now, insisted he was happier in the classroom with the kids and had no desire to swap his eight-year-olds for an office job and PTA meetings.

Grace was glad that Heidi had Elliot. They were soulmates and had found a wonderful balance within their little family. Her daughter was content to be a homemaker and mum and, until the children were all in full-time education (including the six-month bump she was carrying around at the moment), Heidi had no

2

desire to go back to her career as a nurse. The idea of juggling shift work, looking after a home and soaring childcare costs for three small children didn't appeal to her and for the sake of a few more pounds, she wasn't prepared to sacrifice their happy lifestyle. Although they weren't exactly rolling in it, the Lambe family had all they needed for now, with their camping holidays, a beat-up Volvo estate and a house that was in serious need of some TLC.

Grace looked away from the patio activity towards the end of the long garden and saw Seth guarding the bonfire. Each year he had the task of bringing a disused oil drum home from work and loading it with wood (and whatever rubbish they found in the garage). Then they'd set it alight and enjoy a self-contained bonfire of their own. Seth was loving his role of Fire-Starter-in-Chief and the official Prodder of the Wood, in full view of his adoring nephew who worshipped the ground his uncle walked on.

Finn, her five-year-old grandson, was sitting on a bench with his little friends, crunching on a toffee apple, totally transfixed and gazing, from a safe distance, into the flames of the fire. Finn was the quiet, thoughtful grandchild who lost himself in his story books and the land of make-believe. He frequently scared Heidi to death by talking to Mr Grumpy, the old man who sat on their stairs (whom only Finn could see) and had a gang of imaginary friends who kept him company in his play tent.

Grace silently observed the guests from her deckchair, most of them she'd known for years; a mixture of Elliot and Heidi's neighbours and friends. Normally, she would've enjoyed a catch up and a chat with any one of them, but tonight Grace just wasn't in the mood for conversation. It had nothing to do with Bonfire Night, or those assembled in the garden, the problem lay with her and she knew it. She was turning into a moody, cynical forty-five-year-old and was even beginning to get on her own nerves. Forcing a smile as one of the guests said hello, Grace's eyes searched for Amber, the career girl, engagement ring hunter and on occasion, her most unpredictable and unsettled child.

Amber worked in a bank. She loved her job, clothes, shoes, nights out, holidays with the girls, and men, not necessarily in that order, but all were of high importance. Along with Seth she still lived at home, apart from the two doomed (never talked about) occasions when she thought she'd met Mr Right. Amber floated out of Grace's door one Saturday afternoon in a Doris Day haze, straight into the arms of 'The One' and his loft apartment love nest. After only eight months (a world record as the first lasted only two) Amber got bored with domesticity *and* Mr Right so came stomping straight back home again. They were now immune to the bin bags in the hall, departing or returning, the tears and tantrums if she was dumped and then the swearing of oaths never to let a scumbag man get under her skin ever again. Without fail, before long, Amber would meet the next hunk-of-her-dreams and the whole cycle would begin again.

Amber had a good heart and a bubbly personality but Grace feared it was becoming tainted by disappointment and high expectations. She also suspected that her flame-haired daughter secretly yearned to settle down and was conscious of getting left behind in the Committed Relationship Race. There was some hope on the horizon though as her latest conquest seemed very decent, polite – and besotted; he appeared to have staying power. Lewis had been on the scene for almost two years and apart from Amber having to share him with his other love, a high-flying job in the investment arm of a bank, Lewis showed no signs of getting bored.

On the down side, there was no hint of him inviting Amber to move in with him or, much to her annoyance, producing an engagement ring either. Seth teased her mercilessly on the subject, saying that she was so desperate to get hitched that any notable date during the year had her convinced that Lewis was going to propose. There'd been a right to-do when Seth circled

4

on the fridge calendar, with a drawing of a diamond ring, every religious and non-religious event, plus bank holidays, birthdays and even the lunar eclipse. Amber didn't see the funny side and had a huge paddy, ending with the offending calendar being shredded and chucked in the bin. Fingers crossed, Lewis might really be 'The One' and Grace hoped that this time Amber would get her man – then they'd all get a bit of peace.

Grace couldn't spot her daughter anywhere so, obeying her rumbling stomach, headed inside for some food and a top-up. As she entered the kitchen, Grace was passed by a hastily retreating guest, who rolled her eyes and signalled with a nod of her head that something was up before scarpering with her plate of chilli. The steamy kitchen smelt of exotic food and would have been a welcoming place had there not been a huge row going on between its four walls. Amber and Heidi were at full throttle, but stopped abruptly when they spotted Grace in the doorway. Prior to this, all she had gleaned from her unintended eavesdropping was that Amber thought Heidi was selfish and in return, Heidi insisted that Amber was irresponsible and heartless.

'Okay, so are either of you going to tell me what you're arguing about this time, or are you going to stand there looking like naughty children.' Grace looked from one to the other and waited patiently, as she had done so many times before, for an answer.

'It's nothing, Mum, honest, just forget it. Are you going to have something to eat now? The chicken provencal is lovely.' Grace didn't miss the glare that Heidi gave Amber, like she was warning her to shut up and leave it.

'Actually, Mum, we need to tell you something. Heidi, as usual, seems to think that because she's the oldest *and* Earth Mother of the Year, that *her* Christmas plans and perfect family come first. Apparently, I just have to fit in and toe the line because I'm obviously of no consequence and to be honest, flaming sick of it!'

Amber folded her arms across her chest defensively which told Grace that her daughter sort of knew she was being unreasonable.

'I don't understand, what plans, and it's the beginning of November, how can you be arguing about Christmas already?' Grace made her way over to the stove and took a plate from the side.

Heidi sighed deeply and began wringing the tea towel, her hands always became restless when she was nervous, which is why Grace sensed she was about to hear some kind of bad news.

'I *was* going to mention it, Mum, but I've been waiting for the right moment. The thing is… Elliot's parents have invited us to Lincoln for Christmas. It was completely out of the blue and if I'm honest neither of us are particularly happy about the prospect. But we've never spent it with them and felt it would be a bit mean to refuse.' Heidi's cheeks were flushed pink and her eyes slightly watery.

'And Lewis has asked me to go to New York with him for Christmas. We talked about it last night and he emailed me the details at work today. The hotel is near Central Park and looks amazing. We're going to go to the theatre on Times Square and do the whole sightseeing and shopping thing. Then, Heidi just goes and spoils it all by saying I'll have to stay here because Seth's going skiing and now, because she's going to the in-laws from hell it means you'll be on your own.' Amber turned to face Heidi, her red hair always looked even fierier when she was annoyed, and while she was on a roll she continued.

'Why can't you go into Lincoln for New Year? It's not as though Elliot and his parents are close, and from what you've said, they're a right pair of miseries anyway.'

Heidi opened her mouth to respond, but Grace had heard enough and raised both of her hands and called time on the conversation.

'Okay, stop right there, both of you. For a start, will you try to remember this is supposed to be a party and there are children around. And, you can both stop treating me like I'm some kind of saddo who needs to be looked after. I'll be fine by myself at Christmas. You seem to forget that even if you two aren't there, I've still got my dear sister and her family to cater for and how could I forget Uncle Terry and Aunty Evelyn.' Grace turned back to the stove and stirred the chilli, giving herself more time to think.

While two sets of eyes bore into her back, Grace gathered her thoughts before turning to face Amber and Heidi. 'It's just one day and I will have plenty to do, so you can both stop arguing because you have my blessing, or whatever you need, to go and do whatever you want to at Christmas.' Grace felt quite pleased with herself for keeping the peace and thinking on her feet, even though her heart was telling an entirely different tale.

'But, Mum, you love Christmas and having us all round for dinner and now it'll be just you and the mad relations. I won't do it. I'm not going. I'll get Elliot to ring them tomorrow and say we can't make it.' Heidi looked adamant.

In the meantime Grace noticed that Amber kept quiet, looking quite pleased that her sister had caved in and probably had no intention whatsoever of cancelling her trip.

Grace's mind was working overtime, desperately trying to prevent a fall-out of epic proportions and either daughter feeling guilty or miserable at Christmas. 'Heidi, listen to me. We will have a new arrival next year so we can celebrate Baby's first Christmas together. If we take it in turns and you go to Elliot's parents as planned this year, then I'll have everyone all to myself twelve months from now. How does that sound?' Grace looked hopefully at Heidi who seemed to be slightly less traumatised and was mulling the proposal over.

Just to be on the safe side, Amber then decided to offer an olive branch too, or at least show a bit of concern for her mother, otherwise she might appear heartless and lose Brownie points to wonderful Heidi. 'That all sounds really sensible, Mum, but you'd still be stuck with Aunty Martha and those horrible kids. Uncle Jimmy just sits there drinking and breaking wind all day, not to mention the other two grinches.'

Grace knew Amber was speaking the truth but she'd nailed her colours to the mast and couldn't back down now so instead, let her continue.

'And what about Christmas Eve? You love doing the presents and all that, you always say it's your favourite bit and Christmas morning will be awful. Who would you swap presents with?' As Amber said the words the reality of them began to sink in and she really did start to feel bad, helped along by a creeping sense of nostalgia which pricked at her conscience.

Then Grace brought the whole thing into perspective. 'May I remind you of last year's Christmas Eve. Your soft focus, rose-tinted version is obviously different from the one I remember. As I recall, I spent all evening in the kitchen ON MY OWN! I was left peeling veg and stuffing the turkey because you and your brother were otherwise engaged at some fancy nightclub in town. Yes, I did enjoy putting the presents under the tree but not at 2am in the morning, because that's how long I waited up for you both to come home.' Two bright pink spots had now appeared on Grace's cheeks from the sheer exertion of her persuasions.

'And as for swapping presents, you and Seth were slightly the worse for wear the next morning and finally surfaced from under your duvets just before Christmas lunch. So please forgive me if the scene you have in your head is different from mine but that's how *I* remember it. If I'm honest, after suffering a very long and drawn out Christmas Day with ungrateful, farting, picky relatives, I was bloody relieved when it was all over.' Grace was a bit overcome with emotion after her little speech and as a consequence had gone right off her food.

After burying all the hurt and disappointment of last year's

Christmas in the 'Uncomfortable Truth Department' of her brain, until now, Grace had managed to convince herself that this year it would be different when in fact, it looked like it was going to be a whole lot worse.

Amber huffed loudly before marching over to where her handbag lay. 'Well, thanks for that, Mum, you've made me feel really great. Just rub it in why don't you? I'll just ring Lewis right now and tell him to cancel the holiday. There's no way I can go after you've laid a big fat guilt trip on my head.' Amber dragged her phone out of her bag and dramatically flipped open the cover.

'For goodness sake, Amber, less of the drama queen act! I don't want you to cancel anything, just go on holiday for heaven's sake. I'm a big girl and if I don't fancy staying in England for Christmas, I might even shock you all and go on holiday instead.' Grace was desperate so plucked the idea out of nowhere.

Heidi piped up next. 'But where would you go, and who with? And what about the Klingons, they always come to you, what would they do?' Heidi looked shocked and at the same time couldn't imagine her mother going anywhere on her own, let alone for Christmas.

'I might go away with Layla. She's always asking me to go on a girl's holiday and never shuts up at work about what a great time they have. The firm is closing for the whole Christmas break so I might just tag along. As for my sister and her family, well, I think it's about time Martha got off her bum and did her bit for once, so she can have the other Klingons this year, it'll make a nice change for all of us.' With that, Grace grabbed her goblet and took a bottle of wine from the rack.

Turning her back on her daughters, she undid the cap and poured the red liquid into her glass which gave her time to think and calm her slightly trembling hands. Well, she'd really gone and done it now, setting her daughters free while at the same time backing herself into a tight corner.

If Grace stayed home this Christmas, after the liberal serving of home truths she'd just dished out, her kids would both be left with a miserable image of her slaving in the kitchen and sobbing into her sherry under the pine tree. It was also obvious from their stunned, silent reaction to her holiday idea that neither had any objections to her binning the relations or heading into the sunset with Layla for a holiday. The fact still remained that even though she knew that her friend and work colleague would be thrilled to include her on the trip, Grace didn't really fancy a jolly to Gran Canaria with a group of crazy single women, ten years her junior. Neither did the compulsory, inebriated rampage around the clubbing hot spots of Puerto Rico hold much appeal, either.

Since Layla's partner, Geoff, had left her for a woman he'd met at the squash club, she'd thrown herself into not looking back and living life to the full. This included making up for lost time, in every sense of the word, and test driving whoever she dragged into bed at the weekends and especially when she was on holiday. No, a Christmas break with Layla was not on the cards but until she had time to come up with Plan B, Grace decided to go with the flow and hope that Heidi and Amber didn't interrogate her further or, see through her smoke screen and realise she was telling fibs.

Grace was soon saved by the bell, or Skye to be precise, who burst into the kitchen with excited eyes to announce they were setting off the 100 banger firework that Uncle Seth had brought. Doing as they were bidden, the three women left the kitchen to watch the show. One of them, however, was suffering slightly from delayed shock and near starvation and knew that when she got home, had rather a lot of thinking to do.

CHAPTER 2

Walking through the smoky streets of Market Harborough, Grace allowed the relentless drizzle to settle on her hair and shoulders, completely oblivious to the booms and crackles overhead as she made her way home, alone. She was immersed in thought, recalling the conversation she'd had earlier with her daughters. Grace forced herself to look straight ahead, making a conscious effort not to take a sideways glance and gaze through the windows on either side of the road.

She knew exactly why she was doing it and that it was slightly immature. Perhaps she was just feeling sorry for herself, but tonight Grace had no desire to see the cosy glow from other people's sitting rooms or hear the excited voices of families in their back gardens. For now, she wanted to think and wallow around in the mood that had been creeping up on her for weeks. She needed to dissect her situation and try to work out what this awful feeling of restlessness and resentment was all about. And while she was at it, she'd put the world to rights, have a one-woman bitch-fest and indulge herself in some self-centred melancholy.

There had been no reason either to walk the four streets from

Heidi's house unaccompanied. Amber would've given her a lift, but Grace really didn't want to listen to her daughter's excited plans for New York. If she'd had the patience to wait for Seth to extinguish the bonfire and then eat the leftover chilli, assorted cakes and whatever else he could lay his hands on, they could've made the short journey together as they had on many other occasions.

But as she set off with an empty stomach and two rather large glasses of red wine swishing around inside her, the only thought Grace had was to get home and be somewhere quiet. Here, she would make cheese on toast and curl up on the sofa with the one person in her life she could totally rely on. Someone who was always there to keep her company and seemed genuinely pleased to see her the minute she walked through the door. After clomping up the path Grace turned her key in the lock before calling out for Coco, her reliable, loyal, and totally gorgeous chocolate Labrador.

An hour later after demolishing half a loaf and two cups of sweet tea, Grace sat in front of the telly with the sound turned down, watching the images on the screen while she fed popcorn to Coco, one of his favourite treats. When her husband, Ben, moved out, the kids had clubbed together and bought her a puppy after she'd let slip that one of her regrets in life was never having a dog. Ben was anti-pet of any kind and he'd always forbidden it so, in a unanimous show of rebelliousness, they decided they would give their mother, and themselves, the treat they all deserved. On her forty-second birthday they proudly produced Coco. In the three years since becoming a member of the family he'd given them unconditional love, a reason for Grace to take long walks and keep fit, plus a few chewed-up shoes and his fair share of little accidents on the kitchen floor.

As Grace stroked Coco's soft fur, her mind wandered from the TV screen and the weather forecast to the niggling voice in her head, reminding her that she still had an issue or two to resolve. It was time she said the words, faced facts, got her finger out and made a few changes in her life. *'Okay, okay... I admit it,'* she told herself, *'I'm sick and tired of sitting here on my own, night after night, staring at the telly and these four walls with nobody for company apart from my dog. At the moment I'm just somebody's ex. Not to mention a mother, a grandma, and chief cook and bottle washer for kids who'll eventually leave home, and me. What will I do then?'*

What Grace really wanted to say and, until now, couldn't bear to accept, was that even though she had so much more in her life than others, it simply wasn't enough. She packed plenty of activities into seven days, just to keep herself occupied. But despite this, her job and family, at the end of the day when she climbed the stairs at night and turned off the light, Grace was incredibly lonely. Thinking back to married life, she sometimes wondered had it really been so bad?

Grace and Ben had met when they were seventeen. Heidi arrived just as they turned nineteen and was followed in equally spaced succession by Amber and Seth. Their marriage was happy and stable, not exactly rock and roll but they rumbled along quite nicely together for twenty years. It wasn't until they approached their forties that gradually, things began to change.

There were no affairs, bitter rows, or even bad atmospheres which would affect their children or even draw attention from friends and relatives. Looking back, Grace realised that they had unwittingly gone from being sex mad lovers to devoted parents and then somehow, along the way, settled for routine, stability and being their other half's best friend.

After an honest, sit-down, soul-searching conversation, Grace and Ben both agreed that they needed to try and put the 'Oomph' back into their relationship. Without further ado and with great anticipation, they booked a fortnight in Kos, both desperately hoping that strolls along the beach at sunset, intimate dinners for two and some secretly stashed lacy lingerie, might just do the trick.

Unfortunately, a combination of factors exacerbated their already tenuous relationship and two long weeks spent in one another's company simply made them feel trapped. Their sunset strolls had to be curtailed as the Greek mosquitoes absolutely thrived on Ben's blood. Any part of uncovered flesh became fair game and liberally munched on, leaving him tetchy, itchy and covered in pussy spots.

Their rampant lovemaking plans took a nosedive after the fourth day. Despite having the air-conditioning permanently on full blast, the whole performance was too hot and sweaty and involved far more energy than either of them could muster. After reaping the benefits of everything an all-inclusive break has to offer combined with a long day in the searing heat, most nights they just flopped onto their twin beds and conked out.

The novelty of getting dressed up for dinner and being waited on hand and foot soon wore off and their romantic dinners became a non-event as they sat morosely, picking at their food, devoid of conversation or merriment. Both ended up spending most of the meal wishing they were with someone else or, sitting at one of the other tables where everyone seemed to be having a right old laugh or at the very least, glad to be there.

When Grace's fair skin turned the colour of a lobster she was forced to hide under a sunshade and couldn't face another hot, sweaty day on the over-hyped Three Island Excursion, so after being assured she'd cope without him for a few hours, Ben went alone. Sadly, after a delicious kebab on the beach in the company of his jolly shipmates, Ben was struck down with a case of Delhi belly and spent a traumatic sailboat ride back to shore and then two days on the loo.

By this time, the writing was on the wall for their second-chance honeymoon, which was gradually becoming the holiday from hell.

Ben spent the rest of the trip playing crazy golf, eating chips and bread rolls, avoiding mosquitoes and chatting in the bar with a nice bunch of Geordies he'd met on the boat trip. Most worryingly, he seemed quite happy to spend time away from his sunburnt, moody wife.

Grace felt much the same and set up camp on the balcony of their room, a cool, quiet, Ben-free zone. Here, she took her mind off her frustration and disappointment by reading her novels (which were far more interesting than her husband) or sadly watching everyone else down below having fun. After tolerating dinner with Ben, cringing as he circled the buffet table like a shark in search of plain, E.coli-free food, she spent the rest of the night wide awake, searching her soul for answers.

While she listened to the sound of her inebriated husband snoring like a camel and the annoying laughter of the happy people down below, making their way back to their rooms where they would no doubt make mad passionate love, Grace pondered on her life and wondered what the hell was in store for the rest of it.

As for the lacy underwear – which remained unworn and dejected – she exchanged the lot for some fleecy pyjamas and three packs of sensible knickers the minute she got home.

After the holiday debacle, things just went from bad to worse. There was a gathering storm, swirling about offshore, laced with negative emotions and bitter, black clouds. Ben irritated the hell out of Grace who could no longer hide it, in fact, she didn't even try. They picked and grumbled about everything from clothes being left on the floor to the lack of teabags in the cupboard, the leaky tap, over-cooked beef, taking the bins out and hairballs in the shower. All those quirky, little things which were once slightly annoying and mildly amusing became major international incidents. Funny little habits and tiny failings which they'd ignored and rolled their eyes at for years soon morphed into huge issues that ruined their day and lingered through the night. Time dragged on and nothing changed apart from the fact that everything Ben did or said grated on Grace and, presumably, vice versa.

Everything, from the way he pronounced some words, laughed at unfunny things on telly, ate his food and slurped his tea, to how he tucked his polo shirts into his jeans and always chose the wrong socks to go with his shoes, just drove her mad. When he spoke, or made any attempt at conversation, she tuned out, nodding where she thought she ought to and feigning interest in more or less everything he said. Whereas in the past she'd closed her eyes to his idiosyncrasies, they were now waving big red flags in her face, drawing attention to themselves and goading her to react. For example, Ben reckoned he was a wine expert; sniffing and slurping, pretending to guess what fruits he could detect or commenting on hints of woodiness and intense liquorice notes. Grace knew full well he read the label first or, if it was in a foreign language, would have a sneaky Google and try to impress their friends.

Out of some kind of childish need to get one up on him and with a perverse sense of pleasure, Grace bought the cheapest, nastiest bottle of plonk she could find at the supermarket and decanted it into a bottle of expensive burgundy. At dinner that night, she watched with immense enjoyment as he swirled, sniffed, then grimaced after he tasted the vinegary bitter liquid which he'd just described to Heidi, Elliot and Cecil from next door as smooth and robust, with hints of red berries and peppery spices.

Grace realised their marriage was becoming toxic and worse, it was poisoning her. She hated the way she felt about Ben. She hated herself more. It wasn't meant to be like this, it wasn't what they promised each other all those years ago.

Still, despite the 'cold war', they soldiered on but the urge to fight for their marriage or even the desire to find a solution had finally deserted them. On one rainy September afternoon, after they'd endured another awkward Sunday lunch, Ben came and found her in the kitchen. As she noisily loaded the dishwasher he took a seat at the table and told her calmly and firmly that he thought it would be for the best if he moved out, just for a while. Maybe a trial separation might be just what they needed, to see if they missed each other, or worst-case scenario, they could manage on their own.

'I don't want to go, Gracie, but we can't carry on like this, can we? It's making me miserable all the time and I haven't seen you smile in ages, well not at me anyway. Thing is, I used to look forward to coming home but now it's like a cloud is hanging over us and I'm buggered if I know what to do about it.' Ben's arms rested on his knees, both hands clasped together, watching Grace intently.

Grace couldn't look at him any longer, it was too painful and anyway her vision was all blurry so she fiddled with the wrapper of the dishwasher capsule, sucking in air while trying to make shaking hands do as they were told. When she turned she saw tears in Ben's eyes too and knew he was right, she had to put him, them, out of their misery.

'I'm sorry, Ben. God you don't know how much. I don't want you to go either but you're right we can't go on like this... I've even thought of counselling, maybe we could try that.' Grace had no idea why she said that because even she knew that holding a bouncy ball while you gave your other half his chance to speak without interruption wasn't going to ignite a spark. Maybe it was guilt, or cowardice.

At this Ben shook his head. 'I don't think all that mumbo jumbo will sort us out, Grace, do you? We've known each other since we were more or less kids and if we can't sort it out together and be honest, there's not much chance of a shrink putting us right.'

'That's the part that is so frustrating... we don't even argue, I don't hate you, Ben, in fact I still love you but there's something missing so I agree, I don't think a counsellor will be able to wave a magic wand or teach us anything we don't already know.' Grace swiped away her tears and wiped her hand on her jeans, watching as Ben stood and pushed his chair under the table, just like she had trained them all to do.

'Well, I think that settles it. I'll chuck some stuff in a bag and then make myself scarce. Let's not say anything to the kids tonight. I'll just slip out while Seth's watching telly. Tell him I've gone round to our Kenny's and then tomorrow when we've slept on it and are less emotional we can decide what to tell them... is that okay with you?'

Grace couldn't speak or move. Her feet were welded to the floor as she saw Ben reach out and felt his hand rub her arm gently, before he turned and left the room.

The simplicity and lack of resentment in his words had made Grace cry. In that life altering moment she realised how much she loved this kind and decent man who had never let her down, the steady rock of their family. How ironic that now he was leaving, she wanted more than anything to be able to love him the way she once had, all those years ago. If she could have had one wish, right there and then, it would be for the days when he made her laugh till she cried. To go back to their nights of passion and for the butterflies that used to live in her chest to return once more so they could flicker like crazy the second she saw his lovely face.

Ben never came back, just like Grace knew he wouldn't. He took his freedom in the kindest way possible. Nobody was terribly hurt by his departure because he was always a regular visitor to the house, fixing the leaky tap or collecting Seth for a driving lesson. At first, the kids had hoped he would come home but were not overly concerned when he didn't, as unlike the break-ups they'd witnessed with their friends' parents, nobody had been wronged or seemed outwardly distressed.

Ben saw his children and grandchildren every weekend and was always invited to birthday parties and major events. Everyone behaved maturely and he still met Seth once a week for a catch up at the pub. Amber, true to form, was the only one to offer mild resistance after shedding what Heidi described as, attention-seeking tears.

Ben spent a short period lodging at his brother's, then rented a small flat and seemed to cope well with all that looking after himself entailed. To Grace's amusement, he now treated her like his female best mate and would often phone up and ask for cooking advice and even what to wear when, to her shock, he started dating again. In an awkward conversation (thankfully by phone) Ben confessed to joining an online dating agency and if it wouldn't upset her too much, he thought he was ready to find himself a girlfriend.

Grace had to admit that for at least twenty-four hours she was quite put out that the man who had been 'hers' for all those years was soon going to belong to someone else. Ben was still good-looking and very eligible and the green-eyed monster in her was certainly consumed by wistful regret. It served one good purpose though, it gave her a huge kick up the backside.

Reeling from what could only be described as a dose of ironic self-pity, Grace decided to take stock and revamp the jaded, forty-something, stuck-in-her-ways, grandmother look that she'd got so used to. Taking a new broom to her life, she started with a new image and had her auburn bob cropped into a cute pixie style and, with the help of Amber, chucked out anything mumsy or ten years out of style. She was then banned from buying any of her clothes from the supermarket when she did the weekly shop and was fully refurbished with the help of Amber and Primark.

Once the physical transformation was complete, Grace set

about on her inner self. She began power-walking with Sandra, her neighbour from across the street who wanted to lose a few pounds and get fit. They spent many a happy hour putting the world to rights as they stomped around their designated route. They even joined a gym and to everybody's surprise and Sandra's husband's delight (she'd lost two stone) had kept up their twice weekly visits for the past two years.

Not resting on her laurels, Grace had forced herself to go on spa weekends, city breaks, one dreadful hen night, Christmas shopping in Belgium, karaoke competitions at the pub, the theatre, a ballet and a tour around the doughnut factory (with the grandkids). Along with babysitting and sleepovers with Skye and Finn, Grace just about managed to fit in going to work at the local water treatment company, where she enjoyed her job in the admin department, sitting alongside her friend Layla.

Grace was quite popular with everyone and it had also come to her attention that she was considered to be a bit of all right by most of the male employees, even getting a few wolf whistles now and then from the younger members of staff.

On the romance front, since Ben left there had been nobody else, not that she would admit to anyway. Her one and only sordid, embarrassing, drunken fumble had been permanently erased from her memory. Now and then Layla brought it up, just to watch Grace cringe as her cheeks burned cherry red. Apart from that, it was consigned to the past, filed under 'Big Mistake'.

The event in question occurred after the work's Christmas party, which was held in a large hotel in Leicester. There was nothing unusual or special about the venue. It was modern and quite plush, and they'd done well to cram as many round tables as humanly possible into one room. After serving glasses of Buck's Fizz (ninety percent orange, ten percent cheap fizz) they professionally herded in the giddy staff from local companies and fed them a four course, slightly average, trendy version of a luke-warm Christmas dinner.

Grace had been separated from Ben for just over a year and was both excited and determined to have fun with Layla and their colleagues. She felt fabulous in a deep plum, silk dress, which clung in all the right places and showed off her long slim legs. Once the feeding frenzy was over they all headed for the disco and, buoyed by the free-flowing, extremely cheap wine they'd consumed, Grace and her merry gang danced the night away.

At some point they were joined by a group of men from one of the neighbouring tables. After a lot of jigging about, a tall, handsome, well-built man with close cropped dark hair and a cheeky smile offered to buy Grace a drink. After a few very strong-tasting glasses of vodka and Coke, they eventually moved into the lounge for coffee so they could hear each other. Grace could remember thinking he was really interested in what she had to say, at the same time as registering the knowing winks she received from Layla as she passed to go to the loo. She vaguely recalled accepting his offer to take their drinks upstairs, kissing in the lift, ordering more vodka and Coke from room service and unbuttoning his shirt. The next thing she remembered was waking up at 4am, stark naked with a pounding headache accompanied by the awful sensation of being on a spinning bed and wishing the walls would stay still.

Forcing down nausea, Grace managed to lift her head from the pillow and slowly turn over. Focusing on the lump of flabby, pale man flesh that lay by her side, shame and horror washed over her as she tried to remember the events of the previous evening, or even his name. As she lay there in mortified silence, Grace spotted a tattoo on his right arm which had previously been covered by his white dress shirt. A big red love heart flashed like a beacon and through the middle, written on a yellow banner was the name Pam, and it told her all she needed to know.

Her conscience swam through the haze of last night's vodka fumes and screamed scornfully, *'You slept with a married man!*

What a mug, what a slut, how could you?' To add insult to injury, the snoring lump then grunted in his sleep, turned on his side, broke wind (loudly) and revealed the *pièce de résistance.* Inscribed on his back and rubbing salt into fresh wounds were the names of, whom Grace could only presume were his two children, Jaden and Kyle. In that very instant, her inebriated, throbbing brain began to think clearly and told her she had to get away. Silently sliding from the bed onto the floor, Grace assured herself that tattoo-man was divorced and he saw Jaden and Kyle all the time, they were happy kids and his ex-wife was shacked up with a millionaire and had moved on.

While scrabbling for her discarded clothes and desperate to regain her dignity, Grace heard the noise from his mobile phone as it vibrated on the bedside table. Curiosity got the better of her, so she crawled along the carpet and looked at the screen, reading the message that well and truly killed the cat. Four missed calls and eight texts from 'My Pam' meant that Jayden and Kyle's daddy was in fact a total shit and his poor wife had probably spent all night wondering where the hell her husband was.

Dressing quickly, Grace took deep breaths, praying that she wouldn't wake Mr Trumpy or throw up all over him (which he deserved) as she struggled into her clothes and frantically searched for her other shoe. Thankfully, the corridor of the hotel was empty when she peeked outside the door and without looking back, closed it quietly, and made a run for it.

Never in all her life had Grace felt so humiliated or ashamed. All she could think of as she asked the smirking receptionist to call her a cab was that she wanted to go home. She tried to hold her head up and ignore the knowing look the doorman gave her, and knew full well what was going through the taxi driver's mind as they made their way through the sleepy streets of Leicester.

The final blow came as she reached her front door and let herself in, only to be met head on by the pungent smell of burnt toast and frying bacon. Seth and his two mates were happily tucking into breakfast after their own night out on the tiles. Her son was most impressed that his old mum had got in after him and even offered to make her a brew and a bacon butty. Feeling the swell of nausea, Grace brazened it out and waved cheerily from the hall, insisting she wasn't hungry and needed to sleep, then fled up the stairs.

When she woke later that morning (praying it had all been a terrible dream) with the headache from hell and a huge love bite on her neck, Grace swore off men forever. True to her word, that's how her life had remained ever since, a barren wilderness, bereft of romance and even a hint of man-related excitement and now, she was thoroughly sick of it.

Grace was irritated by her own reminiscing because her stroll down memory lane had done nothing to alleviate her mood and only made her feel worse so she turned off the TV and decided to call it a night.

As she lay in bed later, listening in the dark to the intermittent booms and cracks of leftover fireworks, Grace wondered how she'd managed to get to this. She was alright-looking, she'd even put herself in the 'attractive' category (on a good day when she'd made an effort). She was intelligent, had interests and hobbies, a decent job, nice friends, who, after the split from Ben hadn't taken sides. She had a lovely little family, a roof over her head and a bit of money in the bank. Everything had been alright until the phone call. Up until then she had plodded on and not felt the need to examine her life or indeed, taken much notice of her innermost feelings.

Turning on her side, Grace tried to force her eyes to close and stop her mind from raking up the past and overthinking her life. It was all Ben's fault. Why couldn't he just have left things the way they were? Why did he have to say that word, to alter the lovely balance of things and bring unnecessary turmoil to her world? He'd made everything sound so formal, too final.

A few weeks previously, he'd rung her late one evening and Grace could tell straight away that he was nervous, stalling for time and needed to get something off his chest. In the end, she stopped him mid-flow because she didn't really want to know how much it was going to cost to have new tyres fitted on his car or that they were building a Lidl near his works. *Dancing on Ice* was due to start and she needed to have her tea and biscuits ready for the live vote-off.

'Ben, is something wrong? You've been going round the houses so whatever it is you rang for spit it out. What's up?' Grace didn't know what to expect but he was like this when he met Janice, and then not long after, when she moved herself into his flat.

'Okay, well, I'll just say it then. I was wondering, if you've no objections, because it has been a while now since we split up, and I don't want to upset you or anything, so just say if I do.'

Grace was getting impatient and not really concentrating so chivvied him along.

'Ben, just get on with it will you, what on earth do you want?' Her tone was harsher than she had intended, but at least it spurred him on.

Ben gave a nervous cough, cleared his throat, then spoke. 'I want a divorce, Grace. Me and Janice are thinking of getting married so if it's alright with you, I think we should make things formal, get the ball rolling and all that.'

There was an embarrassing silence where Grace could've sworn she heard Janice whisper something, and had wrongly presumed Ben was alone. Before she even had chance to recover, Ben hit her with another request.

'Oh, and there's one more thing. It's about the house. I know I said it was fine for you all to keep on living there but Amber and Seth are both working now, so perhaps it could be remortgaged and you could buy me out. No pressure, it's just an idea. I wouldn't expect you to sell up, it's your home too, but the money would help me start over.'

The silence was once again deafening.

Grace was stunned. Her legs and hands shook and her mouth went dry. After managing to make her lips work she somehow forced out a limp reply. She told Ben that it was fine, just a bit of a shock and she would ring him when she'd thought it through properly, then quickly ended the call. As she pushed the button to disconnect, within the darkest recesses of her brain and deep inside her leaden heart, something changed and her world tilted on its axis. In that pivotal moment, as he'd said those grown-up, alien words, Grace realised that a huge important chunk of her life had just ended.

CHAPTER 3

It had been Grace's decision to remain single, despite hints from Amber and Heidi that she should start dating. They both insisted they wouldn't mind if she got a boyfriend and encouraged her to get out there and have some fun. Instead, she found it much easier to stick to the well-trodden path of being the Best Mum in the World, a Top Gran – and celibate.

Grace had so far resisted all matchmaking attempts by her friends, especially Layla, as the whole scenario was just too cringy. She'd let her guard down just once, appearing as the spare part at her friend's birthday dinner. Just as they were sitting down to eat, Layla shouted, 'Surprise… guess who's turned up at the last minute,' cue: Baldy Dave from work, who hadn't had a leg-over for years and spends his Sundays watching aeroplanes through his binoculars. No thanks!

Then there was the roving rep from the chemical company. He took a shine to Grace once he knew she was single and became a complete pain in the neck to the point of being weird and obsessive. Along with a banal, pointless phone call each morning, he sent her flowers on Valentine's Day, followed by a card and chocolates on her birthday (Layla's big mouth was to blame there) and a very rude, jokey Christmas card. He also seemed to think the way to her frosty heart was with a free box of industrial strength toilet cleaner, so when he finally transferred to the north-east office, Grace breathed a huge sigh of relief and her nervous twitch vanished, however, she did miss the free samples and having the cleanest, lemon-fresh loo for miles.

It was now one week after Bonfire Night and three weeks since the 'divorce' word was mentioned. Nothing more had been said and she knew that Ben was leaving her to come to terms with his request.

Just admitting that he knew her so well had caused her bruised heart to contract. The familiarity of married life had returned to haunt her and every day she would drag from her memory another snippet from the past or be reminded of Ben's many good points, because for now, he still was her husband, if only on paper.

Still, Grace couldn't resist and felt like she was exorcising a ghost, she needed to purge herself of Ben and their life before she could finally let him go. The question that ran like acid through her brain cells was so simple, why now, when it was too late, could she only remember the good things? She pictured their very first home and smiled. Here, Ben would get on with stripping the walls as soon as he came home from work, no matter how shattered he was, insisting he was going to turn their tiny flat into a palace.

Heidi's birth flashed up next. Ben slept on the floor of the hospital room all night because he didn't want Grace to be scared or alone. Their first family holiday to Norfolk came into soft focus. The tent blew down (twice) and it howled with rain but they all cuddled up in one sleeping bag while Ben made them laugh and cooked tinned food on a two-ring stove. The list of happy times was endless, and snapshots of their life played on a continuous loop, flickering before her eyes, starting in black and white and gradually blossoming into full colour, just as their marriage had done.

As Grace pulled into the car park and made her way into the office, real life took precedence so she shook away the past and forced herself to focus on the day ahead. It was Monday morning and she was determined that this would be the start of a new Her. No more brooding and sulking, it was time to make some decisions and concentrate on the here and now.

By lunchtime, it was clear that a mountain of perfectly processed orders and a succession of politely answered phone calls were not going to be sufficient to fend off the gloom that was waiting in the wings. The depression hung about while Grace ate her lunch with Layla.

The atmosphere was ruining the dubious joy associated with eating soup and tuna sandwiches at your desk, and more than likely resulted in Layla bravely broaching the subject of the 'D' word and also, the as yet unsolved Christmas situation.

'So, have you spoken to Ben about seeing a solicitor or are you letting him sort it all out? Perhaps he's changed his mind and wants you to make the next move, he is a bit of a wimp when all is said and done.' Layla opened her can of Coke and put her feet up on the desk, pondering Grace's predicament before continuing.

'I bet that Janice cow is pulling his strings, she's too pushy that one. It's like she's had a game plan from the very beginning the snidey witch.' Layla opened her packet of crisps and nonchalantly munched away while she waited for a reply, happy to have stirred things up.

'No, he's not mentioned it and neither have I, not even to the kids. If he wants a divorce *he* can sort it out and if Janice is behind it all then that's his fault for being a pushover. I know they've been on holiday for a week so I'm expecting another call now they're back. There's no point in being awkward but I'm not going to go out of my way, either.' Grace stirred her soup thoughtfully, ignoring the rain cloud hovering above her head.

It was true what Layla said about Janice. Grace remembered clearly the first time her name was mentioned. Ben slipped it into a conversation while he was collecting Skye and Finn from Heidi's. He was ten minutes late and Skye had been pacing the hall, totally unimpressed and eager to get to the park because Grandad was never late and she was fuming. As he ushered them out of the door Ben apologised to Heidi, saying with a twinkle in his eye that he'd been for lunch with someone called Janice and it all went really well.

Naturally, the word spread to Amber who told Grace and before they knew it, the name Janice was liberally mentioned by a loved-up Ben at every opportunity. The general consensus was that their dad was acting like a lovesick teenager, which at first they found amusing, however, when he invited the three of them to dinner so they could meet his new girlfriend, from what Grace had heard, by the time dessert was served the smile had been well and truly wiped off their faces.

Grace had relished every morsel from the fated dinner, related in great detail by Amber who thought that at thirty-two, Janice was cloying, jealous, opinionated, and far too young for her father. Basically, Amber couldn't stand her. This didn't really surprise Grace as Amber had always been a bit of a daddy's girl and liked to be the centre of his attention.

She then mentioned that Seth thought Janice had an annoying laugh, like a whinnying horse, a big bum and worse, she didn't let him get a word in edgeways when he tried to chat to his dad about football. In the end Seth had given up and let her rabbit on about her job as a dental nurse, her holiday in Egypt and whatever else *she* thought was interesting.

Amber said that Heidi took the huff when she showed her some photos of the children and Janice haughtily advised that Skye would soon need a brace on her gappy teeth and Finn looked a bit on the pale side. Janice's withering prognosis was that Finn was likely to be lacking in vitamin D and probably didn't eat enough fruit and vegetables which also accounted for him being rather small for his age.

In her summing up, Amber was convinced that Janice was off her rocker and by criticising Heidi's children and as a consequence her parenting skills, she may as well have shown a red rag to a psychotic bull!

Before they all knew it, 'our Jan' as the kids now un-lovingly referred to her, was moving out of her mother's house and into Ben's flat. They'd since been on holiday to Canada to visit her father and last Christmas, much to the disgust of his children, Ben spent all of his time with Janice and her family and a thick red line was drawn in the sand by Heidi, Amber and Seth.

Amber was adamant that 'our Jan' was a man hungry, gold-digger whose biological clock was ticking and soon, there'd be the patter of tiny feet and just the thought of it made her feel sick.

Heidi merely kept the peace so that Skye and Finn stayed in touch with their grandad. Even they didn't like Janice, mainly because she was really strict and sweets were totally banned at Ben's flat and maybe forever if she had her way.

Seth just chose to ignore Janice completely and got on with his life, meeting up with his dad at the pub for a pint or to watch the match. This was until recently when Ben announced that next year he wouldn't be renewing his season ticket for Leicester City as he and Janice wanted to go to Australia, the money he saved (by missing matches with his son) would come in handy.

Grace just listened to their gripes, rolled her eyes, and stayed out of it, but it did bother her slightly when Amber scathingly announced that her dad was having some kind of mid-life crisis. To her shame, Grace had a bit of a giggle when she received a text from Amber saying Ben was wearing RED Converse High Tops when he picked her up from the station and was sure he'd dyed his hair because it was definitely less grey than before. When he swapped his beloved Range Rover for a racy convertible, Grace was slightly perplexed and even cringed a bit when she heard he was going to a Paloma Faith gig. Apparently, according to Amber, over forties go to concerts and shouldn't be allowed to say 'gig' plus, she was convinced that Ben didn't have the first clue who the singer was, anyway!

Despite the alarm bells in Grace's head, common sense told her there was no point in speaking to him about how the kids felt as it was clear he was in love. That concept alone had freaked her out at first and yes, she was a teeny bit jealous. She was also secretly quite pleased that the kids didn't like Janice which she knew was slightly immature but judging by all of the evidence, thoroughly justified. According to her wise friend Layla, it was a completely natural reaction and she'd get over it eventually. But had she?

Layla had finished her sandwiches and as she wiped crumbs from her desk, interrupted Grace's meanderings.

'And what about Christmas? Have you chosen martyrdom and the bosom of your family over hedonism and a wicked holiday with me and the girls? I've told you, you're welcome to come with us, it'd do you good to get back in the saddle and shake the cobwebs out of your knickers.'

Layla's cheeky smile and carefree outlook on life always managed to make Grace laugh and it snapped her out of her maudlin thoughts.

'No, I haven't decided yet and I know, before you say it, I'm running out of time, but I just can't seem to get my head straight or be enthusiastic about anything at the moment. Everything seems such a mess.' Grace was surprised when she heard her own voice crack slightly and a tiny tear tried to escape from the corner of her eye.

Layla, never one to miss a trick, had spotted the dip in mood and decided to take control of the situation.

'Right, well it's about time we made a start on sorting a few things out and besides, I'm getting sick of sitting next to a misery guts. It's been ages since we've had a laugh, even at Baldy Dave. If you don't cheer up soon I'm moving my desk over to the dark side of the office, even Mavis from logistics is more fun than you, and she's practically a nun.' Layla was eating her Twix, biting off the top layer while she watched Grace's face for a glimmer of interest.

'I don't know where to start. What do you think I should do about Christmas? I was slightly put out when Seth mentioned his skiing trip, but I could live with that knowing the girls would be around. Now, I've been royally dumped by all of them and it looks like I'm stuck with the Klingons. If I'm honest, I'm dreading it and haven't got a clue what to do. No offence, but I don't really fancy coming on a snog-fest with your lot. I'd put a downer on everyone's holiday and the last thing you want is your old-fart friend spoiling things. So, come on, brains, help me out.' Grace felt she might as well be honest, rather than ruin Layla's much awaited holiday.

'Well, for a start, no offence taken by the way, but you can stop feeling sorry for yourself right this second. I know you thought you were doing the right thing by letting your chicks fly off but you still have the option of slaving over a hot stove and playing Monopoly with your sister. Let's face it, you could be totally alone like some poor sods are at Christmas so luckily for you, that's not really the case, is it?' Layla let her honest words settle for a moment and then swiftly soldiered on.

'Let's play pretend… if you could have a Christmas of your choice, what would it be? Just let your imagination run riot or in your case, get a bit giddy. I don't want you having a funny turn.' Layla peeled her tangerine and squirted juice all over her blouse while Grace started thinking.

'Well, I've never fancied a sunny Christmas, you know, partying on the beach and all that, but at the same time, I wouldn't want to go the whole hog like Seth and spend it up to my eyes in snow and ski boots. It all sounds far too energetic and soggy. So what other options do I have? A Christmas cruise means guaranteed company but also involves eating dinner at a round table and making polite conversation with complete strangers. I might hate them *and* I'd always be the odd one out *again*. Plus, there's Coco to take into consideration. There's nobody to look after him, apart from Cecil next door, or Ben, who doesn't even like animals. No way is Our Jan getting her hands on my dog. She can keep my husband but Coco is a no-go area.' Grace felt the grey cloud thickening and a downpour of carefully held back tears threatened to break through at any moment.

'Well, now we're getting somewhere, I think.' Layla could hear the anguish in Grace's voice so was doing her best to find a solution.

'We've established that wherever you go it has to be dog friendly and not too cold, hot weather is out of the question anyway and you need somewhere you don't feel pressured into meeting strangers. I know... what about going to the seaside, maybe you could rent a caravan?' Layla looked quite pleased with herself, at least it was an option.

Grace perked up a bit. Her mind started to take on board the possibility of getting away from it all, and taking Coco would mean she would have company. They spent plenty of time together, just the two of them, so she knew she'd be fine with her faithful friend. But then, as the image of a draughty caravan by the sea sprang to mind, with the wind howling across the cliff tops as it rattled the walls, Grace realised she'd actually quite like a bit of luxury, so rejected that idea. Still, it would be lovely to get out of the city and breathe fresh air, go for long walks and have a complete change of scenery. Images

33

of wintry lanes and log fires set her mind racing with possibilities.

Grace made Layla jump when she had an idea. 'I know. What about a cottage in the country? Coco would love it. We could go for bracing walks or just slob about and have a rest. It'd have to have a log fire and a telly, and not be too isolated, that would give me the creeps. Apart from that, I reckon me and my faithful hound could cope quite well looking after ourselves and, for once, not be rushing about like an idiot dishing out sprouts and turkey. What do you think?'

Grace was on a roll and looked expectantly at Layla for the thumbs up.

'I think it's just what you need. A trip away and something to plan for will be empowering. The kids will be able to get on with their Christmas, guilt-free, especially if they know you are having an adventure of your own. They might worry a bit so you'll have to act like you do this all the time and it's no big deal. Your sister and the rest of the rellies won't be too pleased though, but they'll just have to look after themselves for a change – like it or lump it! Don't you dare back down when they start moaning and try to make you feel guilty or else they'll have me to answer to.'

Layla was obviously still hungry and began searching her desk drawers for something else to eat so Grace threw her a chocolate muffin and marvelled how the blonde bombshell sitting opposite could eat and drink whatever she liked and still have a figure to die for. Perhaps it was nervous energy or her nocturnal activities that kept her slim, but whatever it was, just listening to tales of Layla's eventful love and social life wore Grace out.

True to form, once Grace had made up her mind, there was no stopping her eager friend and before she knew it, Layla's PC was humming into life and Google was ready for action.

Layla's fingers were poised above the keyboard, awaiting instructions. 'Right, now all we have to do is find the perfect place. It's short notice but I'm sure there will still be vacancies somewhere. Here we go, what shall we type in?'

'Just put, cottage rentals in the countryside, Christmas break, or something like that, and let's see what comes up.' Grace wheeled her chair round to the other side of the desk and waited for the search engine to do its thing.

Layla clapped excitedly when the page appeared showing link after link of Christmas lettings, so she clicked on the first one and typed in the criteria for Grace's stay. One hour later, they were still at it, in between doing a bit of work and keeping an eye out for Graham, their boss. There were lots of whispered messages passed across their desk each time they found a prospective cottage, then the details of all possibilities were duly noted so that Grace could check them out properly when she got home later that evening.

It was 4.57pm when Grace finished working on her spread-sheet and before switching off, thought she'd just take a quick peek at the lettings page. It didn't do to be the first one to turn off their PC and head for the door so both she and Layla always lingered a bit, until somebody else made the first move. As Grace scanned through the list, passing over the ones they'd already checked out, something caught her eye. There, near the bottom, was an advert which was slightly different from the others, it read:

CHRISTMAS COTTAGE RENTALS
ESCAPE TO THE FRENCH COUNTRYSIDE THIS
YULETIDE AND LEAVE THE WORLD BEHIND.
OUR COSY GÎTES WITH LOG BURNING FIRES ARE
NESTLED IN THE BEAUTIFUL VALLEY OF THE LOIRE.
FULLY EQUIPPED AND CLOSE TO ALL AMENITIES,
VIBRANT TOWNS AND PICTURESQUE VILLAGES, YOU

CAN EXPERIENCE RURAL FRANCE AT ITS WINTRY BEST.

PETS WELCOME. CALL FOR DETAILS AND AVAILABILITY.

Grace was instantly hooked. She looked up to tell Layla but spotted Graham hovering about so scribbled the details on her pad and stuffed it in her bag, then closed the page and logged out. There were bubbles of excitement fizzing in her chest as she relayed the advert to Layla on the way to the car park. They were still there as she drove home, mainly because her friend had been just as enthusiastic and thought that going to France was a brilliant idea.

'This way, the Klingons won't be able to tip up unexpectedly, or worse, invite themselves along on your holiday. All you've got to say is there's no room at the inn. End of story. The kids will be a bit surprised and might be worried about you driving on the wrong side of the road and all that, but I bet they'll be dead proud of their boring old mum. Sorry, I meant stuck in her ways, scared of change, on the verge of being boring, not really *that* old, mum.'

Layla laughed as she received a crack around the head and watched as Grace jumped into her car, eager to get home and back on the internet.

By 7pm, Grace's fizzy bubbles had popped and her dreams of Christmas in France lay in tatters, along with the ripped up piece of notepaper that she'd destroyed and chucked on the floor after discovering that all four gîtes were booked and not available until spring. What made it even worse, was that Rosie, the owner of *Les Trois Chênes*, had sounded lovely and seemed genuinely sorry that she couldn't fit her in.

To rub salt in her wounds, before she rang, Grace had taken a virtual tour of the cottages, which were cosy and luxurious, as was Rosie's lovely hotel next door which served the most gorgeous food. Stupidly, Grace had also Googled the area and saw all the lovely places she could visit while she was there, or not, as was now the case.

By the time she'd taken Coco for a walk through rainy, litter-strewn streets, not crisp, wintry lanes that wound their way through the Loire countryside, Grace's strop had reached mono-lithic proportions. She managed to feign interest in Seth's pre-ski exercise regime and Amber's new red wedges and then hold a semi-sympathetic conversation with Heidi who was full of a cold and thought that Finn was coming down with it too.

After dispensing sage medical advice, half-watching Seth's contortions while Amber paraded up and down in her shiny shoes, Grace knew she was running out of patience so took herself off to bed. Even here, peace of mind and even the hint of sleep spitefully evaded her. The night went on forever as she tossed and turned, tormented by shattered dreams and fuzzy images from the internet.

Tuesday, when it dawned, well and truly dragged its feet and was determined to rub Grace's nose in a puddle of misery. Even though she had no desire to continue her search, Layla insisted that they press on and she shouldn't let one disappointment get her down. Unfortunately, the gods were working against them both and decided to strike a plague upon their computers, rendering them completely useless for a full day. Not only did they feel like their arms had been chopped off, it appeared there was almost nothing anyone could do without the appliance of science. The day droned on and on while they waited for the technical whizz person to arrive and sort their lives out. Then, just as Grace thought her life couldn't get any worse, Ben decided to ring her.

At first, she ignored his calls but Ben persisted so she put her phone on silent, knowing full well what he wanted but was in no mood to discuss their divorce. He was obviously determined to get through and tried to speak to her on the office line so Layla stepped in, heading him off each time.

She told him that Grace was on the loo, had gone for sandwiches, was in a meeting, up a ladder, on the phone to Japan, cleaning the office windows and by call number seven, Layla lost the plot. After letting out an exasperated sigh, she informed Ben, in hushed tones, that Grace was bang at it in the stockroom with Baldy Dave and just couldn't be disturbed but could leave a message for when they were finished. It was the only time all day Layla managed to make Grace laugh, which is more than could be said for Ben who didn't sound remotely amused.

Finally, Graham gave in and at 3.30pm he told them they could all go home. With a silent cheer, Grace grabbed her coat and after half-heartedly promising Layla that she would continue her holiday search that evening, headed despondently out of the gates.

After letting herself in, Grace didn't notice the flashing light of the answerphone straight away and when she did, decided to ignore it. She knew it would be Ben trying to track her down, most likely terrified he'd have to admit to Janice that she'd given him the slip. Grace knew deep down that it would be better to get it over with as soon as possible, otherwise, he might call round to the house and that was the last thing she needed right now.

She stalled for time by loading the washer and making coffee, then let Coco out and had a wander round the garden with him, just in case Ben rang again. She was just about to get the ironing board out when, lo and behold, the peace was interrupted by the shrill sound of the phone, resigning herself to the inevitable, Grace lifted the receiver, took a deep breath and said hello.

'Hi, is that Mrs Shaw, it's Rosie calling from France, we spoke yesterday. I hope I'm not interrupting anything, is this a good time to talk?'

Grace was momentarily nonplussed, relieved and intrigued all at the same time, then gathered her wits so said it was fine and to fire away.

'Oh good. Well, I'll get straight to the point. I've been trying to contact you all day, you see first thing this morning, I had a cancellation! It was quite out of the blue but the family I had booked in can't make it. His wife needs an operation and her name came up on the waiting list so she's going to be out of action all over Christmas. Anyway, I wanted to give you first refusal as you sounded so disappointed last night but before you decide, I need to tell you that the gîte I have available is a bit bigger than what you wanted, it sleeps up to eight. You can view it on the website but it might not suit you, so have a look and let me know.'

Rosie came up for air and gave Grace the chance to speak.

'I'll take it. I don't care if it's too big or how much it is. I've been so fed up since yesterday because I'd set my heart on coming, even before I rang, which I know was totally stupid. So please, can you book me in, with red pen and in capitals.' Grace's heart was hammering in her chest and the fizzy bubbles had returned.

Rosie laughed. 'Okay, okay, you're in. And I will give you a reduction as it's last minute and you are helping me out. I doubt I'd be able to let it at such short notice, unless France in December is suddenly the place to be. I'm just happy that I've cheered you up and it's all worked out well. For both of us.' Rosie was laughing as she spoke, obviously delighted to hear that she'd made someone's day.

'I really don't expect a reduction, but thank you anyway. I'll send you an email confirming the dates I'll be arriving once I've booked a ferry, is that okay?' Grace's head was spinning, her brain working overtime already.

'That's fine. Just drop me a line tomorrow and I'll be in touch with any other details I think you'll need. Have a lovely evening,

Grace, is it okay to call you by your first name, we don't stand on ceremony here?'

'Of course it is, and thank you again, Rosie, speak to you soon.' When she hung up, Grace did a bit of a jig up and down the hall, observed from the kitchen by a bemused Coco who was waiting patiently for his tea.

'We're going on holiday, Coco, just you and me. We'll have a big adventure. You can chase French rabbits and sleep in front of a lovely fire. I'm so excited and you would be too if you knew what I was talking about.' Grace ruffled Coco's ears then kissed the top of his head.

'Right, let's get you some food then I'm going to ring the kids. It's time I started making some plans.' Grace poured dog biscuits into the bowl and as she mashed up the tinned meat, embraced the new positive feeling washing over her.

Layla was right, she actually felt empowered, and while she was on a roll, Grace decided to give Ben a call and exert herself. Janice might be pulling his strings but for now she was still Mrs Shaw, Ben's oldest friend and the mother of his children. It was about time Our Jan backed off and realised that Grace wasn't going to be railroaded into anything. Plopping the bowl on the floor, she patted Coco's head then picked up her phone and rang Ben.

CHAPTER 4

G race valiantly battled her way through Tesco and the throng of busy shoppers, who, it seemed, were caught up in a festive panic buying session. It *was* the second to last shopping weekend before Christmas after all and from the frenzied way the staff were restocking the shelves from huge, over-laden pallets, a world-wide food shortage was imminent. She'd only gone in for some extra wrapping paper and a roll of sticky tape but now Grace was going to be waiting in the self-serve queue for ages.

She wondered if she could sue the store for misrepresentation as there was absolutely nothing express about this checkout. As she shuffled her way forward, feeling quite ticked off with all the people in front of her who had rammed a small trolley worth of food into a basket, Grace's mind wandered to her forthcoming holiday.

By this time next week, she'd only have four days to go before her voyage across the Channel to France. The butterflies in her stomach had a little flutter and she had to hide the self-satisfied smile that came to her lips every time she thought about her trip.

❄

Grace had begun her preparations by ringing Ben. She was determined to get the uncomfortable stuff out of the way before throwing herself into making plans and telling the kids where she was going.

Ben seemed flustered when he answered the phone and Grace wondered if he'd been having his ear chewed off by Janice. She heard her in the background and caught the comment 'it's about time too', which narked Grace straight away, making her even more intent on unleashing a few home truths on her lily-livered husband when the time was right.

'Sorry I've not returned your calls earlier, Ben, I've been rushed off my feet today. So, what did you want that's so urgent?' Grace wasn't going to make things easy and guessed that Jan was listening because the TV had been turned down.

'I was just wondering if you'd thought any more about, you know, what I mentioned a few weeks back. Is it okay to go ahead and all that?' Ben sounded nervous and Grace heard a loud 'tut' of annoyance from Janice.

'Oh, you mean the divorce and wanting me and your children out of our home?' Grace let the words and sarcasm sink in before she continued.

'Yes, I have given it some thought, Ben, and it's fine. If you want to make arrangements to see a solicitor just go ahead. I'll tell the kids after Christmas that you and Janice need the money so we might have to remortgage or sell up. It might put a dampener on things if I mention it beforehand. Anyway, I've got a lot on at the moment and will be away over the Christmas period so I won't have time to get the ball rolling until the New Year. I'll need to see a mortgage advisor and my own solicitor so if it's alright with you, I'll do it as soon as I get back?' Grace took a breath and waited for Ben to take silent instructions from his puppeteer.

'Right, yes, that's fine, Grace. No big rush, the New Year will suit me too. And I don't want you and the kids thinking that I'm pushing you out of your home. I'm sure we can come to some amicable agreement about the equity in the house. The last thing I want is for us to fall out over it.'

Ben sounded genuine and Grace's heart softened until she heard Jan, who just *had* to stick her nose in.

'As long as she knows that we've got plans too and we're not prepared to wait forever for her to sort her life out.'

Grace's mouth was agape, shocked at Janice's bare-faced cheek and not only that, she didn't even care that she'd be overheard.

When the sound on the TV went up and his other half had said her piece, Ben set about apologising.

'Sorry about that, Grace, Jan doesn't mean it, she's just a bit eager to get things organised and was hoping I'd have it sorted by now.'

Unfortunately, his words fell on very deaf ears, the damage was done and Grace had seen red.

'For God's sake, Ben! Stop making excuses for her. Can you not see what she's doing and how you are beginning to look? I've kept my opinions to myself up till now but while you may be a pushover, I certainly am not! Who does she think she's talking to? And, while I'm on a roll, when her appalling attitude starts to affect our children and your relationship with them, I won't stand by and just allow it to happen, enough is enough.' Grace was livid and all the things that Amber, Heidi and Seth had told her suddenly bubbled to the surface and were about to be boil over.

'I don't know what you mean. What have the kids said, are they upset with me?' Ben sounded alarmed and slightly incredulous.

'Yes, Ben, they are upset with you but they are totally sick of Janice. They think you've changed since you met her and if I'm honest, I think you are losing sight of who you are and being manipulated by someone who is only concerned about themselves. I was glad that you'd found someone new and if it really is love, then the very best of luck to you. But when it comes at the expense of the kids' feelings, I have to step in.'

Grace heard a door close and could tell that Ben had moved out of the room where Janice was and now, she had his full attention. His next words confirmed this.

'Grace, I have no idea what you're going on about, what have they been saying?'

Taking a deep breath, Grace let rip. 'Well, let's start with Seth shall we? He's our most easy-going child and you've even managed to hurt his feelings and let him down, all in one go. How many times have you cried off meeting him after work for a pint since you met Janice? It's always with some lame excuse and he's not stupid, Seth knows it's because she wants you home and begrudges you an hour with your own son. And then, if that's not enough, just because you and Jan want to go to Australia, match days with his dad are coming to an end. I'm so cross about that. You've been going to the football since he was seven years old. That's sixteen years of father and son time, no more memories, those happy times are over, just like that.' Grace clicked her fingers for an added dramatic sound effect.

She wasn't finished, either. 'Well, I hope you are prepared for a guilt trip at the beginning of the season when you realise your son is up in the stands without his dad and while I think on, what on earth are you thinking of going to Australia? You'll be eaten alive by bugs and you're scared shitless of snakes, you're going to hate it!' Grace was in full throe and continued quickly before she forgot anything and lost momentum.

'Then there's Skye and Finn. You've always been so reliable and have never let them down or made them feel second best, but even your grandkids are starting to feel pushed out. Saturday has always been "Grandad Day" and they can't wait for their morning at the swimming baths and then the park. To my knowledge, you've cancelled three times lately and when you do show up, you're either late or cut the day short because *she* needs to go somewhere. You also know damn well that Heidi doesn't let them have sweets and saves their ration for when they are with you, but since Jan has been tagging along, you don't take them to the newsagents for their bag of toffees, *or* for a burger because a certain person thinks that anything remotely fun, or tasty, is bad for them! Who does she think she is?' Grace paused for breath, then continued. 'Our Heidi is a very good mum who feeds her children healthy food but also allows them to have the odd treat. It's condescending of Janice to act like she knows best and nobody is going to upset my grandkids, do you get that? For God's sake grow a spine, Ben, and remember who your priorities are and where your loyalties lie. If she's going to spoil the day, leave her at home, otherwise you will ruin the relationship with your grandchildren, not to mention your son.' Wow, thought Grace, this home truth lark feels good.

There was a moment of silence before Ben spoke.

'I really didn't know they felt like that. But Janice wants to be included and feel like a part of the family, she's only trying to help. She's not a bad person like you're making out. She wants to spend time with me at the weekend too, so I have to fit everyone in. It's not like I've just dumped the kids, I still see them and things are bound to change a bit, it's only natural.'

It sounded like Ben was going on the defensive but it didn't wash with Grace.

'Ben, it's about as natural as your hair is these days. Oh yes, don't think it's gone unnoticed that she's even changing the way you look, let alone act. I know that Amber isn't exactly objective and can err on the side of jealousy, but sometimes her opinions and observations do hold water. If you were having some kind of mid-life crisis and independently wanted a crack at your second youth, go for it, who am I to judge? But from where I'm standing it sounds like Janice is trying to remodel you and you're starting to look silly. If she's not happy with you how she found you, then that's a real shame. There's nothing wrong with having a makeover, it's not just women that need a new image, but, Ben, grow old gracefully. Don't have the lads at work laughing at you behind your back because you dye your hair or wear clothes you don't feel comfy in. Don't let the kids lose respect for you either because you've always been the best dad and grandad. Janice could ruin all that so easily.' On hearing her own truthful words, Grace felt a bit mean and was slightly annoyed that she'd even had to say those things. She actually felt sorry for him now!

Ben began to speak until they both heard the voice of doom approaching. Janice had caught him on the phone so instead of responding to her accusations and opinions, he ended the conversation quickly and cut Grace off.

Since then, she'd not heard a single peep from him so left him alone to ponder on her words and got on with making plans for Christmas.

All three children were quite taken aback by Grace's decision to go away and, as predicted by Layla, they voiced their concerns on a number of issues. Firstly, her navigational capabilities and driving skills were thoroughly questioned. Would she even find her way to Portsmouth, never mind the prospect of driving on the wrong side of the road? Next, the fact that she would be spending Christmas Day alone caused immense concern. Apparently, Coco didn't count as company so it did take a while to convince them that she would be fine. Grace had skilfully painted a wonderful image of their mother having huge lie-ins, walks in the countryside, gourmet food up at the hotel and the laziest, most self-indulgent Christmas Day ever.

Once she'd produced the photos of her rustic accommodation and the places she intended to visit, they seemed semi-placated but just to test the water, Grace gave them an alternative and also an ultimatum. If they were still unhappy about her trip then *all* of them would have to cancel their plans and spend Christmas with her, because she point-blank refused to be home alone with the Klingons, so it was their choice. Finally, as Grace expected, they gave in.

Seeing as she was owed loads of holidays and her company was shutting down for most of the Christmas break anyway, Grace had no problem booking time off work. With two whole weeks at her disposal she was due to leave for France on the Thursday before Christmas. Everything was arranged. She'd bought and wrapped everyone's presents, which she would give to them before she left. The children insisted that Grace take her gifts with her so she could open them on Christmas morning and then made her promise to ring them all in turn as she opened their respective presents, it would be as though they were in the room.

The only person to take real umbrage was her sister Martha. Grace thought this was a bit rich, seeing as she had never even offered to do the honours at Christmas let alone help out on the big day, or contributed anything of any use. The only thing she brought was a bottle or two of Lambrini for herself and a crate of beer for Jimmy. Not forgetting her two very annoying, insolent, ungrateful twin sons, Jacob and Jeremy, who, in Grace's opinion, had not improved in the manners or the conversation department during the fourteen years they'd been on the earth.

Their windy father, Jimmy, was capable of consuming vast amounts of food and lager, but incapable of processing it through his digestive system in a quiet manner. Consequently, large amounts of wind frequently and loudly escaped from his two main orifices, much to the horror and disgust of everyone gathered.

Using her initiative and following sound advice from Amber, Grace rang her Aunty Evelyn first and after explaining her own plans, she sort of invited Ev and Uncle Terry to Martha's for Christmas dinner. Evelyn was the world's number one moaner and her husband wasn't far behind. They had special dietary needs for various minor illnesses and were a trial from the second they walked through the door, commandeering the television and the day's viewing schedule. Grace only put up with them out of respect to an older generation, ignoring her own family's pleas to bolt the door while patiently accepting their idiosyncrasies, plus, they were her last remaining link to her mother.

Grace missed her mum and dad more than she could say and Christmas always brought with it a touch of melancholy along with so many happy memories of them both. They had passed away within eighteen months of each other and, at the time, Grace thought that she'd never get over losing them. But as the years went by, her heart began to heal, mostly with the love and understanding she received from Ben, that, and the distractions of bringing up three children.

After her mum died, Grace became the head of the family by default and Martha, being plain bone idle and always on the lookout for an easy ride, was happy to let Grace take the lead. Naturally, Martha was shocked and outraged when she heard that this year, Christmas was going to be on her.

'What do you mean you're going away, where to and what about your lot? You can't just abandon everyone.'

Martha sounded completely flabbergasted as she listened to Grace explain, with great delight, the whole thing.

'So, it looks like this year, you get the chance to be the hostess with the mostest and take care of Aunty Ev and Uncle Terry. I've just reassured her that you wouldn't leave them on their own at Christmas and she said she'd give you a ring later on and arrange what time Jimmy should pick them up.' Grace sniggered to herself as she listened to the stunned silence at the other end of the phone.

'Well, I suppose there's nothing I can do about it now but my Jimmy won't be pleased if he can't have a drink on Christmas Day, so it looks like I'll have to stay sober and run them home again. Those two tight arses won't pay for a taxi so that's my day totally ruined. I'm going to be rushed off my feet and they won't even think of chipping in for the food and drink. I'll have to stump up for the lot and you know Uncle Terry gets on my nerves. I can't believe you'd rather be on your own than with your family, but if you insist on having some kind of mid-life adventure and driving off into the sunset, I suppose I'll just have to put up with them.'

The irony of her own selfish words seemed completely lost on Martha and only made Grace all the more determined to go.

When she finally hung up the phone, it hit home just how relieved she was because this year, Grace was free. She knew it wasn't going to be plain sailing and despite her bold plans, there had actually been a few moments as she lay in bed at night, when she suffered a crisis of confidence. What if it was all a huge mistake? What if she hated France or being alone in a big gîte in the middle of the countryside? It could be haunted, or a mad axeman might roam the woods, looking for a stupid, single woman and a soft dog to chop up. Would she find her way there, or feel the odd one out in the restaurant and worse, freeze to death because she couldn't light the log fire? Thankfully, as is usually the way, by morning and after a good night's sleep her worries miraculously vanished and the thrill of an adventure, along with her new-found spirit of independence, spurred Grace on.

Finally, having reached the front of the queue, Grace placed her items on the shelf, just as a weary checkout supervisor sauntered over to utter the immortal words, 'Do you know it's cash only at this till, love?' Seeing as Grace had about seven pence and a book of stamps in her purse and her patience had finally ran out, along with any remaining Christmas spirit, she handed over her basket and told the shocked assistant exactly where she could stick the two rolls of wrapping paper and some sticky tape, then stomped out of the store.

By the time Grace had eased her way out of the car park which was rammed full to capacity and swarming with irritable drivers waiting to pounce on every available space, her heartbeat had returned to normal and her stress levels were slowly receding. After popping into the first convenience store that she spotted, to buy whatever rolls of paper they had left, which happened to be for kids and decorated with Santa saying 'Ho Ho Ho', she made her way home.

Grace wanted to wrap up their next door neighbours' present, which was a lovely wooden bench. They'd all chipped in and thought it would be fun to cover it with paper and put it in Cecil's garden on Christmas morning, but as they wouldn't be here she was going to give it to him this afternoon when he came for Sunday dinner.

Cecil was their oldest neighbour and over the years had become more like an uncle to her and the kids. On the day they moved in, almost twenty years ago, a younger, sprightlier Cecil had helped Ben move their furniture and his wife, Peggy, had made cups of tea and sandwiches for all of them. Over time, they had become good friends and to Grace, having them next door gave her great comfort, especially when her own parents died. Cecil was always on hand to lend tools to Ben and tell him where he was going wrong with his DIY, or keep an eye on the garden when they went camping. Peggy minded the kids if Grace had to nip out and patiently taught Heidi to knit and sew. They were always included in family events and Grace fondly remembered both of Peg and Cecil's daughters setting off to the church on their wedding day on the arm of their proud dad.

When Peggy passed away, both of his daughters wanted Cecil to move in with them but he had resisted. He'd lived in his home for fifty years and it held too many precious memories, so he stuck to his guns and stayed put. Even Grace worried that he would be lonely and promised Lauren and Rachel that she would keep an eye on him, so for the past seven years, Cecil had been a regular for Sunday dinner and always welcome for a cup of tea and a biscuit. Grace would accidentally-on-purpose make too much casserole or lasagne and have just enough pastry left for an extra pie, which was gratefully, and knowingly, received by Cecil.

Not that he was a burden and he had done well to retain his independence and self-esteem. He still went to the local pub a couple of nights a week to play dominoes in the snug with his mates, and his old bones could just about manage a game of bowls. Despite Grace offering to help, Cecil kept to a routine, washing and cleaning for himself and did his own shopping.

Grace regularly assured Cecil that Peggy would be so proud of how he had coped but noticed the sad, wistful look that flitted across his face whenever her name was mentioned. She knew only too well that Cecil would do anything to have her back and missed his wife more than he could say.

Shaking off her gloom, Grace tried to be positive and be glad for Cecil. He was still independent and rarely ill, apart from the odd cold and the curse of arthritis. He was visited regularly by his daughters and grandchildren and had a small group of friends who he could pop out and visit. Still, she felt sad some days when she saw his solitary row of washing on the line that now lacked the vibrant, flowery blouses and dangly tights which blew gaily in the wind when Peggy was alive. Sometimes, at night, if she was reading, Grace could hear the blare of Cecil's telly through the walls. He always took his hearing aids out after his dinner so turned the sound up full blast but then, when silence fell and she knew he'd switched it off, Grace imagined him making his weary way upstairs, alone.

Seth told her that sometimes he'd see Cecil at the front window, sitting on the edge of the bed, just watching the world go by. Grace knew only too well what it felt like to go to sleep alone and when insomnia struck, spend hours wishing for the first chink of morning light to arrive and offer hope. During the day there was company, people to talk to and many distractions which helped push painful memories and depressing thoughts away. In stark contrast, during the lonely night hours, with an empty space in the bed to taunt you and a brain too full of worries to rest, you were regularly haunted by the past.

Grace remembered Cecil once saying that for a while, he resented the couples he saw together and felt like walking over to remind them how lucky they were, and not to take anything for granted. Now, Grace knew exactly how he felt and despite the generation gap, both of them had ended up single, even if it was for entirely different reasons. In her own way, Grace understood how it felt to be lonely and alone. The difference was, she had a choice, maybe Cecil didn't.

As she pulled into the drive, Grace saw the lights were blazing next door so she decided to ask Cecil to come round a bit earlier. He could watch telly with Seth while she cooked dinner and wrapped his pressie up in the garage. They were going to suggest that Cecil put his new bench in the front garden so he could chat to the neighbours and watch everyone go by, rather than do it from his bedroom window.

One thing was for sure, Grace was thoroughly sick of her current single status and after her holiday, her New Year's Resolution might just have to involve internet dating or, God forbid, putting herself at the mercy of Layla and her matchmaking skills. Whichever one she chose, anything was better than this.

CHAPTER 5

Amber lay on her bed flicking through a travel brochure, gazing longingly at images of the hotel in the Big Apple where she would be staying with Lewis. She knew everything there was to know about New York and had saved all the details on her phone so she could sneak a peek whenever she wanted.

The itinerary of their trip was ingrained in her memory anyhow, from their accommodation to the cruise they would take on the Circle Line around Manhattan Island, then shopping at Bloomingdales, Saks Fifth Avenue and Macy's. They were going to a cool diner to eat ham and eggs and maple syrup pancakes for breakfast, have lunch in the Hard Rock Cafe and dinner at The Four Seasons. Lewis had promised her a carriage ride in Central Park and Amber was praying it would snow, she was also praying for something else but after Seth's relentless sarcasm, she'd kept her wishes to herself.

All the girls at work were green with envy about her relationship with Lewis, however, she'd played the trip down, wanting to appear cool and quite accustomed to being whisked away on a first class jolly by *the* most eligible, good-looking guy that ever walked into the bank.

Amber did feel guilty about leaving her mum and had tried to persuade Lewis to go away for the New Year but his appointment book was literally heaving, so it had to be Christmas. She nearly passed out when Heidi said she was going to Elliot's parents. Why would anyone wish to spend time with the Grim Reaper and his wife? Thankfully, it had all been sorted out and her mum was going to have an adventure of her own, nevertheless, Amber would bring *the* best mum in the world a fab present back from New York. The idea appeased her conscience slightly yet no matter how hard she tried, she still couldn't erase a misty image of her mum, all alone on Christmas Day.

Amber knew that mums always put their kids first and that hers in particular would never let any disappointment show, or play the sympathy card. For that reason she was having trouble reconciling the thrill of her upcoming trip with concerns for her mother. Was her mum really excited or simply sacrificing herself for the good of her children? When these thoughts surfaced, the misty image became quite clear and made Amber's heart contract so she forced them away and focused instead on her secret mission. It was the only thing that made her feel better.

Amber knew it was imperative that she went away with Lewis. New York had to be perfect so she could seal the deal and secure their future. She was head over heels in love with him and on one or two occasions, had sensed he was going to confess his true feelings for her but the moment always passed and she was left hanging. Amber knew that her family thought she was pushy, man-mad and self-absorbed, but if that's what it took to realise her dream then so be it because at the end of the day, she wasn't asking for the earth. All she really wanted was what her mum and dad once had, a happy home and a little family. The difference was, that when Amber finally got her prize, she would learn from their mistakes and do absolutely anything to make things work, and never let Lewis go.

✳

Seth was downstairs in front of the TV, trying to ram everything for his holiday into a rucksack. He'd bought the largest one they had in Argos and he was still having trouble getting it all in. As he'd never been skiing before it was a bit difficult to know what to take, especially as the lads had planned lots of après-ski activities and he wanted to look his best for the hot chalet maids he'd been told about. When he emptied the contents onto the floor for the third time and all of his toiletries rolled out and under the sofa, Seth admitted defeat and decided to wait for his mum to get back from Tesco, she'd sort it out.

The minute he thought of Grace, and then surveyed the carefully ironed clothes she'd left in a pile for him, which were now crinkled and in a right mess, Seth's heart plummeted. He felt so bad about going away for Christmas and had tried really hard to convince the lads that the New Year would be the best time to go, but they all had to be back at work or had other commitments, so it had to be then. The only thing that eased the guilt was the fact that his sisters, and niece and nephew would be here, then that all went tits-up and now they were going away as well.

Seth really wanted to go skiing and was looking forward to it, yet at the same time would have been just as happy staying at home for Christmas. Even though his dad didn't live here anymore, he thought his parents had done a great job of staying friends and, since the split, the big day hadn't been ruined. He really admired them both for not tearing each other, or the family, apart and his dad even came to theirs for Christmas dinner, until Janice came on the scene, of course. Seth didn't mind admitting to anyone that he liked the familiarity of being around his family, and the traditions of Christmas Day, so this year it would all be a bit weird and for want of a better word, sad.

Seth was a big kid at heart and looked forward to opening his presents whatever time they finally got round to it. Skye and

Finn would turn up, in full-on hyper mode and fizzing with excitement, then once they'd calmed down he'd play endless board games with them or watch a festive film. The best bit was his mum's epic Christmas dinner that went on forever and then they would just spend all night watching telly, eating chocolates, mince pies and turkey sandwiches. He could even cope with the Klingons, especially as his twin cousins provided fair game for him and Amber, and their Uncle Jimmy was a comedy show in his own right.

Along with the rucksack dilemma, his mum's solo expedition was pecking at his brain and Seth was really worried about her going all that way on her own. For a start, she'd end up with about a hundred speeding tickets as she was totally oblivious to traffic cameras and just zapped about in her own world. The only reason she hadn't been booked near where they lived was because Seth had drummed it into her where all the speed cameras were when she took him for driving lessons.

Then, there was her abysmal map reading so Seth was borrowing a satnav from his mate – it was the only way she'd make it to the ferry port, let alone France! And the thought of her driving on the other side of the road, well it gave him the hot sweats. She was always going the wrong way in car parks despite the big, white, pointy arrows on the ground and God help her at roundabouts. He could guarantee she'd get confused and then there'd be carnage. Maybe he should make a sticker for the dashboard saying 'MOTHER – STAY ON THE RIGHT' or something on those lines.

Once his mum finally arrived at the cottage Seth knew she'd be fine and it would be nice for her to have a rest from looking after everyone and putting them first. His heart took another nosedive and Seth prayed that when it came down to it, despite all her bravado, that she wouldn't be lonely. Just the thought of her alone on Christmas Day was awful, so he cheered himself with the notion that he would bring her back a fab present from the Alps to make up for everything. Perhaps he could fit one of those cuckoo clocks into his rucksack. Hearing her key in the door Seth pushed his maudlin thoughts away and gathered all his bits and bobs into a huge pile, then decided to make his mum a nice brew before she got started on his packing.

Heidi wiped her swollen eyes and tried to pull herself together before Elliot and the kids got back from the park. It was the conversation with her sister-in-law Helen that set her off and now she was in full flow and could barely contain her anguish. Consequently, all the anxiety about her forthcoming stay with her parents-in-law, plus the debilitating guilt and sheer desolation she felt at abandoning her mum at Christmas, had finally got the better of her. Heidi had only rung to let Helen know that their gifts were in the post and should arrive soon. However, by the time she got off the phone, she was quite literally dreading their imminent trip, thanks to a few well-meant survival tips, courtesy of her sister-in-law.

Elliot's brother, Nathan, had always resented the fact that his older brother flew the coop and basically left him alone with their overbearing, pious, cold-fish parents. Over the years, he had never been able to find the courage to fly free, not until he met Helen, who slowly but surely managed to ease him away and limit the control his parents had over him. Once their two children were born, Nathan seemed to blossom and grow in strength and with Helen by his side, finally fledged.

They still maintained regular contact with Gordon and Vera, since they lived in the same village on the outskirts of Lincoln, but limited it to birthdays, Christmas and Bank Holidays, as more frequent visitations would have resulted in brutal murders. The same, dismal routine had continued until Helen and her syndicate at the supermarket where she worked, won the lottery.

It wasn't a life changing amount but just enough to give the house a face lift, buy a bigger car and, best of all, book a trip to Disneyland for Christmas. This meant that the senior Lambe's were home alone for the festivities and now, Heidi and Elliot felt duty bound to step into the breach.

Helen had warned Heidi that she had to be firm and stick to her guns where Gordon and Vera were concerned. There was no way she would ever agree to spending Christmas in their gloomy, stuck-in-the-seventies, rambling house, so always insisted they came to them for the day. Helen said enduring occasional mealtimes that were frugal, monotone and devoid of normal conversation was bad enough, so she couldn't imagine Christmas Day being much different. Not to mention the fact that they were so stingy they probably wouldn't even have the heating on, so Heidi should wrap up warmly or take thermals, just to be on the safe side.

By the time Helen had imparted her wisdom then hung up, Heidi was under no illusions whatsoever about what to expect from their parents-in-law, and the tears she'd held back for weeks burst their banks. At seven months pregnant, Heidi was in full bloom and enjoying her pregnancy but after a scare at eight months when she was carrying Finn, she was being over-cautious and slightly apprehensive. Her mum was her best friend, her rock and confidante who made Heidi feel safe so the last thing she wanted was to be parted from her, just as she was approaching the eight month stage again.

Heidi, the kids, and Elliot especially, loved going to her mum's on Christmas Day because from what he'd told her, the ones he remembered from his youth were polar opposites to the relaxed atmosphere at Grace's. Heidi knew it wasn't exactly perfect because there was always the inevitable tension with the twins, or grumbles from Great Aunty Ev. The house looked like a bomb had hit it by teatime and Amber and Aunty Martha always fell out about something or other. But as soon as she walked into the hall, it smelt and felt like Christmas and gave her that wonderful, priceless sensation of coming home. Not just the cinnamon candles or the dinner that was cooking in the kitchen, it was the noise and the mess and the scramble while they all opened presents. Most of all, it was the person that held it all together, who averted any crisis and calmed whoever's row, and that was Heidi's lovely mum.

Heidi couldn't bear the thought of Grace being alone at Christmas and had even suggested she came to the Lambe's with them – anything just to keep her close. But it would be like stepping on Gordon and Vera's toes and besides, Grace hadn't been invited so Heidi wouldn't dream of asking, it simply wasn't done.

Another downer was that now Heidi wouldn't even be able to do her Mega Boxing Day tea, which she looked forward to. Adding insult to her injured heart, she had spent all year saving up her Iceland points so she could put on a good spread. It was also her chance to cook for Grace and pamper her a bit but now it was all ruined. Worst of all, Skye and Finn were not a bit impressed with the plans – they weren't too keen on Elliot's parents, previous family visits having been tense. The kids were very observant and had instantly picked up on the atmosphere between their dad and strange grandparents.

Finn was also very concerned about Mr Grumpy, who, to Heidi's dismay, had taken to sitting in the chair on the landing. According to her son he wasn't very pleased that they wouldn't be there for Christmas and said he would miss them. Heidi really wished Finn wouldn't impart these nuggets of information on her because it freaked her out. She also secretly wished, that whoever Mr Grumpy was, he'd sod off outside and sit in the garden. The only thing Heidi could think of to appease her son was that if Mr G got really fed up he could always go and sit in the play tent and spend Christmas with the rest of Finn's invisible mates.

Heidi heard the sound of the creaky gate and then the children's voices as they ran down the path. Blowing her nose and checking her reflection in the mirror, she thought she'd just about get away with it. If Elliot did comment on her red eyes she'd blame it on hormones, as usual. To cheer herself up, Heidi decided that while they were in Lincoln she was going to look for an extra special present to give to her Mum after Christmas, something that would let her know how special she was, to every single one of them.

Ben was having a rubbish weekend. Janice was driving him up the wall and in his darkest moment was beginning to wish she'd never moved in with him. They'd spent all afternoon traipsing round the garden centre with her mother, despite the fact that they lived on the third floor of a block of flats and didn't even have a balcony. He'd planned to watch the Grand Prix and lose himself in *Escape to the Country* but the way he was feeling, even Outer Siberia wouldn't be far enough away from Janice at the moment. Since his one-way heart to heart with Grace the other day, he'd been doing some serious thinking and even a bit of soul-searching.

At first he was a bit offended by Grace's harsh words and honesty. He'd somehow fobbed Janice off by telling her they were talking about the kids and arrangements for Christmas and the travels of their brood. Even that narked him, the fact that he couldn't have a quick conversation in private about his own children.

That night, Ben lay in bed going over and over what Grace had said. Try as he might to convince himself that she was being over-dramatic or making a mountain out of a molehill, deep down, he knew she was on the money with her observations. Grace had no idea that they were just the tip of the iceberg because, in truth, Janice was taking over every aspect of his life, even down to his diet and his fuddy-duddy eating habits, as she called them. As far as Ben was concerned, there was nothing wrong with enjoying traditional English food but even this was seen as an irritation; his beloved pie and chips had been replaced by a range of recipes taken from Janice's organic cook book.

After Grace's tirade, he had plucked up the courage to ask Mike, a friend and colleague, if he thought that dyeing his hair was a bit naff and had any of the lads mentioned it. Mike went a bit red and then told him that actually, it did look a bit weird and the younger mechanics had taken to calling him Tom Jones. Ben was mortified. Just as Grace had insinuated, the lads he had trained up since they were kids and, up until now, respected him, were starting to see him as a joke.

After Mike made an excuse to leave, probably worried in case he was asked any more awkward questions, Ben had looked desolately from his office onto the car park below where his eyes came to rest on his shiny convertible. He hated that poncey car (chosen by you know who) and longed for his lovely Range Rover which had been his pride and joy. Ben remembered the day he'd collected it from the showroom and they all went for a day trip to the seaside, the kids, oohing and aaghing at the smell of new leather and the big bouncy off-road wheels. This realisation came as a bit of a shock, and then, without warning, something inside him snapped.

Ben was sick of being told what to wear and resented the fact that Janice had more or less binned most of his old but quite acceptable clothes. He did feel like mutton dressed as lamb in his red Converse and hated being dragged round Asda every Satur-day. Grace had managed to do the family food shop, solo, for twenty-odd years so it was beyond him why Janice couldn't cope by herself. Now, it was glaringly obvious that the excursion was intentional and specifically designed to prevent him from being with Finn and Skye.

Then, there was the way she rolled her eyes when one of the

kids rang him, like they were a nuisance or something. And he did want to go to the match with Seth, he loved football, and his easy-going son even more. As for Australia, the real reason for the trip was to visit Janice's sister. Grace was right, he did hate snakes and after being eaten by mozzies in Greece, the thought of the creepy crawlies which inhabited the land of Oz made Ben's tasty blood run cold.

Why should he sacrifice the relationship with his son, and Leicester City for reptiles and giant bugs? Then there was the subject of divorce. It wasn't even his idea and come to think of it, he couldn't quite remember how he got talked into proposing to Janice either, he only knew it might have been in the same way that she manoeuvred her way into his flat. One minute she was cooking the odd romantic meal, then her toothbrush appeared in the bathroom cabinet, next it was her clothes in the wardrobe and before he knew it, she was rearranging the furniture and his life. Ben put his head in his hands. Oh God, what had he done?

As he pondered on his predicament, he noticed the tofu salad and bottle of carrot juice that Cruella had packed for his lunch and Ben realised that the inoffensive, plastic container kind of summed up his situation. Every day he ate food he hated and when he went home, was trapped in a box with a woman he didn't even like anymore, let alone love. Not only that, Grace and the kids were annoyed with him. He was about to get divorced, then married, and worse, force his family out of their home, just because Janice wanted a new build and, God help him, probably a baby too.

His scrambled thoughts soon turned to Grace. How he wished they could have saved their marriage. He liked to think they did try but sometimes, Ben thought, they could have tried just a bit harder or maybe had a go at counselling rather than giving up and running away. He knew deep down that the spark had gone, that they were better at being friends than lovers but some couples carry on like that for years. What was wrong with making do, going through the motions, circling around each other and forging separate lives under one roof? Why did they have to be so honest with each other? They could've lied to themselves and pretended everything was okay, soldiered on for the sake of the kids and saved all this upheaval. Perhaps they were just selfish. Still, what was done was done and as much as he wished it were possible, he couldn't change the past.

Ben got up and made himself some strong coffee. He needed to clear his head and think straight. As he stirred two heaped spoonfuls of sugar into his tea (he'd been put on sweeteners at home by the Chief Inspector of the Misery Police) Ben felt like the loneliest man in the world. He had three great kids, two wonderful grandkids and a bloody brilliant, soon to be, ex-wife. The uncomfortable fact that he had somehow hooked up with a bunny-boiling control freak, threatened to ruin all of that. As Ben drank the hot liquid and focused on his ridiculous sports car, his life gradually came back into focus. While the caffeine swam through his veins, a small glimmer of hope and much awaited chink of illuminating clarity filtered into his brain.

It was useless wishing for Grace and the happy years, they were gone for good. He had even enjoyed his foray into the land of the singleton and the unexpected excitement that dating had brought. There was still life in the old dog yet and it was unfair on him, or Grace, to resign themselves to a future lacking love and even a bit of lust. One thing was for sure though, Grace was his best friend, the mother of his children and he had loved her since he was seventeen years old, he still did if he was honest, just not in the same way.

He was NOT going to let Janice destroy that, or the relationship he had with his kids. He didn't want that car outside, he hated sushi, loved sugar in his tea, checked shirts, Leicester City Football Club, Johnny Cash and Saturdays at the swimming baths with Skye and Finn, oh and sherbet lemons. He'd finally had enough and the worm turned. He was going to order a kebab for his lunch when the lads went to the chippy and he'd have a cream bun and a can of pop as well. And a Mars Bar!

If Janice didn't like the way he looked, or his family, or pea and ham soup, she could bloody well sod off. There were plenty more fish in the sea but before he could get out onto the ocean and catch a new one, there was the small problem of an annoying, clingy, great white shark that he had to shake off the line first.

CHAPTER 6

I t was Thursday, December 18th and quite mild for the time of year as Max loaded his car and attached his bike to the metal rack on the boot. He ticked off the list in his head: tickets, passport, wallet, briefcase, then ran back up the path and checked that his front door was locked – just in case. It had all been a bit of a rush to get ready in time. He hadn't planned to leave until the Saturday morning, however, events beyond his control had allowed him to get away early and make the most of the holidays, which was why he was up and about at the ungodly hour of 5.30am.

Thanks to the dodgy Victorian heating system at the school where he worked, the classrooms and halls had plummeted to temperatures deemed unsuitable by Health and Safety, which meant they were closed until the new term in January. Most of the teachers were still in work, marking coursework or lesson planning, but Max had managed to escape.

This was mostly down to the fact that the headmaster was one of his oldest mates and many years ago, his best man. Therefore, Max held Don solely responsible for not leaving him tied to a lamp post or failing to send him to John O'Groats on a mail train. Had Don not been negligent in his role of best man, he would've rendered Max incapable of making it to the church to marry Carmel, thus, wasting fifteen long, tortuous years of his life. It was a mistake that Max took great delight in reminding his guilt-ridden friend of whenever he needed a favour and, usually with a wry smile of resignation, Don could be relied upon to cut him some slack.

As he set off from Cambridge, Max felt his spirits lift and all his niggles and worries began to evaporate. He loved going to France. It was one of his favourite places and since his divorce four years ago he'd spent each summer there. He enjoyed sightseeing from his bike, taking in the variety of landscapes and passing through towns and villages on cycling tours with his club. In the evenings, they all took a well-earned rest, soaking up the atmosphere of cobbled squares, which were bathed in the setting summer sun, whilst sampling the delights of French cuisine.

It was the recollection of these happy memories that resulted in Max's spur of the moment decision to book a room for Christmas at a small place he'd stayed in on the way back to the port. The owners, Rosie and Michel were a great couple and he'd reserved a small gîte until the New Year. The hotel would be open up until Christmas Eve and he was looking forward to a few nice dinners and seeing them both again.

Since making the booking, there had been a few moments when he questioned the rationality of his actions but now he was on his way, Max was sure he'd made the right choice. During the drive down to Portsmouth, while listening intently to the travel updates on the radio, Max processed the events that had led him to be travelling across the Channel to spend the festive period alone. He certainly wasn't in the 'bah humbug' category of Christmas haters. He actually embraced the season of goodwill and enjoyed the buzz that it brought to school and at one time, his own home, with his wife, Carmel, and son, Jack.

Those days seemed so long ago now and Max had learned that it was imperative to separate the truth from fantasy. It was the best way to get through any disappointment and face the future, because looking to the past only reminded him of how deluded he had been. If one good thing was to come out of his marriage, apart from Jack, it was that he would learn from his mistakes.

They had met when they were both twenty-four, Max was beginning his career as a history teacher and she was embarking on the long road to becoming a solicitor. Once Carmel had achieved her goal, she agreed to get married, mostly because it was on her tick list and part of the grand scheme of things. They already had a nice home and were comfortable financially, so it seemed sensible to take the next step.

At twenty-nine, they finally tied the knot and had the full shebang: a big white wedding and a luxurious honeymoon in the Maldives. Max hoped that a baby would soon follow but to his dismay, Carmel resisted, insisting that it wasn't the right time and taking maternity leave was frowned upon within her company. He had to wait five long years for Carmel to deem it socially and professionally acceptable to reproduce and finally, Max was rewarded for his patience with a son.

Regretfully, that was as far as his dream of having a large family went. Carmel hated everything about pregnancy, and childbirth even more. It sometimes struck Max that his wife didn't seem all that enamoured with motherhood either, an unsettling concern which he forced to the back of his mind. When Carmel threw herself straight back into her career the minute she could squeeze herself into one of her power suits, his fears were further compounded. Max consoled himself in the knowledge that he had a son, a beautiful, high-achieving (extremely trying) wife, a home that wouldn't look out of place in a glossy magazine and a job he loved.

They trundled along for another seven years or so, reaping the rewards of Carmel's highly paid job, she was a divorce lawyer and worked for a firm that wasn't at all shy when it came to their fees. They took three lovely holidays abroad a year and more or less didn't want for anything in the material sense. Both of them enjoyed life to the full while at the same time, they were unconsciously drifting further and further apart.

While Carmel loved her office and job, Max loved the outdoor life, playing rugby and in particular, cycling. He was a member of clubs for both and was fortunate to have a decent group of friends with whom he participated in extracurricular social events and weekend trips away. He *should* have realised that Carmel was far too accommodating and possibly, near the end, quite relieved that he was off to Wales cycling or taking part in a rugby tournament in Scotland.

Similarly, his wife had her own friends and hobbies which entailed weekends at a spa, shopping trips to the city and girls' only holidays. Before long, it became necessary to sit down together and check Carmel's diary in order to arrange family time.

Max had always been irritated by her lack of parenting skills and sometimes, non-existent maternal instincts. She was adept at arranging Jack's timetable and childcare needs, but Max often suspected that it was more to do with allowing herself freedom rather than genuine concern for their son. He was the one who collected Jack from the nursery, the childminder's or doting grandparents' then gave him his tea and waited patiently with Jack for Mummy to come home.

You would've thought Carmel was the most perfect parent in the world when she breezed in, just in time for Jack's bath, a quick cuddle and then a bedtime story, making promises of treats at the weekend and special kisses for her best boy. Jack adored her, despite the minimal effort she put into caring for him and whenever Max mentioned the words 'quality time', he was rebuffed with the age-old excuse, that *she* provided everything Jack needed and their little boy wanted for nothing.

When Carmel hit forty, there may as well have been a tsunami whipping its way across Cambridge, wreaking havoc in their lives and turning their world upside down. Jack was seven and thankfully oblivious to the change in his mother. To him, she was beautiful, generous and made sure he had everything he wanted, which amounted to toys, the best birthday parties any child could wish for, play dates with his friends *and* she let him stay with his grannies and grandads whenever he wanted.

But Max knew Carmel was changing and whatever was going on in her head and possibly other areas of her increasingly secret life, it was starting to seriously affect their marriage. It began with her physical transformation. She had always been pretty and quite glamorous really, but suddenly it seemed that what God had given her just wasn't enough. Whether she was scared of getting old or being bypassed by the younger, prettier women at the office, Max never found out, because by the time she was forty-four his once naturally beautiful wife had breast implants, lip fillers, tattooed eyebrows, and hair extensions. And worse, their love life was practically non-existent and neither was any other kind of life if the truth be told. There was neither communication nor interaction, apart from the necessary coming together of minds to organise the collection or distribution of their son.

Max was at the end of his tether and felt like a man marooned on an island, even when he was sitting on the sofa watching TV while his wife ignored him, drank her wine and sent texts to whoever was at the other end of the phone. By the time Max finally plucked up the courage to ask her what the hell was going on, and if she was having an affair, Carmel pipped him to the post.

With stealth-like planning and calm execution, she was waiting for him when he came home one Friday evening at the beginning of the Easter holidays. With practised ease and the coldness of a professional quite used to addressing the legal counsel of some poor sod who was also losing his family and his life, Carmel proceeded to tell Max exactly how it would be.

'I'm taking Jack away for a fortnight and when I come back it would be best all round if you are gone. There's no point in dragging things out any longer, I want different things from life and we've just run our course.'

It later transpired that Carmel had failed to mention that one of the things she needed was the senior partner of her law firm. She also didn't see any need for a big fuss and was quite sure they could handle it all like adults. After self-righteously declaring that Jack would be fine and unaffected by the divorce, Carmel sanctimoniously announced that she was prepared to share him equally, starting from when they came back from holiday.

'Here, I think this might be of use. I've taken into consideration your salary and I think you'll find I've been fair and sensible. You need to bear in mind your responsibilities to Jack and find somewhere to live as soon as possible, that way his routine won't be disrupted. Two of the landlords on there are friends of friends so I'm sure you'll have no trouble, and I've opened a separate account for payments, just so everything is nice and neat.'

Carmel handed Max a typed breakdown of proposals for the separation of their joint finances and his expected contributions to Jack's upbringing. He noticed, with incredulous bemusement, that she had already made enquiries into suitable alternative accommodation on his behalf, and had helpfully ringed her personal favourites. Two weeks later, like an obedient puppy, Max moved out of his home and into an apartment within walking distance of Jack's school and as far away as possible from Carmel. Despite the protestations of his mates (who thought he was a right mug) he knew that resisting her would be completely futile, so he gave in. Max didn't have the energy, resources or the inclination to fight for his marriage and was sensible enough to recognise a more than worthy adversary in court.

After the shock and awe wore off and he'd managed to replace the rug that was pulled from under him, bitterness and resentment set in. He was forty-four and had lost everything. He saw Jack every weekend (which he knew suited Carmel down to the ground) and sometimes during the week if convenient to her. They had father and son holidays, educational day trips, pizza and DVD nights, and as far as he could make out, Jack really was coping and seemed happy enough, even with meeting Hugh, Carmel's bit on the side.

Before he knew it, four years jogged by and at forty-eight, Max had reached a turning point in his life. Jack was fourteen and even though they were still close, he needed his dad less and his teenage friends more. Obviously, Max was useful in the taxi driving and pocket money department, but most of the time he had to compete with coursework and the doe-eyed girls who hung out in the park; he was frequently the loser in the battle for his son's attention. Max couldn't quite put his finger on when he became unsettled and things started to change, because for ages, he thought he was doing fine.

After the divorce, he knew he was faced with two choices, sink or swim. Carmel may have stolen most things from him, but he was buggered if she would take his self-esteem. Fuelled by lingering bitterness and desperate to avoid disappointment, Max threw himself into rebuilding his life. He concentrated hard on filling it up, first with his son, then sport, teaching and, obviously, women.

He was pleasantly surprised where the female population was concerned and had no trouble meeting new people, either with or without the help of his friends and a very productive dating agency he saw on TV. He'd had a mixture of successes and a few near misses, but soon learned the ropes.

PATRICIA DIXON

It was imperative to sort out the desperate from the clinically insane, and the secretly married ladies looking for a bit of excitement from those with a ticking biological alarm clock. Then there were the fibbers who said they were approaching forty when in fact they were desperately fighting off sixty. More worrying, and a greater cause for concern, were those who wore so much make-up it was hard to tell if they'd finished their A levels or not. Maybe he was just punishing Carmel for breaking his heart, or at the very least, for giving him the illusion that the vows she'd taken on their wedding day meant something. Because they meant something to him – every single word.

Max tried to embrace all the positives about being single as it made his predicament easier to bear. He got a second crack at the whip where romance was concerned and had few responsibilities, apart from his monthly maintenance cheque, paying his bills and getting himself to work on time so he could educate his pupils (which he enjoyed anyway). Max didn't have to mow the lawn, talk to the in-laws, take out the bins, paint the fence, or any other mundane task allocated to him. He was free to make independent choices, raise or lower his own expectations as he wished. Max could eat curry from the carton, let the pedal bin overflow, watch *Top Gear* all day dressed in his boxer shorts, wash his bedding once a month (unless he was entertaining) and drink cheap instant coffee.

On the romance front, he avoided women with children under sixteen as he saw enough of them five days a week, and those in their thirties, who were hoping to hook a fertile specimen for breeding purposes. He didn't encourage meeting their families or tolerate a spare toothbrush in the holder over the sink and didn't agree to a romantic break to Alicante, either. Max thought he'd got it sussed with his casual, honest approach and always made it clear that he was *not* looking for commitment or even companionship, just some fun, a few laughs and whatever else the night may bring.

72

Unfortunately, he took his eye off the ball with Melissa, the new school secretary who he stupidly offered a lift home after a night in the pub. Melissa was alright-looking, slim, dark-haired and funny. She was even more entertaining after a few lager and limes and before he knew it, they were in his car, then on the sofa and when he woke up the next morning she was in his kitchen, making breakfast. Melissa turned out to be a rash that every single cream in the chemist couldn't get rid of, because Max tried, he really did try!

When he showed resistance to her charms, she sent him provocative notes which were borderline obscene. Melissa then took to bringing saucy messages into his lessons, pretending they were urgent and from someone or other, always leaving with a sultry pout and a cheeky wink, in full view of his very observant year elevens. Max knew she spied on him when he was on yard duty; he could feel her eyes burning into his head from the window. He'd even taken to paying one of the sixth formers to do his photocopying rather than go anywhere near her office.

He'd tried to tell her, the morning after the night before, that it was better to be 'just friends' and to keep what had happened between them hush-hush. Melissa was having none of it. The constant texts and phone calls almost wore him down, capitulation seemed the easier option. But Don, who was amused by and aware of the situation (especially the frilly knickers she left in his form room desk) begged him to resist and sagely warned his paranoid friend that she'd have him for dinner if he gave in.

It was the 'casserole in the staffroom incident' that broke Max. Because when he spotted her offering, lovingly left on the beverage table next to the custard creams, his name emblazoned for all to see on another dreaded note, securely stapled to the tinfoil, he FLIPPED!

Max marched straight down to Don's office, consumed by rage. During a slightly hysterical, bordering on desperate, conversation, he accused Melissa of sexual harassment, mental cruelty, stalking, being a pervert and guilty of writing obscene material that could cause offence to minors. She was making his life a misery and if he had a nervous breakdown he'd sue the school for neglect – and that was a promise!

'I mean it, Don. That nutter could teach Glenn Close a thing or two and I'm glad I haven't got a bloody rabbit because it'd end up in the stew. Yesterday she came into my year ten class and asked me to meet her in the gym at lunchtime... not out loud, it was written on one of her kinky notes. I nearly choked when I saw what she wanted to do on the vaulting horse and that little shit Edwards just had to point out to everyone that I'd got a cherry on. He's getting detention next week, and a D in his next essay.'

'Come on, Max, you've got to see the funny side and she is a bit of a looker. You should think yourself lucky having such an ardent admirer, but don't tell our Steph I said that otherwise I'll be in the pot with your rabbit.'

'I haven't got a sodding rabbit!' Max held his head in his hands, just in case it exploded all over Don's desk.

'Alright, just relax.' Don held up his hands in mock surrender. 'Now, why don't you take a seat and tell me what Melissa's been up to and I'll see if I can sort it out.'

Max huffed and pulled the chair out then seated himself in front of Don who he could tell was trying hard to keep a straight face.

'And there's no need to take a sarky tone with me. I'm not one of your self-righteous parents come to get their little angel out of trouble... and if you don't sort that headcase out I am going to dob you in to Steph and that's a promise.' Max folded his arms in defiance, then unfolded them when he realised he looked just like that little shit, Edwards, from year ten.

When Don stopped laughing (and crying a bit too) he managed to take some notes in order to convince his sweaty, red-faced friend that he was taking his complaint seriously. Once he'd calmed Max down and shuffled him off to last period, he sent for Melissa. In one of the most uncomfortable conversations he'd had in many years, Don gave his sullen secretary a verbal warning before she flounced off in a manner worthy of his most troublesome pupils.

Melissa left Max alone for seven whole days. For one joyous week he was relaxed, twitch free and unafraid of opening the register in case a note floated out. Then, just as he thought she'd moved on and had got the message, she began to take her revenge. Max had to give her credit where it was due though, because she was extremely thorough and must have put hours of thought into her very professional, one-woman, terror campaign.

It began with bizarre pizzas topped with disgusting combinations that only a psycho would order. After that he received an assortment of Chinese and Indian takeaways, which then progressed to skip firms insisting he'd ordered the biggest one in stock and numerous taxis tipping up at his door at various, unsociable hours of the day. It took ages to persuade the paramedic he wasn't suicidal or suffering from a schizophrenic disorder before he would leave and he was suddenly inundated with brochures for all manner of vague and slightly questionable products which gave him nightmares.

Melissa must have arrived at school extremely early to draw the face of the devil on his roll down whiteboard and taken great pleasure in snapping the nibs off all his pencils. Max could also have done without the smelly fish she'd taped under his desk or both of his bicycle tyres being punctured on the wettest night of the year. He fumed and cursed all the way home, soaked to the skin and battered by hailstones. Max swore then that he was off women for life and that when he got proof it was her, he was going to have her arrested or sectioned, or both.

Luckily for Max and the rest of the male teaching staff, Melissa ran out of luck the night she decided to pour paint all over his car. After tipping black gloss across his bonnet, she foolishly decided to drive home with one and a half bottles of Merlot inside her. Three zillion times over the limit and with traces of her dastardly deed all over her fingers, Mad Melissa was stopped by an eagle-eyed police officer when she drove through a red light in the town centre. After watching the CCTV footage of her wilful damage, her zooming through a red light and verbally abusing the police officer before throwing his hat into the middle of the road in temper (which was squashed by a lorry) the judge banned her from driving, gave her points on her licence and sixty hours of community service. She was then unceremoniously sacked from her position at the school.

For one whole year since the Melissa period, Max had been happily single, totally celibate and quite prepared to jog along with his peaceful, woman-free existence for the foreseeable future. And then one day, out of the blue, his feelings changed. Don blamed it on the male menopause, which at first Max laughed off, telling his friend that it was a figment of spiteful female imagination and their desire to burden the male population with one of their illnesses.

'There's no such thing, just like a mid-life crisis. They're just phrases that are designed to make men look stupid when in fact, there's sod all wrong with wanting a Ferrari or a hair piece.'

'You don't need a hair piece.' Don stopped mid-dart-throw and looked confused.

'I know I don't, I was just giving you an example, just throw the dart.' Even seeing Don miss the double didn't cheer Max up. 'I just think there's more to life than all this plodding because that's what I'm doing, treading water and being Carmel's lapdog and Jack's contingency plan. I need to change, or find a challenge but either way, something's got to give.'

'Well as long as your challenge doesn't entail you going on the hippy trail round Marrakesh because I've got nobody to replace you. You're not thinking of leaving... are you?' Don's hand hovered mid-air, the dart poised but redundant.

'No, I'm not going to abandon you... I don't think I could stand my own company as I backpacked around the world, I'm too bloody depressing for a start, not to mention cursed.'

When Don finally threw and scored a treble, Max held up his hands and simply mouthed – see.

When his feeling of being in the doldrums escalated into full-blown misery-guts syndrome, Max had a quick Google, just to check that Don was definitely barking up the wrong tree. After he ruled out menopause, Max decided to give himself a good talking to, or at least try and work out why he was so unsettled. He had a good job, a nice apartment in a converted warehouse that was stylishly furnished and fully equipped with boy's toys. Apart from his job, weekdays were quiet but bearable. He could mark coursework, go for a run, or if he felt like it, just slob around the flat doing whatever he liked. At weekends he'd play rugby or cycle, have a night out with the lads and go for a curry, spend time with Jack (spotty-girlfriends permitting) or visit his sister or their parents for Sunday lunch.

It was during a mammoth washing up session at his sister's house, that he spilled his guts about how fed up he was, and his little sister treated him to one of her 'say it like it is' home-truth sessions. Nadine's observations and analysis of his current crisis, whilst slightly harsh, had a ring of truth to them.

'Well I think you just need to grow up and stop shagging about because from where I'm standing you're simply punishing every woman you meet for Carmel's endless inadequacies. You need to decide whether you want an STD or a proper girlfriend who you can build a relationship with – and if you act like a normal human being it's highly possible you'll succeed.'

Nadine took the soggy tea towel from Max and hung it over the radiator to dry before adding, 'You've just got too used to sitting in your posh flat night after night, thinking you've got it made. Everyone needs someone to love, Max, and now you're pushing fifty, you'd best get your finger out otherwise you'll end up a lonely, bitter old man.' Nadine stood on her tiptoes and kissed Max on the cheek then left him to ponder her words.

As Max drove home that night, Nadine's advice swam through his brain and was impossible to ignore, however hard he tried. They had stung a bit, but definitely hit home. For days after, while he lay in bed at night, drank his tea in the staffroom or tried to concentrate on the causes of the Second World War, the gloom that had settled all around him wouldn't lift.

He hadn't even considered that he might be lonely, how could he be? He had loads of friends, things to do if he wanted, people to chat to at work or on the phone and was always being invited for dinner or weekend barbeques. Most of the time, he declined. His mates were a good laugh and their wives or girlfriends always welcomed him into their homes, going out of their way to make him feel comfortable and fit in. But that's what bugged him. He was getting tired of being the odd one out, the charity case who they felt sorry for, who was casually positioned in the middle of the table so he could join in and be included, not plonked at the end of the row like a spare part.

This was precisely when Max had his eureka moment. He'd hit the nail on the head. He was the odd one out. The friend they felt sorry for, the irritating, partner-less bloke that they couldn't leave out but caused them a dinner party, seating plan conundrum. Max realised that lately, he'd been subconsciously avoiding social gatherings because it was easier to turn down an invite than to make the effort and cheerily pass round the bread rolls, and, worst of all, go home alone. He worked it all out during the Russian Revolution while year ten diligently completed their fact sheets. As his students pondered the predicament of Czar Nicholas, Max took stock of his whole life.

It *had* become far too easy to retreat into the safe environment of his flat and daily routines. If he so desired (apart from interacting at work and with Jack) it was perfectly feasible to avoid contact with real-life people. He could shop for everything he needed online without even stepping outside his front door. On the occasions he ventured into the supermarket, he'd use a self-service checkout, thus ruling out the need to make conversation with the chirpy assistant. He hadn't been to his bank for years, he managed his affairs online and last Christmas he'd bought every single present from Amazon.

The word 'Christmas' sparked new anxieties and he could foresee exactly how it would pan out this time around. He would sit at the table and fake being jolly. His mother would give him the breast of the turkey and an extra roast potato to make up for the fact his ex-wife and child were elsewhere. His sister Nadine, husband Nick and their daughter Ellie would kindly include him in all their jokes and cracker pulling. He would wear his paper crown and be thankful for his three-year-old niece who made up the numbers to a nice round six, preventing a gap in the chairs and the silent message the empty space conveyed. At the end of a day of merriment, he'd be loaded up with gifts and leftover turkey, enveloped in too-tight hugs from his mother and face the rest of the night alone.

Max knew he was getting down to the nitty gritty and forced himself to face the truth head on. Yes, he still enjoyed going to rugby practice or the cycling club but after the activity was over and the changing room banter ended, what did he have? Once he'd waved off his mates who all had someone to go home to, Max was left with the rest of the evening to navigate. By the time he'd microwaved a ready meal and watched the news, he was pretty much done. Max pictured himself as he opened the door to the apartment. No cooking smells came wafting down the hall, no noise from the TV or radio. No cheerful voice shouting out 'hello' and no one with whom to impart the immortal words 'Hi, honey, I'm home'.

He'd forgotten what it was like to chat over dinner or have someone to listen to him grumble about work, or simply laugh with. Admittedly, Carmel wasn't exactly a domestic goddess or his spiritual rock, but at least for a while, she was there, some company and a reason to go home at night. Max missed having a special name in his phone, at the top of his contacts list, someone to buy gifts for, to take out to dinner or stay in with. He needed closeness and human contact but in a more honest, mutually beneficial, long-term situation than a one-night stand.

Since Melissa, Max realised he'd not only lost confidence, he'd slipped into his own version of self-enforced solitude. His one-man routine had crept up on him and was threatening to swallow him whole, he knew he had to change. Exactly how, was another matter entirely.

By the time he got home the Bolsheviks were long forgotten but his worries remained, and when Max let himself into the flat, the silence engulfed him. By the time he'd scrambled some eggs and eaten a tin of rice pudding, Max had come to a decision. He was going to burst out of his shell and change the course of his life. He was sick of being single but there was no way he'd go down any of the routes he'd previously taken. Instead, he would let fate take its course and if he did stumble upon someone wonderful along the way, all well and good.

After two cups of tea and a packet of Jaffa cakes, Max was feeling proactive and ready for action. He started by ringing Nadine so he could commence with step one. His sister was integral in the grand scheme of things because at the weekend, Max was going to buy himself a dog.

80

CHAPTER 7

Five months had passed and even if he did say so himself, Max thought his attempts at self-preservation and reinvention had gone quite well. Nadine worked from home and already had two golden retrievers of her own, so he hoped that one more member of the canine community to keep an eye on during the day wouldn't be too much of an ask. Once he'd explained why he wanted a dog and felt that it was unfair to leave a puppy in the flat all day, she willingly agreed.

One month later, Max was the proud owner of Ginger, his very own red setter, new best mate and trusty companion. Max dropped Ginger off on the way to work and collected him from Nadine's in the evening. He was an excuse to take long walks in the park and have a friendly chat to the other dog walkers on his regular route. He made frequent trips to the supermarket, and the butchers for the odd meaty treat – online grocery shopping was now banned in favour of the old-fashioned way.

It was quite nice to have someone to talk to in the evening even if they weren't exactly the greatest conversationalist in the world. Ginger always seemed politely interested in what he had to say and they enjoyed their nights in, watching TV on the sofa and playing fetch in the hall. Max agreed wholeheartedly with Nadine that Ginger wasn't a substitute for a real human relationship but for now, his dog was very good company and lifted his spirits no end.

Ginger was also a magnet where Jack was concerned. Max tried to ignore that since the puppy's arrival, his son had become a much more frequent visitor to the flat and even turned up with his friends which was nice. It gave Max the opportunity to get to know his son's mates and talk to the faces beneath the beanie hats. And then there was the cycling.

Max wanted to find a common bond or hobby that he and his only child could participate in, and since the 2012 Olympics, cycling had become a cool sport, probably due to Bradley Wiggins being 'a bit of a dude' as Jack said. Following a visit to the cycle shop, trying out different bikes and accessories, Max left the store a few quid lighter, while his son wore a beaming smile and was the proud owner of a spanking new racer. Since then, they had spent Sunday mornings exploring the countryside around Cambridge and the afternoons at the flat with Ginger, refuelling on pizza and watching a film.

As for women, well, Max was still waiting for the right one. In the meantime, he had struck up a few innocent conversations at the pet shop and in the vets with fellow dog lovers. Had he felt so inclined Max could have pursued one or two but he found it was a refreshing change to just talk. He was also relaxed and confident when he attended a fiftieth birthday party that was liberally scattered with eligible, unattached females, however, on this occasion, Max preferred to enjoy the celebration, rather than scoring.

Step two had been booking a holiday. This year he refused to be the odd one out. No more sad Uncle Max, the spare-part, geeky friend or the lonely son, who sat gratefully waiting for his portion of Christmas pudding. Max decided to free everyone of his burden and take himself and Ginger away for the festive period. He'd kept the number of the place he'd stayed during his summer holidays so after checking out ferry times, Max booked himself a two-week break in France. He intended to breathe some fresh air into his lungs and blow away the cobwebs of the past then return in the January ready to face the New Year head on.

Max took a quick peep behind him and smiled at Ginger who was fast asleep, sprawled out on the back seat of the car. They were almost at Portsmouth and as he approached the terminal he could see the Spinnaker Tower lit up on the coastline and the lights from the ferries waiting in the port. It was still dark and there were hardly any other cars on the road, apart from early morning commuters and other excited travellers heading to the docks.

His boot was loaded with Christmas presents from his family and plenty of warm clothes as they were expecting temperatures in the minus over in France. Max knew that most people would've been dreading a Christmas Day alone, but it was just one day, and he would cope. For the rest of the time he was looking forward to walking and cycling, visiting the historical gems of the Loire and recharging his worn-out batteries.

Pulling off the M27 into the ferry port, a sense of excitement filled his soul. This had been the right decision, he could feel it in his bones and for the first time in a while, Max was actually looking forward to Christmas.

Grace had been forced to stop for coffee at the service station on the A34, but after a double espresso and a wee break for Coco, she was back on her way and wide awake. As she approached the ferry terminal she could see the yellow lights glowing in the goods yards and the cranes overhead moving containers and loading ships. While most of Portsmouth slept, the docks and harbour were alive with passengers and workers, ready for a new day to begin.

Once she'd passed through the check-in booths and Coco had his microchip zapped, Grace let him stretch his legs as she took in some air and her surroundings. There was already a long queue of cars waiting for the 8.15am ferry to Caen and now she was here, she was glad she'd chosen this option. It would be a three hour drive down to the Loire once she got off the ship later that afternoon, but this way she'd have at least an hour of driving in the light to get used to the roads before darkness fell. All the other ferries left later and she didn't fancy driving through the night or taking an overnight boat. Coco would have had to stay in the car or a kennel for twelve hours and for his first time on the sea, Grace thought it would be unfair. Now he could have a good kip and a nice chew bone and they'd be there much quicker.

Grace decided to text the girls and Seth, who was in the Alps, just so everyone could breathe a sigh of relief that she'd actually made it to Portsmouth all by herself. She had just finished setting everyone's minds at rest when the marshals began waving the cars through. She put her car into gear and drove forward, passing the customs sheds before joining another queue in front of a huge ship. Grace felt those bubbles of excitement fizzing inside again and she couldn't wait to get on board. She turned round to stroke Coco who was curiously looking through the windows and she knew for sure that she'd done the right thing; for the first time in months, she was really looking forward to Christmas.

Grace felt a bit mean as she left Coco in the car but promised faithfully to come back later and take him for a walk. Her faithful hound looked unperturbed by her departure and stretched out on the back seat, eagerly tucking into his Jumbone.

The self-service restaurant was filling up as Grace waited her turn at the cashier station. She was really looking forward to breakfast; starting as she meant to go on by resisting the full English menu and opting for French fare, even if it was just coffee, fruit salad and a croissant. There was a sudden rise in the noise levels as a large group of schoolchildren made their way into the restaurant, all wearing 'I Love London' T-shirts or silly hats with the Union flag on. As she turned to look, a male voice behind her spoke.

'Looks like we made it just in time. I wouldn't like to be behind that lot in the queue.'

Grace looked up to meet the face that spoke the words and was rendered temporarily speechless.

She was staring into deep brown eyes, protected by long dark lashes and *the* most gorgeous face she'd been this close to in a long time. He had dark wavy hair, just long enough to be cool but short enough to be classed as groomed and stylish and a hint of midnight shadow was visible on his angled cheeks. She realised that he had caught her on the hop and grappled for something to say as she felt herself blushing like one of the schoolgirls in the queue.

'I know. There must be a hundred of them! I'm so glad I got my croissant first because they'll probably run out, unless there's someone baking away like mad in the kitchen. I'll make sure I'm in here early for lunch, just in case they all come back and they run out of chips.' Phew, that didn't sound so bad, Grace thought nervously, reassuring herself as she shuffled along with her tray.

'Well, I rejected the fruit salad and went for the unhealthy option, but I am on holiday after all so I thought I'd treat myself. Look, I got a bottle of orange, just to balance the books.' The man smiled at Grace as he wiggled his bottle of juice in the air as if to prove his point.

'Oh, well that definitely absolves you of any sin then.' Before Grace could continue the conversation it was her turn to pay. Once she'd handed her money over and picked up her tray, she turned to say bye.

'Enjoy your breakfast and have a good trip, I hope the sea stays flat otherwise all that might be making another appearance,' she said before scooting away to find an empty table and calm down.

Grace was staring out to sea, cup in hand, trying to look cool. She could see 'Handsome Man' out of the corner of her eye and was half hoping he'd come and sit near her. She couldn't believe that the thought had even crossed her mind and knew full well she'd poo her pants if he did. Anyway, he walked in the opposite direction and the moment was lost. Grace concentrated her thoughts on her food and not long after she felt the engines rumble into life and hoped that Coco wouldn't be scared by the noise. With graceful ease, she felt the ship gently pull away from the moorings and begin its journey out of the harbour. Not wanting to miss a thing, she finished her food quickly, drained the last of her coffee, grabbed her bag and made her way to the stairs that led to the upper decks.

Sailing past the grey navy ships and ancient dockyards, Grace allowed the cold December air to fill her lungs as it pinched at her cheeks and made her nose freeze. Passing a funfair and modern apartment blocks along the way, Tudor pubs and old sea walls, the harbour opened out into the Solent and the ship passed the large round forts guarding its entrance. Grace climbed to the top deck and relaxed in the morning winter sun that lit the crests of the waves whenever it broke through the clouds. She sat there quite contentedly, watching the smaller ferries and tugs making their way back and forth and once she'd glided past the Isle of Wight, decided her feet and bottom were getting a bit numb so headed downstairs for a look round the shops.

After passing an hour looking in the gift shop and perfumery,

Grace heard the call for dog owners to go downstairs to the car deck. Eager to check on Coco, she set off down the narrow stairs and into the noisy parking area where she found her dog, fast asleep. Tapping gently on the glass as she peeped through the window, he opened a sleepy eye and began wagging his tail happily when he spotted the boss. A few minutes later they were at the back of the ferry in a small outside area set aside for dog walking. There were a couple of other passengers there already, braving the wind and the swell of the sea as it whipped around the ship. Coco was busy sniffing and seemed oblivious to the other dogs or the motion of the deck under their feet as it rocked to and fro. Grace had noticed that as they ventured further out to sea, the choppier it became so kept well away from the edge. No matter how much she loved her dog, her hands were freezing so once Coco had performed, she decided to put him back in the car where it was warm, top up his water and then head off upstairs.

Grace was trying to make her way back to the car but Coco was hindering her progress by sniffing every single tyre they passed – then she spotted 'Handsome Man' coming her way. Her first thought was wow, he really is fit, and then, bloody hell, I bet my hair looks like Ken Dodd's. Trying to casually tidy herself up before he spotted her, Grace continued onwards, dragging Coco between the vehicles and waiting for their paths to cross.

Max couldn't believe his luck when he saw the redhead from the restaurant. It had only been a brief conversation but when she'd smiled back and teased him about his breakfast, his heart had performed a weird flip-flop inside his chest. Then it was his turn to pay and he'd wanted to respond with something witty but the cashier was eyeing up the huge group of approaching school-children and looked impatient, and before he knew it, the redhead was gone.

While he was paying, a voice in his head was daring him to find a seat near her table. Max could see her from where he stood, she was by the window looking out to sea and drinking her coffee. But he'd lost his bottle and carried his tray in the other direction while the voice in his head shouted loudly, CHICKEN!

Now, 'Red' as he'd nicknamed her was right there in front of him, so it must be fate.

'Hi, fancy meeting you again, is this your dog? Hey, fella, how do you like being on a ship, not feeling sick I hope?' Max bent down to stroke the chocolate Labrador and gather his wits. He couldn't believe his luck.

'I think he's fine. It's Coco's first time on the high seas, or any sea come to think of it, but he seems to be coping. How about your little one, he's gorgeous, it is a he, isn't it?' Grace crouched down to stroke the puppy.

'Yes, Ginger's one of the boys. I think he's doing okay. He was flat out when I got here but couldn't wait to get out of the car. I was up on deck getting some air so I didn't hear the announcement the first time and had to run before they locked the doors again. What's it like out there? It's *so* noisy down here with the engines. I wouldn't be able to sleep with that racket.' Max was desperate to make conversation but knew he had to go outside with Ginger. If only he hadn't missed the call, he could've spent longer talking to those emerald green eyes.

'It's really windy and wet! I was a bit nervous about going near the edge as well, but at least Coco got some fresh air and it's eased my guilty conscience about leaving him alone.' Grace ruffled her dog's head.

When the concierge called out to Max that he should hurry because he needed to secure the doors to the car deck there was no time for him to suggest they meet for a coffee later, or for Red to accept.

'Right, I'd better get a move on, otherwise Ginger will be

crossing his legs for the rest of the journey, come on, boy.' Crest-fallen, Max obediently shot off towards the dog walking area under the scrutiny of a very impatient crew member as Red nodded in agreement before saying a quick goodbye and heading towards her car.

After settling Coco, Grace made her way to the restaurant for some lunch. She still felt flustered and slightly annoyed with herself, but she knew it would be a long drive to the hotel and she needed something to fortify her for the journey. Perhaps, if she was lucky, Ginger's owner might just come along and join her. Grace managed to make her lunch last for about an hour before admitting that he wasn't going to show and even if he did, she'd look like a right saddo if he walked in now. Pride eventually forced her to get up and find somewhere else to pass the remainder of the crossing.

Two hours later, after a rocky ride over the Channel, Grace could see land on the misty horizon. She'd spent the journey in the lounge, trying hard to concentrate on her book while keeping a covert eye out for Ginger's dad. Now, she felt really, really stupid. How cringeworthy was it, at her age, to get the hots for a stranger on a boat? And worse, be sitting there like a lovesick teenager hoping for a glimpse of him? As the ship docked and the passengers were called down to their respective car decks, Grace made a concerted effort to look straight ahead and not search the crowd for his face. On the car deck, she unlocked her door and climbed inside, and just to pass the time until they disembarked, fussed over Coco while averting her gaze from the window.

Max felt dreadful. He'd started feeling a bit queasy just before he went down to walk Ginger, that's why he was on deck, sucking in huge gulps of air and trying to convince himself not to be sick. Unfortunately, his quick visit to the back of the boat and the sight of the rolling waves eventually got the better of him. He managed to get to the toilets, just, where he spent an embarrassing time retching loudly and depositing his fry-up into the loo. Once he thought the worst was over, Max made his way on wobbly legs to the outside decks. He tried to gain his composure, sitting forlornly on one of the benches, eyes closed, facing the front and praying for the journey to be over, soon.

He'd made this crossing many times and had never been sick, but in the past, he'd spent much of the summertime journey in the bar with his friends, oblivious to the outside world and the swell of the sea. This time, in between hanging over the sides and praying nobody down below was suffering from splash-back, his mind wandered to Coco's mum. Max had fully intended to search for her after he'd put Ginger in the car. He presumed she'd be in the restaurant at lunchtime but even the *thought* of food set him off, so he stayed put. He almost froze to death on that bench but it was either that or the men's toilets and he thought he'd look a bit dodgy if he lingered there too long.

As he saw the coast of France appear on the horizon, Max let out a silent cheer. His stomach was beginning to settle so he braved a trip below to buy a bottle of water. Red was nowhere to be seen in the restaurant and owing to the size of the ship and his fragile stomach, he knew it would be a futile search and a bit risky at the same time. Imagine if he found her then mid-conversation, as he offered to buy her a coffee, he went green and then threw up all over his shoes, or hers!

Max waited until the very last minute before he went down to his car, there was no way he wanted to embarrass himself in front of all the drivers on Deck Four. He didn't even have time to search the car windows and see if he could spot her face, then perhaps give her a friendly wave, so when he started up the engine and drove down the ramp, Max resigned himself to the fact that Coco's mum was somewhere ahead, driving into the sunset and would go down in his history as the one that got away.

Grace set the satnav as she waited in the queue for the gendarme to check her passport. If she was honest, she was incredibly nervous about the next leg of her journey and silently dreaded hitting the autoroute. Would it be a disaster, driving in a foreign country and all it entailed, especially without someone sitting beside you to give you confidence or help with directions? But she was here now and she'd just have to get on with it, take her time and concentrate.

Two hours later, Grace and Coco were still alive and had tentatively negotiated the *Périphérique Ouest* and were tootling along the N137, listening to tunes from Radio *Allouette* and the intermittent advice from the chap on the satnav. It was pitch black now and as they headed across country, Grace pushed her concentration levels up a notch while she negotiated the roads. They were soon passing through small villages and towns and despite the need to keep an eye on where she was going, Grace couldn't help but admire the festive decorations that adorned the buildings and houses along the way. Each village had a church, it must have been some kind of French law, because despite the fact that some were quite small, their places of worship were huge in comparison. Without exception, they were either festooned with lights, or garlands, or both. Some had beautiful stable scenes with large colourful statues of the nativity family. Lining the narrow streets were twinkling fairy lights, snowflakes, candles and angels, and as she drove further into the countryside, farmyards and small cottages dotted along the route had decorated their roofs and gardens.

There was still quite a bit of activity in the sleepy hills of the Loire, despite the hour. She overtook slow moving tractors transporting huge wheels of hay and what she suspected were commuters, heading home from the city. Grace wound the window down to let in some fresh air and was surprised by the arctic blast that whipped around her cheeks and hands. The temperatures must have dropped considerably since leaving England and Grace looked forward to her log fire and a cosy bed. The festive displays and warm glows from inside the houses she passed along the way were in stark contrast to the chilly wind and icy lanes outside, but it made her feel even more Christmassy and eager to reach her destination. Feeling secretly very pleased with herself and despite being tired, the fizzy bubbles of excitement and the thrill of expectation spurred her onwards. She couldn't wait to arrive and meet Rosie. Tomorrow, after a good night's sleep, Grace could begin her French adventure.

CHAPTER 8

It was 7.30pm when Grace passed the sign that said *Bienvenue* and then pulled into the gravel courtyard of *Les Trois Chênes* and the quaint hotel was just as it looked in the photos on the website, but so much more magical in the moonlight. The white painted frontage was lit up with yellow-gold rope lights, which ran the length of the building and up the peaks of the roof. On the large porch stood a huge pine tree which twinkled grandly, waiting to welcome you in.

Grace made her way to the entrance but before she could ring the ornate silver bell to announce her arrival, the front door was swung open and a tall blonde with a beaming smile beat her to it.

'You must be Grace, I'm Rosie. Welcome to our little hotel. Did you find us okay? I've been keeping an eye out for you and was praying you wouldn't get lost. Come in and let me get you a drink, or would you prefer to go straight round to the gîte?' The smiling woman named Rosie was effervescent and put Grace instantly at her ease.

'If it's okay with you, I'd like to get to the gîte. I'm dying to see it and I think my dog is getting a bit fed up of being in the car, he's been very patient up until now but even Coco has his limits.'

Grace hoped she hadn't offended Rosie but she really was tired and wanted to get settled in.

'Not a problem. Give me two ticks while I tell Michel that I'm nipping out and then we'll get you organised. Just wait there.'

And with that she was off, leaving Grace to listen to the sounds of a French love song playing on the antique radio in the corner and admire the cosy lounge with its comfy armchairs and huge roaring fire.

By the time Rosie came back, Grace couldn't wait to sit in front her very own log burner and relax.

Once they were back in the car, they turned right, out of the gate and along a dark, very bumpy lane, following a row of thorny hedgerows. Rosie chattered all the way, pointing out the home of their closest friends, Dominique and Zofia.

'They've always got plenty of fresh eggs for sale if you fancy a taste of the countryside. I said the very same thing when I welcomed another new arrival about thirty minutes before you, I sound like a broken record sometimes. And you'll have more neighbours soon because the other two gîtes will be full by the weekend. On one side you'll have some of Zofia's family from Poland, she's also expecting her daughter and grandchildren but couldn't fit everyone into her house so they're using our gîte as an overspill.'

Pausing for a second, Rosie told her to take the next right, through the farm gate and into a field that was actually situated behind the hotel. Driving slowly forward, Grace flicked her lights on to full beam and followed the gravel path that wound around the perimeter.

She spotted them instantly, four stone gîtes of varying proportions, lit up by glowing yellow lanterns on either side of the door. Rope lights traced the shape of their slate roofs and reminded Grace of the little wooden chalets at the Christmas markets back home. It looked like a tiny, secluded village.

'Oh, Rosie, I can't believe this is where I'm staying. They're perfect!'

'Yours is the second one from the end, keep going and park at the side. There's actually a space around the back for cars, but tonight just leave it here while you unpack.'

Parking in front of her new home, Grace got out of the car, desperate to get inside. It really was cold now and Coco was already sniffing the air and getting agitated so she asked Rosie if it would be okay to let him go for a wander.

'Sure, he'll be fine, he can run wild and free here.'

After opening the car door and watching Coco leap from the seat and bound into the darkness, Grace and Rosie stepped onto the veranda that held a wooden table and chairs.

Here, Rosie took a key from her pocket and opened the door then motioned for Grace to look.

'Come inside and see your Christmas cottage. I hope you'll enjoy your stay here.'

A blast of warm air, then the scent of wood smoke and pine oil invaded her senses as she took in the scene before her. The downstairs room was an oblong and sectioned into two by a long breakfast bar. At the rear was a kitchen made from light oak and above the cooking area, overlooking the lounge, was a mezzanine with twisted pine spindles.

Grace took in the lounge area where, set on the stone chimney breast wall was a glass-fronted log burner, which provided the centrepiece of the room. A large coffee-coloured sofa was positioned in front of the roaring flames, flanked by two matching armchairs. A pine coffee table was set between the fire and the seating area and in the corner was a decent size television.

Rosie switched on the chunky cream lamps that stood on either side of the dining table at the edge of the room and then led Grace to one of the doors at the back of the kitchen. In here was a small bedroom with a double bed and mirrored on the opposite side, another room with two sets of bunk beds. In the centre was a small bathroom with adjoining doors.

'We usually have large families here during the summer, that's why I thought it might be too big for you but once you've seen upstairs, I'm sure you'll be happy. Come on, I'll show you.' Rosie smiled and once again, led the way.

The wooden stairs led to the mezzanine level, where, in the centre, stood the most inviting king size bed Grace had ever seen. It was covered in a festive red patchwork bedspread and scattered with big squashy pillows and cushions. There was an antique oak dresser and matching wardrobe and over in the corner, a compact en-suite bathroom.

'So, do you like it, are you sure you will be okay here?' Rosie looked expectantly at Grace.

'I think it's amazing. You've used the space so well and I don't know what you were worried about. I think it's really cosy and I love it up here. It's so warm, you can feel the heat rising from the fire.' Grace went over to the balcony and looked down onto the lounge below and couldn't wait to put her feet up and wind down with Coco, which was when she remembered they'd left him outside.

'Flipping heck, Coco! I hope he's not wandered off.'

Rosie and Grace turned and made their way quickly down the stairs and opened the front door, both calling out Coco's name. Within seconds, two green, shiny eyes appeared in the darkness as he came bounding towards them, tail wagging and tongue hanging out. He'd obviously been having a good time exploring and didn't seem at all traumatised by being left in the wild. They made their way back up the steps, followed by Coco, who, once he was inside and after a good look round his new home, plonked himself in front of the fire and started to nod off.

'Right, I'll be off now. I've left your welcome pack in the kitchen so you should survive until morning. There's a comprehensive booklet in the drawer over there, telling you all about the area and where everything is, but if you need me in the meantime, for anything at all, just ring my mobile number. The Polish contingent should be arriving after lunch tomorrow so you won't be disturbed and can have a nice lie in.' Rosie gave Grace a quick hug and went to the door.

'I'm sure I'll be fine and thank you again for everything, but I don't think I'll be lying-in. I can't wait to see what everywhere looks like during the day. Will you be okay in the dark by yourself, oh, and who will be on the other side of me, you didn't say?' Grace could feel the icy wind whipping around the veranda and pulled the door closed to keep in the heat.

Rosie placed her hand reassuringly on Grace's arm. 'Oh, I'm fine. I'm used to wandering around in the dark and the path is lit by solar lamps, we only live on the other side of those trees, just behind the hotel.' Rosie pointed to a small area of woodland further along the path where a soft glow could be seen through the copse.

'There's a chap on his own in the end gîte and your other neighbours will be my André and his partner, Wilf. André is my surrogate dad and spends the year travelling in a camping car, we English say motorhome, but "when in France" and all that. Anyway, they always come home to roost for Christmas and the worst of the winter, and live in the gîte next door. He'll turn up sometime tomorrow.' Rosie wrapped her scarf around her neck and then turned back to face Grace.

'That reminds me, we're having a get together tomorrow evening for all our guests and the returning wanderers. Please come along. It's very informal and if you want to eat in the restaurant later, I'll book you in. Don't be shy, I promise to look after you and everyone is very friendly.' Rosie lingered, giving Grace time to think.

'I'd love to come and yes, book me a table. I want to make the most of every second, so some French cooking would be perfect.'

Grace was determined to enjoy herself and not be a complete hermit or a stick in the mud, either.

With that, Rosie gave her the thumbs up and set off towards the top of the field. Grace closed the door and ran over to the huge sofa and jumped on it with glee. Coco lifted a sleepy eye, checked on his mistress then slowly rolled over to toast the other side of his body.

Rosie made her way along the path towards home and as she passed the end gîte, the door opened and out ran a bouncy red setter, followed by his owner, wrapped up in a warm jacket, ready to face the frosty night air.

'Hi, Max. Hi, Ginger. Are you off for your night-time walk?' Rosie loved dogs and stroked the giddy puppy before he shot off into the darkness.

'We're not going far. I'm shattered and need a kip so this is his last run round for the night. Has someone else arrived, I heard a car pull in?' Max rubbed his hands together as he spoke.

'Yes, a lovely lady called Grace. You'll be able to meet her tomorrow at my little soiree. Don't forget, seven o'clock, and I've booked you a table in the restaurant for later.' Rosie could see puffs of mist form in the cold air as she spoke.

'Don't worry, I'll be there. I can't wait to sample Michel's food again, now that my stomach's settled a bit. Do you want me to walk up to the house with you, it's very dark?'

'No, I'll be fine. Night night, see you tomorrow, have a good day cycling and take care on the roads.' And with that, she made her way home.

Rosie cut through the copse to see the welcome glow of the lights from her converted barn and smiled smugly to herself. She loved it when a hunch paid off and one of her matchmaking plans started to come together. Rosie had a nose for romance and was a good judge of character as well. From the minute she heard Grace's tentative voice on the phone, she'd sensed a lost soul and could hear the apprehension and then the disappointment in every word. Rosie had been somewhat elated when the opportunity arose to ring Grace back and give her the good news that a gîte was available after all. She had no idea what her excited holidaymaker looked like but when she put the phone down, Rosie just had one of those feelings. Call it intuition, wishful thinking or whatever you like, but Rosie had felt a plan coming on. One of her very handsome, eligible, returning guests would be staying at gîte number one, all alone for Christmas. Now, out of the blue, another single, rather nice sounding female would be residing in gîte number three, so it had to be fate or destiny, didn't it?

Rosie knew she'd been hedging her bets and Grace could've been nothing like she imagined, but the second she opened the door at the hotel that evening and spotted the auburn haired, green-eyed beauty on her doorstep, she knew she'd backed a winner. All Rosie could do now was let the magic of *Les Trois Chênes* do its work and the rest, she would leave in the hands of the gods. Well, maybe she'd give them a nudge here and there, because after all, it was Christmas, such a special time where now and then, miracles really did happen.

Max sat on the veranda of his temporary home, staring out into the blackness while Ginger sniffed and pranced about. He was still a baby really and gave out the odd nervous bark, just to check his dad was still there. Ever cautious, Ginger never strayed too far away from his owner, which Max was pleased about, because it was bloody dark out there and he didn't fancy wandering around on his own looking for a daft dog. He could see the lights in the gîte across the way and curiosity teased his brain.

Rosie said it was a woman named Grace and he wondered what brought someone to the French countryside on their own at Christmas. Perhaps she was the eccentric, reclusive type who hated everything festive so buried herself away to avoid all things merry. Max pictured her to be late fifties and an avid hiker. She was a wearer of stout brown boots and tweedy clothes who could walk for miles a day in complete isolation and looked like hideous Miss Trunchbull from the film, *Matilda*.

Max grimaced, then pulled himself from his imaginings and called for Ginger to come inside. The cheeks of his bottom were feeling the cold and his nose felt a bit runny, so it was time for a warm drink and then bed. Tomorrow, he intended a morning of cycling, then a quick trip to the supermarket, followed by a stroll up to the hotel for drinks and one of Michel's superb meals.

During the summer, he'd met Dominique who was also a keen cyclist and Rosie had told Max he would be at the gathering. He hoped he might fancy a trip out on the bikes over the holidays and it would be an ideal opportunity to arrange something. When he reached his door, Max glanced over at Miss Trunchbull's gîte and imagined what she would look like in her winceyette nightie and rollers. He shuddered and quickly closed the door and fastened both the bolts.

Across the way, Grace was tucking into the most delicious supper of fresh crusty bread, pâté and to follow, ripe Brie and *tarte aux pommes*. Rosie had left her two bottles of wine so, in celebration of her independence and landing on her feet in this perfect little haven, she'd opened the bottle of white from the fridge and was toasting her sense of adventure and *joie de vivre*.

In the spirit of embracing her temporary home, she rejected the English channels on the TV and following the instructions in

Rosie's very concise handbook, she tuned in to BFM and watched the French news channel.

After sending (slightly smug) texts to her nearest and dearest, telling them she had arrived safely at the hotel and all was well, Grace relaxed and soaked up the ambience of her surroundings. Coco snored quietly in front of the fire, which he had claimed as his own personal property while she watched the images on the TV flickering in front of her.

Earlier, she thought she'd heard the sounds of a dog barking and presumed it must be the other guest at the end of the row. Grace pondered on who would be staying here, alone at Christmas, and why? It's probably someone who hates children, or a sad widower who couldn't bear to be around jolly people making merry while he was grieving. Maybe, he was the psychotic axe murderer she'd spent so many nights worrying about at home!

Instinct forced Grace off the sofa to double check she'd turned the key in the lock and to be on the safe side, she pulled both the bolts across. Settling back onto the comfy couch, she told herself to grow up as she dragged the soft throw over her knees and tucked into her desert.

After flicking through the channels, she settled on what looked like the French version of *X Factor* so snuggled down and turned the music up. Nothing was going to spoil her first night in France and if the lonely, axe murdering psycho came a-knocking, she'd set Coco 'The Killer Labrador' on him, that's if sleepy over there could be bothered to get up from the fire.

As she watched the flames dance through the glass window of the log burner and listened to Coco's gentle snores, just as some poor girl got booted off the show, Grace smiled contentedly. She was going to be fine here, she just knew it.

CHAPTER 9

When Grace eventually woke the following morning, it took her a second or two to remember where she was. As her eyes became accustomed to the bright winter rays which shone through the roof light, she yawned loudly and noticed that the air was slightly cooler than it had been the night before. Realising the fire must have gone out, Grace reached over and grabbed her phone. It was almost 10.30am.

Getting out of bed, she quickly threw on her jumper and found her slippers. When she reached the stairs, Coco was lying at the bottom, waiting patiently for the boss to get up. He gave her a slow thump, thump, thump of his tail to let her know he was glad to see her, at last.

'I'm sorry, boy, have you been waiting ages? Just hold on two ticks then we can both go outside and sample the French countryside… I promise to be quick.' Grace ruffled Coco's ears as she spoke.

Grace flicked on the kettle and made herself a cup of coffee, then with her mug in hand, she unhooked her coat and slipped it on before opening the door and letting Coco loose. The poor dog must have been crossing his legs for hours, thought Grace as she watched him sprint across the field. Seating herself on one of the wooden chairs, she looked out at her very own picture-perfect view.

Stretching out to the horizon was a patchwork of fields, all in varying hues of pale, mossy greens through to soft, earthy browns. Dotted here and there were small cottages or farms and a distant church steeple jutted from between the crests of two hills. It was extremely cold, but the presence of the winter sun, as it valiantly tried to warm the land, took the edge off the sharp wind that blew in from the fields.

Turning to her left, she glanced along the row of dwellings and tried to catch a glimpse of the mad axeman at number one. There was a black 4x4 parked in front of the gîte, but no apparent signs of life. Surveying the rest of the large field, she saw a play park, sandpit and a small empty paddling pool. At the far end there were camping pitches and a toilet block, plus a very exited chocolate Labrador, bounding about like a spring lamb.

Shouting for Coco to come back, Grace decided to go inside, relight the fire, take a shower and then head off to the supermarket. She'd already wasted most of the morning sleeping and was looking forward to a bit of French retail therapy.

Max had been up since 8am and after breakfast hit the road early to make the most of the glorious December day. He'd done a circular route of the hotel and surrounding villages and felt invigorated and free. He pedalled along the quiet lanes and smooth roads, meeting the challenges of some steep, hilly sections and then the thrill of the ride down the other side. The clean air filled his lungs and he was oblivious to the chilly weather because his blood was pumping through his veins, providing his own heat source.

His ride had taken almost three hours and Max was mindful

of the fact that Ginger would be missing him and probably needed to go outside. He was also starving and looking forward to getting stuck into his welcome pack as he didn't have much of an appetite the previous evening. Once he'd had lunch, he was going to head off to the supermarket where he intended to stock up for the weekend and treat himself to a few French delicacies, plus a bottle or two of the Loire's finest wines.

Grace had been in shopping heaven. Her car was loaded with provisions and she couldn't wait to get back, unpack, then spend the whole afternoon in front of the fire, reading and eating her way through her purchases.

Before going into the supermarket, she'd spotted a small retail park jammed full of smaller shops selling shoes, clothing and homeware, plus an artisan bakery. On the passenger seat were two rather glamorous looking carrier bags containing a lovely multi-coloured lacy jumper in her favourite tones of purple and maroon, and in the other, a very chic, deep plum, faux suede skirt which was quite short but teamed with thick tights, would show off her legs and still be quite decent.

Along with her new clothes, Grace had splashed out on food and her supermarket carrier bags contained an assortment of cheese, fresh pasta, cooked meats, pâté and a box of petite breakfast pastries and sticking out of the top, a long thin baguette dusted in flour. There were also a few bags of crisps and some speciality chocolates to enjoy while she sat in front of the fire, she *was* on holiday after all.

The clinking of glass gave away her more liquid purchases. Grace thought it would be nice to offer Rosie a drink if she called in, or maybe one of her neighbours. There had been a large display of Loire Valley wine in the supermarket, along with a very helpful young male assistant (he thankfully spoke good English and seemed pleased to be practising his language skills) who explained each one in great detail. During her sampling session, Grace's mind automatically flitted to Ben and she decided to take home a selection for him, it was Christmas and the spirit of giving swam through her veins, along with the delicious red wine she'd tasted.

Grace had a bit of everything in the box and tried hard to remember what she'd been told. There was an earthy red Malbec and a fruity Pinot Noir. A crisp, dry Sauvignon Blanc and a slightly fizzy Muscadet. For aperitifs or with dessert, she had a light, bubbly, fruity Crémant de Loire. Grace laughed at herself, knowing full well that by teatime she'd have forgotten everything. Passing a lone cyclist along the way took her mind off wine and she made sure to admire his very tight bottom and toned physique before pulling out and overtaking, carefully.

She was parking her car at the back of the gîte when her phone rang in her bag, but by the time she'd found it, the caller had rung off – it was Heidi. Grace had an uneasy feeling and decided to get her stuff inside, let Coco out for a quick wee, then ring her straight back. Literally minutes later, she watched her dog through the window and waited for Heidi to pick up.

'Hi, Mum, how's it going?'

Grace knew her daughter well and sensed tension in her voice. 'I'm fine, love, are you okay, is something wrong?'

'No, not at all. I just wanted to hear your voice. I miss you already and I think I'm just a bit hormonal and needed a chat.'

Yes, there was definitely a hint of emotion there so Grace tried to jolly her along. 'Well, I'm all yours. How are the kids, are they looking forward to going to Lincoln tomorrow?'

And that was it. Heidi burst into floods of tears and she gulped, hiccupped, sobbed and did her best to explain her woes to Grace, who could do nothing more than listen.

Half an hour and one potentially huge phone bill later, Grace had managed to calm her daughter and seemed to have eased her troubled heart. It had all stemmed from a short phone call with Heidi's mother-in-law.

Gordon and Vera were regular churchgoers and the mainstay of their local Methodist chapel and as a result, expected their son and his family to participate in the Christmas programme whilst in Lincoln.

Heidi knew full well that religion had been a long-standing bone of contention between Elliot and his parents. He'd had his fill of his father's puritanical way of life while he was growing up and wouldn't stand for being told what to do now he was an adult. After the call, Heidi had built up a miserable scenario in her head where there would be conflict and tension between father and son. She knew the kids would rather stay at home than go to Lincoln and were already missing their Grandma Grace, and Elliot had been like a bear with a sore head all week because he didn't want to go, either. The combination of all these factors naturally resulted in Heidi getting into a right old state.

Grace had managed to reassure her that Elliot was quite able to deal with his father which, when they thought about it sensibly, probably wouldn't even be necessary, as neither Gordon nor Vera would risk spoiling the holiday by making an atmosphere, especially for the children. All Heidi had to say to the in-laws was that it was far too late for Skye and Finn to attend midnight Mass with their grandparents, so they were all off the hook on that score.

Apart from that, Grace knew that deep down, Heidi was scared of encountering problems with the baby and not having her mum on hand if she needed her. After pointing out that Heidi was blooming and there was no reason to expect complications but, if the occasion arose, she could be home within twenty-four hours, Grace managed to calm her daughter down. Taking heed of her mum's advice, Heidi changed the subject. She wanted to know all about the gîte and her mum's shopping trip then, after both promising to keep in touch, they said their goodbyes. Opening the door, Grace searched the field for her faithful hound and called out for him to return.

'Come on, boy, let's get some food and put our feet up. I've got a right old tale to tell you, get inside you crazy dog, it's freezing!' Grace was momentarily distracted by a cyclist who had appeared at the top of the field, then focused on Coco as he galloped up the steps, quickly closing the door behind him.

Max cycled into the field and noticed the door closing on Miss Trunchbull's place and then remembered she'd be up at Rosie's later that night. *I bet she drinks pints and smokes a cigar and tells rude jokes*, mused Max as took his bike round the back, then went to let Ginger out. He was looking forward to the evening and dinner in the restaurant. First he needed to refuel after his ride so once he'd watched his dog gambolling about the field and putting thoughts of his gruesome neighbour aside, he called Ginger back and made his way indoors.

Grace was a bit nervous. For a start, she didn't have a clue what to wear. Rosie had said informal, but what did that mean in the countryside? She was going to be dining in the restaurant later so thought she should make a bit of an effort. But then she hated it when you turned up somewhere only to realise that you're the overdressed guest, but nobody wanted to be the scruffy one, either. In the end, Grace decided that jeans were definitely out, but she wanted to save her new skirt for tomorrow and her trip to the Christmas market. She settled on her slim black chinos and a soft, winter-white jumper with a sparkly v-neck.

Approving of herself in the bedroom mirror, Grace checked the clock and saw it was 6.55pm, time to get her boots on and set off. She was putting on her coat when her mobile pinged and was pleased to see a message from Seth. Going by his previous texts, he was having a ball and by all accounts the resort in the Rhône-Alpes was everything he and his mates had been expecting, which meant masses of snow and fit girls. But when Grace began to read the message, her heart sank. The text said simply:

MUM DON'T PANIC. BROKE MY ARM. COLLIDED WITH A TREE. HOSPITAL VERY NICE. ALL SORTED AND IN PLAS-TER. ON WAY BACK TO CHALET WITH NICK. GOT PAINKILLERS SO WILL BE OKAY. TEXT YOU TOMORROW. PLEASE ENJOY YOURSELF AND DO NOT BE STRESSING. LOVE U. X

Of course, Grace instantly started to stress and after annoying the living daylights out of Seth by firing off a list of 'Mum' questions, she was eventually placated and convinced he really was alright. Still, how he'd cope on the slopes when he was one of the walking wounded, she couldn't imagine. His snowy holiday was probably ruined now, which made her feel very sorry for her son. Giving Coco one last stroke, Grace sighed and wound her scarf around her neck, then set off up the track.

A full silver moon lit up the dark sky and the frost covered field, which was comforting as Grace was a bit edgy about walking through the copse of trees on her own. She thought briefly of the bitter, widowed axe murderer, then told herself off for being stupid but sped up, just in case. As Rosie had said, the bright lamps illuminated the path and the trees, so once she was on the other side, the lights from the house, then further up the track the gaily decorated hotel, made the short walk less worrying.

There was a large motorhome in Rosie's drive, which Grace presumed must belong to André. The Polish neighbours still hadn't materialised, unless they'd arrived while she was at the supermarket and she'd missed them. For a moment, she had an attack of nerves and wavered at the door, too shy to go in, then pulled herself together and rang the bell which within seconds, was immediately opened by Rosie.

'Grace, there you are. I was wondering where you'd got to. I thought you might have changed your mind, come in, it's cold. Let me take your coat and get you a drink.'

Before she knew it, Grace was inside, her coat had been swiftly hung up and she was being introduced to the group of people gathered in the lounge.

First, there was André, a huge bear of a man with a smiling face and kind eyes. He had a very fashionable beard and long, wavy, salt and pepper hair. He shook her hand energetically then introduced his partner Wilf, who was much shorter and had a rugged, Scandinavian, outdoorsy look, which was complemented by his handlebar moustache and a blonde-grey ponytail.

André insisted she took his seat on the sofa then introduced her to the rest of the crowd while Rosie brought her a glass of sparkling Crémant. Finally, Grace met the Polish family who *had* arrived that morning while she was out, but had spent the rest of the day at Zofia's. All were very friendly and spoke good English, wanting to know where she was from in England and were thrilled when they found out she was from Leicester as they also had family there.

Everyone was chatting animatedly when a petite blonde woman entered the room. Rosie proudly introduced her best friend, Zofia, and began looking around for her husband Dominique who she was told was in the bar, chatting with someone called Max, about cycling.

Two little girls and an older boy were playing in the corner and Grace learned that this was Sabine, Rosie's daughter and the other two were her cousins, Oliver and Lily. Their mother, Ruby, was the housekeeper at the hotel and might make an appearance later but she was waiting for her partner, Dylan to arrive. He was driving up from Bordeaux for Christmas.

Grace began to relax, sipping her Crémant before sampling the tasty hors d'oeuvres of tiny toasts spread with pâté, along with rolled pieces of crêpes filled with garlic cream cheese. Rosie, true to her word, remained by her side and was chatting with André about dogs and Seth's broken arm.

It seemed that André and Wilf had stayed in Val D'Isere and had tried their hand at snowboarding but actually preferred the culinary, less energetic après-ski activities.

'We have decided it is much more fun to watch people from the bar than risk our lives on the slopes. I cannot do the snow-board, it is like sliding on a serving tray and a ridiculous idea and when I saw the video of my skiing, I decide straight away that I look like the chubby clown in my snowsuit and stupid hat. I was like the human bowling ball and knocked over a whole group of children in one attempt and was banished from the nursery slope. Next, Wilf dropped his ski from the chairlift and nearly killed the man below and had to stay on because he would be beaten to death, so went up and down all day, round and round, like a mad person. So now we are retired from sport and instead are voyeurs, it is safer for all concerned.' André took a sip of his wine as Rosie tittered.

'Well I wish I'd known all this before Seth went skiing, but then again it wouldn't have stopped him... he'd have thought I was being overprotective or dramatic. Perhaps I should send him a text to remind his friends to make sure their skis are fastened properly, just in case.' Grace had visions of some poor skier being given the chop.

'I'm sure Seth will be fine, Grace, and he can have another go at skiing next year. You're only young once I suppose. Anyway, it's just André that needs his wings clipping... I've already forbidden him from trying to be an action man and made him promise to take it easy after an unfortunate jet-ski accident had left him incapacitated. But did he listen? Of course not.' Rosie raised her eyebrows in the direction of André who in turn, winked at Grace.

Grace warmed to André instantly, and Wilf, who seemed content to let his other-half continue to tell holiday tales and only interjected now and then to embellish the story. She was just agreeing with André that it was a very small world, when they were interrupted in their discussion by loud, laughing voices, coming along the hallway. As Grace passed the bottle of Crémant to Wilf, the proof of Andrés wise comment came walking around the corner with Dominique.

Grace was lost for words and aware that her mouth was agape and she was holding a bottle mid-air. The man from the boat soon came to her rescue.

'It's you! Hi, sorry. I can't believe that you're here. What a coincidence, fancy us both turning up at the same place. Did you arrive on Thursday like me?' The handsome guy was waffling, he sounded flabbergasted but looked quite chuffed at the same time.

Grace laughed at his outburst and was glad he spoke first because it gave her time to compose herself, sort of.

'Yes, I came straight off the boat but you must have beaten me to it. Rosie said she'd just settled someone in before I arrived but I had no idea it was you. How weird, what are the chances of that?' Grace's heart was slowing down and had returned to a more moderate rate, but she could still feel her cheeks and knew they were flushed, but hopefully, not cherry red.

'I'd say thousands to one. If we'd had more chance to talk on the boat I'm sure it would've come out, but I had my head over the side all the way here so there wasn't much chance of that. Anyway, my name's Max, pleased to meet you, again.'

PATRICIA DIXON

Accepting the hand that was offered, Grace introduced herself and tried to ignore the strange feeling as they made first contact. Turning to his left, Max then introduced Dominique before they were joined by Rosie who demanded to know how her guests knew each other.

In between explaining, Grace noticed that she and Max were wearing daft smiles on their faces and in her case, had a very fluttery heart. Once the shock had worn off they joined the group on the sofas and in between enjoying conversation with the others, Grace felt her eyes being drawn to Max who it had to be said, looked even more handsome in the flickering fire light than he had under the fluorescent tubes on the car deck. Eventually, Zofia, along with her friends and relatives decided to make a move *as the aperitif hour* appeared to be over, just as diners began to arrive and make their way to the restaurant. When Grace felt her own stomach rumble, as if by magic, Rosie reappeared, just like a well-practised fairy godmother, albeit a slightly flustered one who it turned out, needed a favour.

'Listen you two, it's really busy in there tonight and I was wondering, would you mind sharing a table? I reserved two singles but you really would be helping me out, just in case I need the space later on.' Rosie looked rather stressed out.

Grace looked at Max who was showing no signs of horror at the thought of sharing a table with her, so bravely spoke first.

'Well, that's fine by me, it's up to Max though, he might want some peace and quiet.' Grace smiled at Rosie and suspected she was being set-up, but didn't mind a bit.

'Yeah, sure. It'll be nice to have some company. Shall we go through now?' Max pointed towards the dining room.

Grace was cheered by the speed in which Max had agreed and it looked like Rosie was relieved, or was she triumphant at her rather obvious matchmaking?

'That's great, just give me two ticks while I reset the table. I'll

112

put you by the terrace doors, it looks lovely with the fairy lights outside the windows.' And with that, Rosie raced off.

'Great, it looks like we can talk properly after all. I hope you're hungry. The food here is amazing and you'll be spoilt for choice,' remarked Max, just as they heard Rosie call their names so after saying goodnight to André and Wilf, headed into the restaurant.

CHAPTER 10

Max was indeed correct because Grace was spoilt for choice and the food was delicious. They had polished off their first and second courses and were having a little rest before they tackled crème brûlée and lemon soufflé. André and Wilf were also enjoying a meal with two other gentlemen who, according to Rosie, were Henri, Michel's brother, and Sebastien, the owner of the bistro in the village. Both of them were André's oldest friends and drinking partners in crime.

Grace and Max hadn't stopped talking since they sat down, apart from when they ate of course, but the conversation flowed with ease, which was a huge relief. They had both talked about their ex-spouses, their children and briefly explained why they were solo in France, at Christmas. Grace hadn't been completely transparent though and put her trip down to the spirit of adventure and the desire to do something a little different, rather than admit the truth. It was too soon to divulge her innermost feelings or failings and insecurities, so for now, she enjoyed Max's company. It was like an unexpected blind date.

'So, what've you got planned for tomorrow?' Max was tackling a plate of assorted cheese while they waited for their pudding.

'I was going to visit the Christmas market in Angers. I had a look at the tourist guides before I left and most of them finish on Sunday, so tomorrow is probably the best day to go. What about you, more cycling?' Grace felt a bit flustered because she now knew that the tight bottom she'd admired earlier that day probably belonged to the man in front of her.

'I've been to Angers, it's a gorgeous city so this trip I fancied a mooch around Tours. I'm really into architecture and the history of the buildings in France so I was going to drive over there in the morning.'

'Is it far? I must admit I was a bit nervous on the way down and I'm slightly wary of negotiating a city, but if I managed to get on and off the boat and here in one piece, I'm sure I'll survive Angers.' Grace was concentrating as she spoke, trying to cut through the squashy roll of goat's cheese without making a mess when Max came up with an idea. His eager sounding voice made her jump.

'I know, why don't you come with me? There's a Christmas market there too. I saw it on TripAdvisor. I wouldn't expect you to look round the buildings if it's not your thing, but there are loads of shops and the Old Quarter is supposed to be stunning. I could drop you off and then meet you later... that'd save you the stress of driving to Angers. What do you think?'

When Grace looked up from the cheese she'd destroyed, Max was studying her face, causing her to go a bit pink. She also sensed he was nervous and probably expected to be let down lightly.

'Are you sure you don't mind? We've only just met and I don't want to intrude on your plans. But it *would* be nice to do a bit of sightseeing and I'd love to pack some culture into my holiday and visit the historical bits of the Loire. I wouldn't expect you to trudge round the market, or the shops though, if it's not your cup of tea.' Grace was secretly thrilled he'd asked her but thought it best to give him a get-out clause, just in case he was regretting asking. After all offering a lift was entirely different to spending a whole day with a virtual stranger.

'Hey, I'm not adverse to a bit of shopping. Can't you tell by my shabby chic, history teacher look? This casual little ensemble wasn't just thrown together you know. It's taken years of staring vacantly into the window at Next and copying what the mannequins are wearing to achieve this level of style. Anyway, they sell all sorts of fancy food and bad for you stuff at those markets, so I can shop till I drop.' Max was spreading Camembert on his bread.

'Okay, let's do it. You can show me the sights and educate me, then we can raid the Christmas market together.' Watching Max tuck in had tempted Grace too, so she scooped up some of the goat's cheese and a sliver of Roquefort.

Looking up, she saw Rosie on approach carrying Sabine who looked sleepy.

'I'm getting off now, this one's overtired and needs her bed. Just give Pascal a wave when you want your dessert. Is everything okay, you two look as thick as thieves?' Sabine yawned loudly and leant on Rosie's shoulder.

'Yes, thanks. Grace and I are taking a trip over to Tours tomorrow.' Max sipped his wine and brushed crumbs from his sweater.

Rosie rocked Sabine on her on her hip as she spoke. 'That's wonderful. It's a beautiful city, you should make a day of it and try one of their restaurants in the evening. The whole place is lit up at night and the food is just superb, but don't tell the chef I said that.'

It was at this point Grace realised they'd have to be back by early afternoon for Coco and Ginger. 'That would be nice but we can't stay all day. We'd have to come back for the dogs. It's not fair to leave them alone for too long.'

'Hold on, I've got an idea. Two ticks.' Rosie scooted off and was soon having a quiet word with André, she was back by their side within seconds.

'Right, it's all arranged. André will do the honours with the dogs so you can go off and have a lovely day out without worrying about them. No arguments, he was happy to help.' As if to prove the point, right on cue, André turned and waved his piece of bread and called across the room.

'Don't worry, your doggies will be fine with their Uncle André. I will take good care of them.' Then he turned and got on with his meal.

'Satisfied?' Rosie looked from one to the other and smiled when both Grace and Max nodded their agreement. 'Just leave your doors closed, no need to lock them round here, we're all trustworthy and St Pierre is the crime-free capital of the world, believe me. Right, come on sleepyhead, we're off!'

Rosie kissed Sabine on the head then turned back to Grace and Max. 'See you when I see you and have a lovely day. Enjoy the rest of your evening.' Then she was gone, waving to the diners and blowing kisses to André and his band of merry men.

Max was preoccupied as he spoke, trying to make eye contact with their waiter. 'Well, that's put us in our place, so now we need to decide on a time to leave. I'm really looking forward to tomorrow... and my pudding.'

Grace, however, was embracing the contentment that had settled on her like a fine mist, along with the thrill she felt when Max looked her in the eye. At the same time, she was trying to remain in control and appear cool. This was *so* out of her comfort zone and literally foreign territory, whereas Max seemed far more confident and comfortable in his own skin. Shaking off her insecurities, Grace told herself to just enjoy herself and her pudding and leave the rest to fate because so far, it had done a grand job and seemed to have things under control.

Grace was glad she had someone to walk back to the gîte with. It was freezing now, definitely below zero and when they stepped out into the starry night, the acute drop in temperature had taken them by surprise, both mentioning it as they buttoned their coats and pulled on gloves. The ground underfoot crunched as they walked onwards and there was a frosty sheen on the branches of the trees as they passed through the copse into the field.

Max didn't want the night to end just yet, but sensed that it would be the wrong thing to do if he asked Grace to come inside for a nightcap. He was still slightly in awe of the fact that the attractive woman he'd spotted on the ferry and thought he'd never see again had been right under his nose for almost a day. For that reason and having the sense to respect the peculiar feeling he got every time their eyes met or she smiled at something he said, Max had no intention of blowing it on the first night. When the gîtes came into view, he made an executive decision.

'Are you going to let Coco out? I'm going to give Ginger a last run about before I turn in. Do you fancy a coffee, we could sit on the veranda and keep an eye on them both if you like? Or do you think it's too cold?' Max thought that he'd pitched that just about right, not too pushy, considerate and safe.

'That'd be nice. They deserve a bit of fresh air, especially as they've been inside all night and we're abandoning them tomorrow as well. Have you got tea though? If I drink coffee this late I'll never get to sleep.' Grace was glad he'd asked and stupidly relieved because she hadn't wanted to say goodnight and the question of whether or not to invite him in for a drink had been playing on her mind all the way back. Now, they could have a bit more time together in the completely, platonic, stress-free environment of his veranda while they watched their dogs.

'Yep, I've got a giant box of PG Tips with your name on. You go and get Coco while I put the kettle on and meet you back here.' Max ran straight up the steps to the sound of woofs from Ginger as Grace headed off to her gîte.

They sat side by side, keeping their hands warm with mugs of tea while frozen puffs of breath swirled around in front of them each time they spoke. The dogs bounded about, blissfully free and clearly oblivious of their owners.

Max, who had numb feet and bottom cheeks like ice cubes was determined to tough it out. He'd pointed out two shooting stars, some bats and what Max was convinced was a space ship and during the whole time, Grace hadn't stopped laughing.

The lanterns above the doors of all four gîtes, aided by the glow from the rope lights on the eaves of the roofs, shone through the inky darkness and set a perfect scene. Ginger kept disappearing into the darkness with Coco and neither came straight back when they were called by their owners, there was far too much to sniff and explore out there on the field.

When Grace heard the eerie night noises, calling from somewhere in the distance, she looked at Max with wide eyes and both got the nervous giggles. There was the piercing screech of an owl, a suspicious rustling in the trees, then, what they thought was a fox calling to his mate. Max volunteered Grace to venture into the void and check the dogs hadn't been eaten by a yeti, saying that he'd stay there and hold the mugs.

'Go on, off you jog. I'm sure your Coco will protect you from the night zombies... and will you tell Ginger that Daddy says to come home.'

'Well I can see you didn't get your Big Brave Boy badge in the scouts. How about we leave the crazy hounds to scare off the zombies by themselves. They don't seem half as scared as you, you big wimp.'

'Well I definitely got you all wrong, and there was me thinking I had a big, strapping lass to protect me if the monsters came out of the woods.' Max began laughing quietly.

'And what exactly does that mean?' Grace put her hand on her hip and turned to face Max.

'Since last night, I've been trying to imagine who was in your gîte and I decided that you'd be a cigar-smoking, Miss Trunchbull lookalike.'

Grace spluttered and whacked him in the arm. 'You cheeky sod! Well, I had you down as a deranged, bitter widower who had an axe under his bed and was planning a chopping-up spree, so there.' Grace smiled into her tea.

The sound of voices singing interrupted their laughter and soon they spotted the glowing beams of a torch, followed by four silhouetted bodies making their way home from Zofia's. This prompted Coco and his trusty young assistant to return from their investigations and check out who had dared to enter their field. With shouts of 'hello, it's so cold' and 'are you mad to be sitting out here?' their neighbours strolled past, waving and stroking the inquisitive dogs.

'You know what? I think they're right. My bum is frozen and so are my toes. I think we should call it a night before we get hyperthermia – or sectioned.' Grace said as she stood up and stamped her feet to encourage some blood flow around her extremities.

'I agree. I think these lights are on timers and any minute we could be plunged into darkness, then the yeti might get us. Those two are getting a bit cocky as well and I wasn't joking about sending you into the wilderness to retrieve them.' Max grinned and winked at Grace as he took the mug she was offering.

'Right then, Mr Wimpy. I'll see you at ten, bright and breezy. Come on, Coco, let's have you in before your paws freeze off.' Grace slowly made her way towards her gîte while Coco lingered with Ginger, then, as if realising he might end up outside alone, chased after his mistress. Perhaps he wasn't so brave after all.

'Night, Grace, see you in the morning. I'll be thinking of you in your rollers and Victorian nightie. And lay off those cigars, they're so bad for you,' Max teased as he patted his legs, signalling for Ginger to come home.

Grace laughed, opening her door. 'And you get sharpening that axe, just in case the yeti comes in the night. Don't think I'm coming to your rescue if he kicks the door in, you big chicken. Night, Max, sleep well.' Taking one last glimpse of him, standing in the lantern light, she waved and closed the door.

Grace loved every minute of the drive to Tours. The scenery was stunning, even in the midst of winter and probably as barren as the land could be. The weather was milder and the sun, when it managed to break through the clouds, shone down on the fallow fields and pruned back vineyards that were scattered across the sloping valleys.

They'd set off promptly at ten o'clock after leaving food and water out for Coco and Ginger, plus both sets of phone numbers for André – just in case. Grace admitted only to herself that she was slightly on the tired side as it had taken her a while to nod off the previous night, simply because her mind insisted on replaying every minute of her evening with Max, dissecting certain sections, and examining snippets of conversation. It was like being a teenager again. Grace was surprised most of all by the unexpected awakening of her feelings but eventually, fatigue won the battle and she slept like a log. Predictably though, she was up with the lark after being woken by the sounds of her phone beeping.

When she managed to focus, she saw it was a text from Seth saying he was fine, a bit achy, and really, really bored. His friends had already left for the slopes so he was at a loose end and it would be a long day, stuck in the chalet or watching everyone have fun from the bottom of the piste. Grace racked her brain trying to think of something uplifting to say or, interesting for him to do. The best advice she could come up with was suggesting he chilled out and watched some DVDs, or wander up to one of the cafes and chance his good arm at chatting up those fit girls he said were *'everywhere'*. Maybe he'd get the sympathy vote and some TLC, which was better than being alone all day. In the end he seemed to have perked up but whether or not it was more for her benefit and he was just being brave, Grace wasn't sure. She was trying hard not to worry about Seth and decided she'd ring him later that night to check how he was, she could always tell how all her children felt, just by hearing their voices.

In the distance, Grace could see the city of Tours appearing from under misty skies and felt a surge of anticipation at what the day may hold. The look of appreciation that Max had given her when she opened her door that morning and came down the steps hadn't gone unnoticed either, it had given her a long-forgotten zap of excitement; she was glad she'd dressed up a bit.

Under her duster jacket and scarf, she was wearing her new skirt and jazzy jumper and looked very festive, even if she did say so herself. With her black woollen tights and knee length leather boots, Grace looked quite chic and hoped she was dressed appropriately for sightseeing and the weather.

Max, she had to admit, was strikingly handsome and Grace thought he'd got it just right after all the hours spent staring at window displays. Even though he was approaching fifty, he could still hold his own in the fashion stakes and looked stylish in a double breasted, grey wool jacket, dark blue jeans and tan laced boots. It did cross Grace's mind that they would look like a rather well-matched couple as they roamed the streets of Tours, then she cringed at her forward thoughts, so instead, concentrated on the road ahead and the breathtaking winter scenery.

They'd decided to go sightseeing first, rather than carry shopping around all afternoon and Max thought the market would look better in the early evening. The journey had taken just over an hour and a half, but the time flew and before she knew it, Grace could see the banks of the Loire and the river below as they crossed the bridge into the city.

They had chatted non-stop about where they lived, their families and work. Max told funny, schoolmaster stories (Grace freely admitted to him that there was little humour to be found in an office that sold water treatments) but had many a tale to tell about Skye and Finn and the Klingons, from whom she'd escaped. By the time they parked the car and began their sight-seeing tour, Grace knew even more about her travelling companion and he her, which perhaps accounted for why she felt relaxed in Max's company.

The first part of the day was exhausting and Grace's feet throbbed from the relentless walking between historical gems. Despite her fatigue and having developed a slight limp, she had enjoyed every second. She also felt rather envious of Max's students and wished that she'd been lucky enough to be taught by someone as gorgeous as him, who made every fact sound excit-ing, mysterious, or just plain interesting.

They started with the Gothic *Saint Gatien* cathedral and then moved on to the basilica, with its crypt holding the tomb of St Martin, before strolling down to the Historic Quarter which was lined with old, timbered buildings. When the pace had slowed, Grace was relieved when Max insisted they stop at *Place Plumereau* so that they could rest and soak up the atmosphere of the city. The busy square was surrounded by restaurants and bars and from there, they watched the hustle and bustle as they ate lunch and reflected on what they'd seen so far.

Once rested, they continued on the cultural section of their visit, wandering the halls of the *Musee des Beaux-Arts* where Grace was thrilled to see, with her very own eyes, paintings by Rembrandt and Monet. Stepping onto the bustling streets, after the darker museum interior, Grace waited while her eyes adjusted to the light as Max packed away the brochures and pamphlets he'd amassed during the day.

Once he'd stashed his haul, Max said he didn't want to push his luck by overloading Grace with culture and hoped she wasn't bored, or pretending to find his amateur tour guide routine interesting. He'd seen everything he wanted to so abandoned the smaller, less significant attractions and suggested they made their way to the *Rue Nationale* so the retail therapy section of their trip could begin.

Dusk was beginning to fall. Grace thoroughly enjoyed window shopping and admiring the glitzy displays at *Galeries Lafayette*. They explored the pedestrianised streets where they found an array of smaller stores selling artwork and antiques, then, as yellow lights began to twinkle on shop fronts and the decorations that were dotted overhead, they made their way to the Christmas market. When the wooden chalets came into view, they both had to admit that the European markets at home looked much the same. The difference was that in the UK you sort of had to pretend you were in another country, whereas this was the real thing and for that reason, the atmosphere was completely different.

The slight dip in temperature may have been a contributing factor to the ambience as it was starting to feel chillier than earlier in the day. The extravagant boughs of greenery that edged the square, trimmed with grand red ribbons, were lit up by bright white stars which were strung across the market place. The cheerful voices of shoppers with French accents, not the twang of Grace's native Midlands, added to the picture-postcard scene. A combination of scents floated on the air, spicy candles, warming cinnamon and the smoky spit roast (Max told her it was boar) emanated from the wooden cabins. Their eyes feasted on an abundance of decorated gingerbread, macaroons and candies, elaborate chocolate creations, not to mention crêpes, meaty baguettes, huge sausages and mulled wine.

Max had forgotten to bring a hat with him so after trying on some ridiculous looking, multi-coloured affairs with ear-flaps and bobbles, he settled for a sensible dark grey beanie. 'What about this? Tell me if I look stupid, but it's got to be better than the one that made me look like I was on *The Muppet Show* or a has-been rock star trying to avoid my die-hard fans and conceal a bald patch.'

Once Grace stopped laughing she assured him that despite his concerns he looked like any normal Christmas shopper who had very cold ears.

'Come on, I'll treat you to some hot chocolate, it'll settle your nerves after all that dithering... who knew choosing a woolly hat could be so stressful. Remind me never to help you pick shoes, we'd be there all day.' As soon as she said the words Grace felt foolish and presumptuous. Like there'd be a next time. But Max appeared not to have heard or noticed because he was paying the stallholder, allowing Grace to relax.

They meandered across the cobbles and along the aisles and soon had a handful of carrier bags, each stuffed with all the things they failed to resist. When Grace stopped at a stall selling tiny statues and commented on the beautifully carved figures and the handmade stable they were displayed in, Max explained that they were *The Santons of Provence*, or little saints.

During the French Revolution, churches were forced to close and their large nativity scenes were forbidden. Instead, people made their own crèches and tiny characters from whatever they could get their hands on and secretly kept them in their homes. In the spirit of revolution, the figures represented all the common people of the village, including their animals. There would be the baker, fishmonger, cobbler and so on. Their manufacture evolved through time, being made from wood, wax and clay and now, many families kept the tradition alive by making their own crèche and filling it with nativity scene *santons*, collected and handed down through the years. Along with the traditional characters of the Christmas story, people now add more colourful statues, or those that have a personal meaning to them.

'They're lovely, so tiny and intricate. You know what? I think I'll buy some and next Christmas, perhaps I could make a crèche with Skye and Finn, they'd love that.' Grace looked to Max for approval, who was nodding enthusiastically.

'Perhaps you could get a few that look like members of your family too, sort of innocent bystanders at the nativity scene, then each time you add a new member of your tribe, you could buy another one. I bet you can get them online so you wouldn't necessarily have to visit France.' Max began searching the stall and picked something from a small box.

'See, I thought so, here's a business card, so even if you don't come back you will still be able to expand your collection.'

Grace was thrilled and gave Max a pat on the back. 'Go to the top of the class, young Max, and give yourself a gold star for quick thinking.' Grace winked and noticed he looked rather chuffed with himself.

It took a while for Grace to pick suitable lookalikes for her family but she knew it would make them laugh because they were all in traditional, old-fashioned clothes. She even bought a dog that sort of looked like Coco, but with shorter legs and hoped he wouldn't take the huff. The stallholder packed them carefully in a box with lots of straw which Grace thought she could use in their crèche when they got it out next Christmas. That seemed such a long way off, a bit like her kids. Shaking the thought away she turned to Max who, ever the gentleman, offered to carry the bag as they set off towards the last row of cabins.

Nearing the end, they came to a display of handmade clothing, brightly coloured shirts, knitwear and flowing dresses and scarves. They were all very chic and slightly retro and reminded Grace of Fleetwood Mac and hippy clothes but with an up-to-date twist. She longingly stroked a fine velvet, azure blue, knee length dress with a softly scooped neckline and long sleeves that flounced at the wrist. It was embellished with silver beads and tiny gems which were scattered over the bodice and A-line skirt. Casually, Grace flicked over the trendy cardboard label and wasn't really surprised by the price tag. Giving it one last touch, she moved away, knowing that she'd spent enough and that the dress, however beautiful, was one extravagance too far.

Max was waiting for Grace as she emerged from the stall. 'So, where shall we eat? Do you fancy one of the restaurants we saw earlier, I'm starving after looking at all that food, or would you prefer to eat here, al fresco? I don't really mind, as long as I'm fed, and soon.'

'What about over there, it looks perfect?' Grace pointed to a cabin serving hot food.

Max was obviously very hungry because he'd already set off in the direction of the cabin. 'Fantastic. Come on, let's get a table and order then I'll bring us some mulled wine, it'd be a sin not to try some while we're here.'

Grace was happy to oblige and smiled as Max guided her through the crowd towards the busy stall to somewhere they could rest aching feet. Best of all, he seemed in no hurry to get back to Rosie's or end their day together.

. . .

They sat in the square eating wild boar baguettes topped with Dijon mustard and drinking hot mulled wine from Christmassy mugs that they could keep as a souvenir. Directly in front of them, under the clock tower, stood a mammoth spruce tree adorned with glowing golden lights that bathed the cobbles in a warm, yellow haze. From inside a nearby restaurant, they could hear the soft strains of accordion music, mingling with the happy chatter of their fellow diners as they ate their meal.

It had been a perfect day, just like the song, and Grace was glad she'd spent it with Max. There had been times throughout their sightseeing and shopping spree when she had the urge to touch him or link his arm. She felt silly and girlish even admitting it to herself but if they did make contact, like when he put his hand on her shoulder to attract her attention, or pull her closer to a stall, she wanted it to remain there. Even as they walked along the streets or between the cabins, when their bodies were forced against each other due to the crowds, she sensed that Max didn't mind but she was still too unsure of the correct protocol and afraid of doing the wrong thing. Maybe Max was shy, like her, which told Grace that their dithering (whilst being refreshing) thus rendered them both incapable of making the final connection and simply holding hands.

Maybe she was getting ahead of herself and he was merely enjoying her company in a purely platonic, easy-going way and would probably run a mile if he knew what she was thinking. Deciding to put her thoughts in a box and turn the key, Grace concentrated on her food and focused on not spoiling the night by overthinking a perfectly natural situation.

Max was enjoying his food, but most of all, being with Grace. It had been the best day he'd had in a long time and as they laughed and explored the city together, it occurred to him that he'd missed doing things like this with someone. It was comforting to turn around and have someone there to share your experience with or ask for an opinion and feel their presence beside you. If he could muster the courage to be a little bolder, he would've liked to hold her hand as they walked along the streets of Tours. They looked like a normal couple, shopping, laughing and eating together, yet an invisible barrier was preventing any physical connection between them and if he could change one thing about today, then that would be it.

God, if Grace knew he was thinking like this she'd most likely prefer to walk back to the hotel rather than get in the car with him. She'd think he was way too pushy and then the day would be ruined. Max resolved to be content with things as they were and not spoil their growing friendship, after all, they still had the rest of their holiday to enjoy and who knew what would happen?

It was getting late and they both wanted to head back and check on their canine companions and not take André's good nature for granted.

As a thank-you, they'd bought him and Wilf a bottle of mulled wine and a box of decorated gingerbread. Grace said she needed the loo before they left so Max offered to wait with the bags while she shot off. Then he made a snap decision.

Gathering up all their things, he raced to the cabin selling the clothes they'd admired earlier, hoping all the way that the blue dress was still there. It was quite a struggle to get his wallet out, juggle boxes and bags and explain to the seller that he had to be quick but he was back where she'd left him, looking totally innocent, by the time she returned. Once he'd casually redistributed their shopping, keeping the blue dress to himself, they set off towards the car park.

It was getting busier now as late-night shoppers swarmed towards the market and it would be easy to get separated so as they headed into the crowd, Max instinctively lifted his arm, indicating that Grace should hold on tight.

When Grace linked hers through his, Max's heart did a weird flip causing him to smile and wonder if she felt the same. While they dodged and weaved through the festive throng, smiling and nodding to the polite on-comers, Max had just one thought. Today had been perfect, just perfect.

CHAPTER 11

W hen they pulled onto the field, Grace remarked to Max
that the sight of the illuminated gîtes still had the same
magical effect as the first time she'd set eyes on them.

Max slowed the car to a stop while they took in the scene and
agreed with Grace. 'Me too. We've stumbled on a gem, hidden
away in the countryside. The weird thing is that even though it
looks totally different in the summer, the feeling is the same, like
a vibe, or is that one of those words that makes anyone under the
age of eighteen cringe when they hear old blokes like me say it?'

'Hey, less of the old. I'm not far behind you but I know what
you mean about a vibe. This place is so relaxing, maybe it's the
Rosie factor, or a combination of Michel's cooking with a
sprinkle of André and Wilf on top. Whatever it is, they should
bottle it and sell it in the hotel. I'll take a crate home with me.'
There it was again, that funny feeling Grace got when she alluded
to the future in any way, a sort of slump mixed with panic, like
she didn't want this to end, whatever this was.

Max, putting the car into gear snapped Grace back to reality
as he reminded her they had their faithful hounds to collect.

'Come on, let's go and get our boys. I bet they've missed us. Is

Coco a sulker? Ginger hasn't learned the sad dog expression yet but he's just a baby. I expect when he's a teenager I'll get full-on, frozen out.'

'Oh yes, Coco actually turns his back on me and you should see the mood he goes in when I throw one of his tatty sticks into the garden… he's worse than my Amber, and that's saying something.'

When André opened his door Grace expected both dogs to come rushing out to greet them with loyal, wagging tails, however, when she and Max popped their heads in the door, both sleepy hounds were snuggled up in front of the fire and looked very at home. To their credit, they did jump up when called and seemed suitably pleased to be stroked and fussed by their owners, then promptly went back to the fire and continued their slumbers.

Coco and Ginger looked none the worse for being abandoned, probably due to the long walk they'd taken through the pine forest where they chased a rabbit. According to André they all had a wonderful time.

'They had many treats from my friend Sebastien who owns the bistro in the village. We passed by earlier and took a few drinks with him. He loves the doggies and they love the big juicy sausages they had for dinner, don't you boys?' André spoke directly to Coco and Ginger who wagged their tails in response. 'So much nicer than those nasty dried biscuits you left, oh and they tell me they are very partial to a bowl of warm milk and honey, it is cold outside, no?'

Max remained silent and looked at Grace who was dumfounded, unable to fathom how on earth André could read Coco's mind or, what had possessed him to give them warm milk and honey, never mind sausages! They would both turn their noses up at dog biscuits in the morning, that was for sure.

'Please, join us for a drink. I have some chestnuts on the fire and a nice ripe Camembert we must sample, sit, sit. I will fetch some glasses.' André obviously enjoyed playing host and Wilf jumped up to fetch plates. Unable to refuse such an enthusiastic invitation, it looked like Max and Grace were staying.

Two hours later, they'd polished off the Camembert and a few bottles of robust Malbec and now Grace was feeling a bit merry. Not only that, after giving in to André and Wilf who insisted both she and Max try the sweet satsumas dipped in dark chocolate and then the chestnuts and cheese, and whatever other delicacies they whipped out from the fridge, Grace couldn't move. They had listened to their host's tales of Christmases past and their travels around Europe but now Grace realised that midnight was approaching and was just about to say goodnight when they heard a knock at the door.

On the doorstep stood the Polish couples. Grace tried hard to remember their names but they were quite difficult to pronounce and the last thing she wanted to do was make a fool of herself or offend them, so she just gave welcome hugs and kisses instead. They had seen that the lights were still on so decided to drop off the boxes of eggs that Zofia had sent over and naturally, André looked thrilled to have even more guests to spoil so they all squashed into the compact gîte and settled down to make a night of it. It was Christmas, after all.

Grace's head throbbed and her brain was a jumble of fuzzy memories from the night before. Did she really drink vodka with gold bits in it? There was definitely some dancing because she remembered being swung around by Wilf during a Polish jig of some kind, and lots of Abba being played. It must have been at least four in the morning before they all went home.

Thankfully, everyone had only a few short paces to go before they made it through the door and she remembered that it had been freezing outside. The gîte was still warm, thanks to her neighbours who had kindly kept the fire going all day and even in her slightly pickled state, Grace had remembered to pop another log in the burner before she went to bed.

Reaching over for her phone she saw it was 8.35am and then groaned as she noticed a string of texts from Seth. She needed to take something for her headache and let Coco outside so she hauled herself out of bed and made her way tentatively downstairs.

It was quite cold so she spent the next five minutes getting the fire going, much to the delight of her dog who wasn't amused that *his* lovely log burner had gone out. Two paracetamols and a strong cup of coffee later, through bleary eyes, Grace began reading the messages from Seth. As she started scrolling through her son's texts, it became instantly clear what was wrong so she took a quick sip of her coffee and rang him.

Seth was fed up with Val D'Isere and skiing and all of his mates. 'It's not their fault, Mum, but I'm the only one in the group who can't ski or take part in any other activities that requires two arms. Everyone went sledging yesterday and I was left in the cafe like a spare part. I feel like I'm a burden. They've all tried to be tactful and not go on about what a great time they've had during the day but even that makes me cringe and feel awkward. They're tiptoeing round me and it's not fair on them. It was a bit better last night but I still stood out like a sore thumb and spent most of the time in the nightclub trying to avoid having my arm whacked.'

'Oh, Seth, I'm gutted for you I really am... but I'm glad the lads are being kind, at least they are trying to include you in stuff. I don't know what to suggest really. At least you are on holiday in a lovely place, and not stuck at home on your own. That's something I suppose.' As platitudes go Grace knew that was extremely weak but it was all she had.

'Mum, do you know how flipping boring it is looking at snow, pine trees and other people having fun? It's doing my head in.' Seth sounded a bit grumpy and impatient.

'Yes, love, I imagine it is, but I really don't know what to suggest. What do you want to do?' Grace got the impression Seth wanted out of there, she was right.

'Well actually I've had an idea which is why I messaged you... but I don't know if you'd be up for it.'

'Up for what?' Grace's head was pounding and she had no desire to second guess her son's thoughts, which he soon made clear.

After much deliberation Seth had decided he might as well go home, until one of his mates suggested he meet up with his mum instead. Seth had mentioned that she was in France so after a quick browse on the internet he'd found out he could fly directly from Geneva to Nantes airport, which, as far as he could work out on the map, was about forty-five minutes from where Grace was staying. So... he was wondering, would it be okay if he jumped on a plane and spent Christmas with her? It was either that or hang about there being a party pooper, or worse, have to spend the day with Janice and his dad. He could be with her by tomorrow afternoon if he got himself organised, so, what did she think?

It was a no-brainer for Grace, how could she refuse? He sounded so fed up on the phone and there was plenty of room there. She heard the relief in his voice when she said yes, laced with a bit of excitement too, and her heart went out to him. How could he even have thought she'd refuse and now, she could look after his poorly arm as well. Grace told him to book the flight and then let her know the details, adding that whatever time it was, she'd pick him up at the airport the next day.

Seth ended the call quickly leaving Grace in peace to warm her toes and drink her coffee. Her headache was easing so she relaxed back on the sofa and absorbed the details of their conversation. It would have been very easy to nod back off but Coco needed to be fed and just as Grace was summoning the strength to get up, she heard a gentle tapping on the door. Coco woofed and shot over, eager to see who was on the other side. It was Max, dressed in his cycling gear and looking fresh and hangover free.

'Hi. I saw the smoke from the chimney so presumed you were up. I didn't wake you, did I?' Max was stroking Coco who then made his bid for freedom and ran into the field.

'No, it's okay. I've been up for a while. I must look a right state and I've got a bit of a hangover. How come you look so bright and breezy, by the way?' Grace felt extremely self-conscious in her fleecy pyjamas and God only knew what state her hair was in. And she probably had streaky panda eyes to match the dragged-through-a-hedge-backwards look.

'You are a vision of loveliness, even with a hangover and I haven't exactly escaped the legacy of André's hospitality either. That's why I'm going for a ride, to clear my head. Anyway, what I came over for, is to ask you if you fancy going up to the restaurant this evening? It's a special Christmas dinner apparently, Rosie mentioned it the other night. It's normally booked up for months in advance but she said she could squeeze us in. What do you think?' Max's face looked eager, and hopeful.

'Okay, that would be lovely. Shall I go up and tell her later?'

Grace was thrilled he'd asked her and the thought of spending more time in his company sent sparks straight to her heart. Then it dawned on her. This would be their last night alone because tomorrow, Seth would be here.

'No, it's okay. I can cycle up there now. I'll call in when I get back to tell you what time. I'll probably be gone an hour or so. Are you okay, you look a bit worried about something?' Max's eyebrows furrowed in concern.

'No. I'm fine. Now clear off while I go and make myself look presentable and find something nice for this evening. I didn't bring anything fancy with me and goodness knows what they wear in France for special Christmas dinners.' Grace was smiling but her heart felt a bit sad.

She watched him jump on his bike, then waved goodbye, admiring his nice, tight bum as he pedalled off up the track. Shutting the door behind her, Grace leaned her head against the timber and closed her eyes, sighing loudly. Just when she'd finally met someone nice, totally by an accidental miracle and things were going from strength to strength, it would soon come to a premature end.

Maybe she was being fanciful and the fun they'd had together was nothing more than that. But she couldn't deny her intuition, or the way he looked at her and that lovely feeling she had last night as they walked arm in arm through the streets of Tours. She sensed he felt more for her than friendship and was in no doubt at all about what was going on in her own head, and heart. Grace thought Max was special and had been sent there by Destiny, or whoever was in charge of Cupid's department.

Unfortunately for Grace, they must have gone on a tea break and took their eye off the ball because while they dunked their custard creams, Seth managed to make contact with a tree and break his arm, totally ruining the plot. Now, her lovely disappointed son needed his mum to cheer him up and was unwittingly going to be a big fat gooseberry. Hearing an angry woof on the other side of the door, Grace jumped.

'Flipping heck! Sorry, Coco, I totally forgot about you.' Opening the door, she let her disgruntled dog inside and watched him walk over to his empty bowl, have a sniff, and then look expectantly in her direction.

Realising it was time she got her finger out, fed the dog and took a shower, Grace brushed away her thoughts of romance and the rosy images of yesterday. Midway through pouring biscuits into Coco's bowl, her phoned pinged twice. One message was from Seth saying he'd booked his flight and would arrive at 2.25pm the following day. The second was from Heidi saying they were on their way to Elliot's parents'. She replied to each of them, telling her daughter about Seth's plans and wishing her a safe trip. Grace truly hoped that Heidi's visit would go well and they'd all have a great time, despite everyone's concerns.

All she could do now was wait and see what would happen with Heidi… and Max. Grace wondered how the latter would react when she told him the news. There was no reason why having her son around should spoil things too much. Seth was an adult and after all, his dad had found someone else, so why shouldn't she? Feeling much more positive, Grace left Coco staring at his dry biscuits and headed upstairs for a shower. A day being fed French fancies had clearly gone to his head.

Letting the warm water refresh her, she told herself it was a blip, a minor hiccup that with careful handling, could be overcome. She would spend a lovely evening with Max and somehow, without being too obvious, give him the hint that she'd really enjoyed their time together then assure him that despite Seth being here, they could still see each other. While she shampooed her hair, Grace told herself firmly that it would all work out just fine and nothing else could possibly go wrong.

Heidi had the heaviest heart, a tetchy husband and two very subdued children sitting in the back of the car and had tried all sorts to jolly them along. She'd sang 'Jingle Bells' (twice) and every single Christmas song she could remember the words to, along with thinking up exciting, fun-packed things that they could do in Lincoln during the next three days. In truth, all Heidi wanted to do was get through the visit to Gordon and Vera's without World War Three breaking out and then skedaddle, just as soon as Christmas Day was over with. To make matters worse, she was truly envious of her brother who it seemed would be spending Christmas with their mum after all.

They'd attempted to put their arrival off until Christmas Eve, but owing to the fact that today was Vera's sixtieth birthday, they'd been guilted into arriving earlier so they could join in her celebrations. Now, they would be arriving just before Sunday lunch and the only thing that softened the blow was being treated to a slap up meal by the Lambe seniors. Some of Vera's friends from the church would also be there along with Elliot's aunts and uncles but despite her rumbling tummy, Heidi was dreading it. From what she'd been told, it appeared that Skye and Finn would be the only children there, so an arduously long, boring afternoon of best table manners and listening to their monotonous yakking was on the cards for all of them.

Skye adored her Grandma Grace and all the things they did together on the run up to Christmas. It was part of the tradition, getting into the spirit of things and building up the excitement before the big day. Heidi knew that hers, as with most children, liked routine and familiarity and her mother provided all this in bucketfuls, for all of them, totally selflessly and in equal measure. Perhaps that's why Heidi was so resentful towards Vera and Gordon. A huge, barbed wire ball of it was stored inside her, unhelpfully laced with thinly veiled disdain and anger, that to date, she had managed to bottle up. The crux of it was that Heidi felt bitter and dismayed at the way her in-laws not only treated both their sons, but their grandchildren too.

Elliot and Nathan had once described in great, depressing detail their unhappy childhoods. Mostly, it had been confined and determined by strict rules, the book of God and parents who should, according to Heidi, have kept their legs crossed and avoided parenthood altogether. They were cold, unloving, and puritanical and had sucked all the joy out of their offsprings' formative years. By the time they were teenagers, Elliot had begun to rebel whereas Nathan chose the path of least resistance and stayed in his room for the duration. His lack of confidence was in stark contrast to the irreverent and rebellious streak shown by his elder sibling.

It seemed that Elliot was so used to having, not only his liberty, but his television, record collection and more often than not, his meals, taken away from him that he decided there was nothing left to lose. As a consequence, he took great delight in disrespecting, disobeying and distancing himself wherever possible from his control freak parents. By the time Elliot was old enough to leave for university, he quite literally ran for the hills and spent three years of unbridled freedom in Edinburgh, returning to see his isolated brother and miserable parents only when absolutely necessary.

One of the topics on which the Lambe family regularly conflicted, was religion. Elliot merely used politics, football, racial equality and their homophobia as a potent blend of herbs and spices to heat up an already volatile relationship and wasn't afraid to goad his parents with any of them. Heidi tended to agree with her husband on almost all subjects, apart from football, simply because she wasn't interested. Now, as Lincoln loomed on the horizon, she had an awful feeling that due to the time of year, religion may just be the catalyst that would reignite the tempestuous relationship between a distant father and his bitter son.

Heidi and Elliot respected and were interested in all faiths, seeing merit in most of them. They thought that some beliefs and traditions were extremely moving and moral, binding communities and families together through times of adversity, but most of all, could give the worshipper comfort and peace which was a rare and precious thing. That said, having had his parents' Christian values rammed down his throat since he exited the womb, Elliot was adamant that his own children would be free from any religious affiliation or parental burden, leaving Skye and Finn free to choose for themselves if, when and whom they wanted to worship.

As time went by and atrocities in the name of many different religions waged relentlessly across the world, Heidi and Elliot were even more convinced that their decision to turn away from faith-based worship was right for them and their young family. They both believed in God and hoped that by teaching their children morals and leading mainly by example, they could inspire Skye and Finn to believe in him too. They explained that being a truthful, kind, loving, helpful person who accepted everyone, regardless of the colour of their skin, or any other name tag they were labelled with, was what they thought God wanted. In private conversations, Heidi told Elliot that the God *she* believed in would be appalled and in despair over what was going on down here on earth, in his name. She also thought he needed to prioritise and make some time to pop downstairs and have a word in the ears of his faithful flocks, sharpish!

It was for these reasons that when Skye and then Finn were brought into the world, but not baptised, holy hell broke loose within the Lambe family. Heidi had her suspicions that the rebellious teenager in her husband did manage to extract some pleasure from his revenge and had served it extremely cold, Ghengis Khan style. However, having heard all of Elliot's miserable childhood tales, she thought he actually deserved a tiny bit of payback at the expense of his parents so turned a blind eye. That said, Heidi was also mindful that her husband may one day have irreversible regrets, when Gordon and Vera were no longer around. Along with the desire for her children to know their grandparents, she had battled valiantly on and secured the tenuous links between them all. Perhaps this short break was an opportunity to get to know her in-laws better, and best-case scenario, they would redeem themselves in the eyes of her husband. It was worth a try, but Heidi knew not to expect miracles.

Now, as the Lambe residence came into view, Heidi wished that she had no morals whatsoever, was the opposite of kind and thoughtful and didn't care one bit what God thought of her. That way, she'd be at home, having homemade mince pies and a cup of tea with her mum, not Sunday lunch with the Grim Reaper and his sour wife.

By first light on Monday morning, all Heidi's fears were being brought to bear. The birthday lunch had been hideous. There wasn't one person under the age of sixty around the table and all were cut from the same cloth, pious, stuck-up, completely devoid of a sense of humour and the ability to have fun. The kids had the most boring afternoon of their lives and spent much of it in fear of doing something wrong, so hardly spoke or ate anything. Luckily, there was a small play area at the restaurant, so Elliot and Heidi took it in turns to take them outside, happily leaving the other in purgatory.

The trouble started when they got back to the house. Vera seemed quite pleased to have been the star of the show and had downed a couple of large port and lemons, much to the annoyance of Gordon who was in a foul mood. Skye had helped her grandmother carry in her gifts and the birthday cake, lovingly baked and iced by one of the Dreary Bunch. As the children had barely eaten, Heidi asked if it would be okay for them to have some supper, maybe a piece of toast or a sandwich. When Vera Pink-Cheeks looked quite put out at having to do a stroke on her big day, Heidi politely offered to do the honours and swiftly shuffled her hungry kids off to the kitchen.

After wolfing down their supper, Skye and Finn were eyeing the cake and not being the shy or retiring type, her son asked when they would be cutting it up. Before Vera could answer, Gordon informed them that they wouldn't be having cake as they had wasted their food in the restaurant *and*, had it been left to him, they wouldn't even have been allowed some toast! Thankfully, Elliot was in the loo and heard none of it so to avoid further discussion on the matter, Heidi announced that it was time they got ready for bed and spirited them upstairs which is when the bedroom incident occurred.

The house was a bit on the chilly side but Heidi had tested the radiators and they were actually turned on, just. Elliot had been sent to the car to collect their things so Heidi went upstairs with Vera. When she opened the door of the first bedroom and after they got over the sight (and smell) of the musty, bleak room, they were hit with the double whammy. Vera announced that this bedroom was for Finn and the one next door, was for Skye. Before her children could burst into tears, Heidi explained that at home, they shared a room and weren't used to sleeping apart, especially in a strange house so if Vera didn't mind, they would top and tail, to make them feel more comfortable. Heidi was quite firm on the matter and while Vera looked slightly wrong-footed, she reluctantly agreed, as long as they didn't let on to Gordon because he would frown upon members of the opposite sex sharing a room, let alone a bed. Heidi watched as Vera tutted loudly and made her unsteady way downstairs then with the crisis averted, began to get the children ready for bed. Jumpers and socks were a necessity despite Elliot turning up the radiators. Skye and Finn were tired and from the looks of them, completely miserable but soon settled down and cuddled up under the cold sheets. After assuring their children that they'd be right next door and they would warm up soon, Heidi couldn't be bothered to go downstairs again because both had seen quite enough of Vera and Gordon for one day, so just shouted from the landing that they were all calling it a night.

It was around midnight when they heard their bedroom door creak open and saw two pale, frightened faces peering into the darkness.

'Mum, Dad, please can we get in with you?' Skye whispered and Heidi heard the tremble in her little girl's voice.

'My feet are cold, Mum. And my nose, and we keep hearing

scary noises. We think there's something in the wardrobe.' Finn was halfway across the room and Skye had already shut the door.

'Come on, jump in the middle. We'll get you warm, cuddle up and close your eyes, no chatting, okay?' Elliot pulled back the covers and let them both in, holding them tight to warm them up.

'Dad, I'm hungry as well. Did you get some cake? Grandad wouldn't let us have any because we wasted our tea. But my tummy is really rumbling now.' Finn was snuggled up under his father's arm and yawned loudly.

'No, I didn't and I don't want any either. If Grandad is too mean to share the cake then he can keep all of it. Try and go to sleep, it will be breakfast time soon.' Elliot sounded furious.

As they lay there in the dark, Elliot with his son's little body squashed close, Heidi just knew his age-old resentment was bubbling to the surface. His next, whispered words confirmed it.

'The miserable old tight arse could've given them a small piece of cake, they're just kids for God's sake. He'll never change, he's incapable of it.'

Heidi could hear Elliot's bitterness and imagined he was reminded of his father's spiteful ways. Then she remembered something of her own.

'Hang on. I think I know what we can eat!' Heidi jumped out of bed and pulled back the curtains to let in some light before rummaging around in her suitcase.

Once she found what she was looking for, she leapt back into bed and snuggled down under the blankets. 'Here, look what I've got. A nice big box of Milk Tray. Come on, we can share these.'

The children squealed in delight and after their mum had opened the box, began tucking in.

Heidi didn't care about the sugar or mention that they were one of the gifts she'd bought for Vera and Gordon and hoped they hadn't heard her rip off the wrapping paper, which was now stuffed inside her case. But Elliot knew exactly what they were and as he leant over and ruffled her hair with his hand, she knew he was smiling and agreed with her course of actions. Once they'd polished off the top layer and made a start on the second, the children's sleepy eyes began to droop and before long, both had nodded off.

Elliot remained awake and Heidi could feel the waves of tension radiating from her husband. This trip had been a huge mistake, she knew that now. It had awakened too many demons and was having a negative effect on all of them. She was dreading tomorrow and would have to try and think of something fun to do, maybe ice skating or a pantomime, anything that would alleviate the awful atmosphere in this house and cheer her family up.

Unbeknown to Heidi, she was wasting her time and should have just gone straight to sleep rather than worrying about day trips or birthday cake. While she made lists in her head, the ticking time bomb inside her husband was primed and about to explode, the very next morning, all over their breakfast.

CHAPTER 12

The first faux pas was to have dared to lie in. According to house rules, they should have been up and about by 8am sharp but after an uncomfortable night squashed into one bed, they all needed some sleep. Leaving Elliot to get dressed, Heidi and the kids eventually trooped down for breakfast at 9.15am only to be met with frosty stares from Vera and the back of Gordon's newspaper. You could have cut the tension in the air with a cake knife until the silence was shattered by a loud voice, barking orders from behind his broadsheet. It caused Heidi and her kids to jump.

'Your mother has just cleared away. We did say that breakfast is at eight and you can't expect her to wait all morning for you, she needs to get on.' Gordon slowly folded his newspaper and glared at them from beneath tortoiseshell spectacles.

'Sorry, Gordon, we didn't realise the time. I hope we haven't put you out, Vera? We don't expect anything warm, the children will be happy with cereal and I'll make Elliot and me some tea, if that's okay?' Heidi thought Gordon was the rudest, most obnoxious man she had ever met and couldn't understand why they had even bothered to invite them, if it was all so much trouble.

When Elliot entered the kitchen, his voice once again made Heidi jump. She was turning into a nervous wreck.

'Heidi, stop apologising, it's only two bowls and two cups to wash up. If it's too much hassle we'll take the kids to McDonald's and get them a nice sausage muffin for breakfast.'

Elliot was being sarcastic but the kids were thrilled and took him at his word because they knew this was only reserved for special treats.

'Huh, junk food for breakfast, why am I not surprised? Vera, get them some cornflakes, they need to eat proper food, not rubbish.' Gordon's pompous voice boomed across the kitchen.

After dishes and spoons were brought and plonked onto the table, the children ate in total silence. Both looked like they were chewing sawdust as their parents drank tea and made polite, strained conversation with Vera. Gordon just read his paper. Finn repeatedly yawned loudly and rubbed his eyes, which Heidi thought wasn't surprising after her kids had been awake for ages, listening to the night noises. The inadequate heating hadn't helped and the chilly room only added to their woes. Heidi knew they were both still a bit tired which didn't bode well for the rest of the day, and they'd probably end up with colds, a depressing thought which was exacerbated by her father-in-law's next words.

'Looks like someone needs an early night. Does he have a proper routine at home or do you let them both run riot?' Every sentence Gordon spoke was laced with innuendo. It was like he just couldn't help himself.

'Oh yes. He's in bed by seven thirty every night. We have a nice story then it's off to sleep. He's been in a routine since he was a baby, they both have.' Heidi was irritating herself now, why should she have to keep explaining or apologising.

Why was he like this? The only thing she could think was that because they weren't used to visitors, it made them uncomfortable and snappy. Perhaps after a day or so they'd chill out a bit, but once again, she was wasting her breath. Heidi's dismal thoughts were interrupted by Skye who out of the blue, decided to pass on an interesting fact about her favourite subject, Christmas. With wide-eyed enthusiasm, the eager seven-year-old swallowed her cornflakes, droplets of milk escaping and dribbling slowly down her chin, then spoke animatedly to Gordon.

'Don't worry, Grandad, we always go to bed *super* quick on Christmas Eve because we have to get up mega early in the morning. And guess what? Mum and Dad let us wake them up whenever we want so we can go down and open our presents. Do you want us to get you and Grandma up too, or shall we just be quiet and let you have a lie in?' Skye was full of it, forcing Heidi to smile lovingly at her naive daughter.

Heidi could see the sheer excitement in her eyes and was proud that even though Gordon was a grump, the little girl was still being thoughtful and in her own way, trying to please him. Heidi couldn't have predicted what was to happen next, in truth, nobody would've believed that a grown man could be so spiteful either, but when Gordon replied, he lit the blue touch paper and right before her eyes, Elliot simply exploded.

'Well, you may get away with that type of behaviour in your own home, young lady, but here, we do things differently. There won't be any running about at all hours while you're under this roof. Your father knows only too well my rules about when you can open presents. Isn't that right, Elliot?'

Gordon looked smugly at his son who Heidi noticed had gone oddly pale. Before anyone could respond, The Grinch continued, directing his comments at Skye.

'You will be allowed to open one present at breakfast and the rest you will save until after church and Christmas lunch. That's how we have always done things and I see no reason to change now.' He then looked away, plucked a pen from his top pocket and began doing the crossword.

Heidi's heart was hammering in her chest, the elephant was in the room and she didn't know how to react for the best. Her mind was working frantically. Should she try to placate her tearful, crestfallen daughter, punch Gordon in the mouth or restrain her husband who looked like he was about to commit murder? In any case, she left it too late.

'Who the *hell* do you think you are speaking to? How dare you talk to my daughter like that when she was trying to conduct a perfectly civil conversation with you?'

Everyone was silent and you could have heard a pin drop in China as Elliot continued.

'Let's get one thing straight, right here and now. You know full well how I feel about *your* church and for that reason, none of my family will be attending the service on Christmas Day. As for presents, they will open every single one of them the second they open their eyes, do you understand? You may have managed to ruin all of *my* Christmases but you are not getting away with it where our kids are concerned.' Elliot looked livid.

The palms of his hands were pressed onto the table as if they were glued in place, which was a relief, because if they came unstuck, Heidi thought they would end up around Gordon's neck. She had never seen her husband this angry – ever!

Gordon spoke next, his smarmy voice laced with disdain and sarcasm, as if he was talking to a delinquent. 'And may I remind *you* whose house this is and that you are our guests. And for that reason alone, I expect you to adhere to our ways and show us respect. Really, Elliot. I hoped you'd grown out of all this nonsense, especially now you are a parent yourself.'

He glanced sideways at Finn and Skye as if to make a point, who, being unused to angry scenes were now filling up with tears, but that didn't stop Gordon.

'Don't you think it's time you ceased this adolescent behaviour. I've always found your mix of anarchy and atheism rather tedious, along with whatever other causes you're banging your drum for. And now, true to form, you've made a scene and upset the children. I hope you're happy because thanks to you, the morning is ruined.' Gordon shook his head and tutted, looking towards his wife as if for back-up. Vera merely looked on, her pursed lips speechless and neither use nor ornament.

Heidi wanted to slap him herself but ever aware of her blood pressure and the precious bump she was carrying around, she quickly leant over and covered Elliot's hand with hers, pleading with her eyes for him to be calm. She knew instantly that it was too late.

Elliot erupted. 'You bigoted old git! How dare you blame this on me? You don't know the meaning of the word parents, either of you. Do you know what, forget it, just forget it. I can't be bothered arguing with you anymore. It's not worth it. You're not worth it!'

Heidi watched on, completely impotent because she could tell that Elliot was on the verge of unleashing all the rage and resentment he'd been storing up for years, bubbling and boiling inside him like a red-hot volcano for far too long.

As Elliot stood up and looked at the nervous, teary faces of his children and the beseeching eyes of his pregnant wife, it occurred to him in that precise moment that he couldn't win. His parents wouldn't listen, understand or care, so why waste his breath? There were many fine examples of their harsh, unfeeling ways festering in his brain but he didn't want Skye and Finn to hear all that. He also knew he couldn't stay in that house for one minute longer though, because if he did, he'd say things that could never be taken back or forgotten.

'Heidi, take the kids upstairs and get our things together, we're leaving. Now! Come on you two, make it snappy.' Elliot was shaking with rage but tried to keep his voice cool and level when he spoke to his family.

He didn't even glance in the direction of either of his disappointing parents, he couldn't bear it. All Elliot cared about now was getting his family as far away from them as he could.

Heidi immediately did as Elliot asked and held out her hands towards her children. Before another word could be spoken, they came around from the other side of the table and grasped on tight. Elliot followed closely behind as they all left the room and made their way upstairs. Heidi packed their things in silence and was surprised by the speed at which the children gathered their belongings and brought them to her so she could zip up the case and they could make their escape. *Actions speak louder than words*, was the thought that sprang to mind as they all trundled downstairs and headed for the front door.

It was blatantly obvious (and probably for the best) that Elliot had no intention of speaking to either of them when he refused to allow his children back into the kitchen, which left Heidi to say goodbye. As her husband loaded the car and the children fastened their seat belts, she went to find her in-laws. Tapping on the kitchen door, she felt slightly nervous about entering but someone had to be the peacemaker, the link between parents and child. Maybe in the future all this could be forgiven and bridges rebuilt.

'Right, we'll be off then. I've left your presents in the hall. Despite what's happened, we do wish you all the best for Christmas.' Heidi couldn't think of anything else to say.

She felt extremely uncomfortable in their presence, it was like being in the headmaster's office and she half expected Gordon to ask her to hold out her hand so he could give her six of the best with a wooden spoon.

It was Vera who finally managed to find her tongue and took to the stage.

'It's not your fault, Heidi. Elliot has always been the same, no respect for his elders or, it seems, the feelings of his family. He's totally ruined Christmas with his selfish belligerence and I am absolutely furious with him.'

Vera walked briskly over to the drawer of her china cabinet, cups and plates rattling on the shelves as she pulled it open sharply and took out four envelopes.

Heidi was furious too, but definitely not with her husband, yet somehow she managed to bite her lip and stay calm. How dare Vera blame Elliot? The sooner she was out of there the better.

'Here, you may as well take these, they're your gifts. Book tokens for all of you, something useful. Perhaps Elliot should spend his on a self-help manual and finally learn to control his temper.' Vera passed the envelopes to Heidi before continuing, her voice terse. 'Please let us know when you've arrived home and until then, have a safe trip.'

Heidi got the impression that Vera was actually dismissing her, like she was a naughty schoolgirl. The bloody cheek of it! Rather than retaliate, Heidi just felt relieved that the lecture had come to an end so smiled weakly and turned to go.

Then she spotted the birthday cake. Two large chunks were missing and she pictured Vera and Gordon last night, gorging themselves on a Victoria sponge while her children's tummies rumbled upstairs.

Swinging around, this time with a voice laced with sarcasm, Heidi bade them farewell. 'Well, thanks for these. I'm sure I'll find something useful to do with them. And enjoy the rest of your Christmas, *and* your cake,' then muttered under her breath, perhaps *just* loud enough to hear, 'I hope it makes you both puke.'

Marching down the corridor, Heidi pulled open the front door and slammed it loudly behind her. Then, as she reached the end of the path, opened the lid of the dustbin and threw the envelopes inside.

'And you can stick your flaming book tokens right up your tight arses.' She said a lot more loudly before getting into the car which was waiting on the street with the engine running.

Heidi fastened her seat belt as Elliot covered her hand with his and squeezed gently. Then, trying to compose herself, she turned to check on her lovely Skye and Finn who looked confused, relieved and slightly nervous, all at the same time. She gave them a big brave smile, a quick wink, then, as Elliot pulled away, she turned to face the road ahead and promptly burst into tears.

Grace was having a lazy morning. She was also blissfully unaware of the drama occurring in Lincoln. Instead, she was warming her toes in front of the fire, sipping fresh coffee and eating warm croissants. She couldn't sleep and had been up since first light, going over and over the events of the previous day, and night. Her mind flitted back over the past twenty-four hours, to when she had her early morning conversation with Seth and told him it was okay to join her for Christmas. Then there had been her dinner date with Max. This time yesterday, she was just boring old Grandma Grace, separated mother of three, dog-owner and typer of spreadsheets. But today, she was reborn and in her place was a modern woman who had thrown caution to the wind and spent a night of passion with a totally gorgeous man.

Grace was mildly giddy, very loved-up and acutely aware of the multitude of emotions swirling around inside her. It was so out of character, bordering on foolish, but last night had seemed so right. She had just clicked with Max, maybe from the moment they met on the ship which was the reason she refused to feel ashamed or embarrassed about sleeping with him. She was a grown woman with a mind of her own and therefore could do as she wished.

If it was just going to be a holiday romance then she wouldn't be the first, or the last, woman on earth to have a fling with a handsome stranger whilst abroad and would deal with the consequences when the time came. But deep down, Grace hoped that it would be more than that and whether she was reading the signals all wrong, or he was a practised love rat and merely stringing her along, she would have to wait and see. However, when Grace replayed the events of yesterday and pictured his face and remembered the words he'd spoken, she was quite sure that it was neither.

The previous morning, once her hangover had eased and she'd showered and changed, Grace began to feel a little more human so decided to get a bit of fresh air and walk up to see Rosie. She needed to check that it was okay for Seth to stay and even though she couldn't foresee any problems, thought it was polite to ask.

Rosie was at home and despite her resistance, Grace was invited in for coffee and a chat. As expected, she was absolutely fine about Seth, saying that the gîte was more than big enough and as the rental wasn't per person, it really didn't matter who stayed there.

Obviously not one to beat about the bush, Rosie then confessed to being an award-winning matchmaker so with a cheeky wink, said she felt duty bound to check on progress where Grace and Max were concerned. Grace was actually relieved to be able to talk about it out loud so as Rosie poured more coffee, she began with their day out.

Grace admitted that she was unsure of what to do about the Seth situation as the last thing she wanted to do was drop Max like a hot potato, just because her son had turned up. That would be mean and unnecessary, however, she'd been single since her split with Ben and felt a bit awkward about introducing someone new. Also, how could she juggle the rest of the holiday, spending time with Seth and also enjoy being with Max? The saying 'two's company' certainly rang true in this situation so Grace looked hopefully at the thoughtful, concerned face of Rosie. Maybe she could come up with the answer.

'You know what I'd do. I'd make sure that tonight, during dinner or after, you tell Max exactly how you feel and then hit him with the news about your unexpected guest. And as for your son, he sounds like a nice lad so I'm sure he's not going to object to you making friends and anyway, there's no reason why you can't spend time with him and Max. Simply explain how you met Max and that you hit it off straight away so you've been spending a bit of time together. I'm sure Seth will welcome some male company and on the flip side, you said you wanted to take things slowly, so now you have the perfect chaperone. Voila, problem solved.' Rosie spread her hands wide and smiled, then passed Grace a slice of brioche.

'You know what? You're right. The last thing I want is to make a fool of myself with Max and then it all goes pear shaped. Seth has to be back at work in a week so I will still have time alone with Max when he's gone home. That's if he wants to, of course.' Grace accepted her cake before adding, 'And I suppose it's a bit of a test as well. If he goes cold on me when I tell him about Seth, then I'll know he was only after one thing. But if he doesn't, well, maybe there's hope.' Grace felt revived by the coffee and her own flash of common sense.

'Brilliant, that's all settled then.' Rosie paused after they heard a car pull up outside, then got up to open the door. 'This will be Anna, no, don't rush off, I'd like you to meet her. She's lovely and one of my best friends. She met her partner Daniel here a few years ago and bought a house in the next village.' Rosie began waving from the door to her friend.

'Stay for one more coffee and we can all swap love stories, this place is magical. I swear it cast a spell over me and Michel and then André and Wilf, and goodness only knows who else over the years. Let's hope it doesn't fail with you and Max.'

In the next breath she was welcoming in her friend, a pretty brunette with a kind, open face and trotting in behind her, came a stocky bulldog who was introduced as Pippa.

Grace spent another hour chatting with Rosie and Anna, and being bombarded with demands for attention from Pippa who apparently had a reputation for being a little diva. She would have happily stayed longer but eventually dragged herself away to catch up with Max who she hoped was back from his ride. Grace was going to take Rosie's advice. In fact she wasn't even going to wait till that evening to drop Max the hint about how she felt. Spotting his bike parked round the back of his gîte, Grace ran up the steps and knocked on the door. There was a few minutes delay before he finally answered.

'Sorry, I only just heard you knocking, I've been over to yours but I thought you might be asleep.' Max was rubbing his wet hair with a towel as he spoke.

'I went for a walk up to Rosie's and we had a coffee. Anyway, I wondered if you fancied coming over for some lunch, nothing fancy. I suppose we shouldn't eat too much if we're going to have a feast tonight, but I could rustle up an omelette if you like?' Grace was suddenly nervous, what if he declined and she was left on the doorstep feeling stupid.

'That'd be great, are you sure? Shall I bring anything, apart from Ginger, if that's okay? He can keep Coco company.'

Max seemed eager enough and Grace was impressed with her spark of initiative.

'I'm sure, and no, I don't need anything. And Ginger will be most welcome. Just come over when you're ready, I'll get going.' And with that, she waved and set off.

Max smiled, pleased as punch she'd invited him and went straight inside to rifle through his clothes, desperate to find something decent to wear. He'd packed for a hermit-style existence and the odd meal in the restaurant, not thinking for a second he'd meet someone he wanted to impress. He'd surprised himself a few times in the past twenty-four hours with the crazy thoughts that were swimming around his head. While he pedalled around the tiny villages, his mind was a whirl and no matter how fast he went or how hard he pushed himself, he couldn't get Grace out of his mind. He hadn't felt like this for years, well, since he met Carmel really and he had to admit it, it was a good feeling. The only problem was, he didn't want to blow things and was battling with stirring emotions, but knew he had to rein them in; otherwise he could scare her off.

Max wished he had someone to confide in or ask their advice, but as the only available ears belonged to his faithful hound, he was on his own. The only sane plan he could come up with was to keep calm and carry on. He was doing alright up to now and as his dad always said, 'steady pace wins the race', so with his father's words of wisdom planted firmly in his brain, Max whistled for Ginger to follow him and made his way over to Grace's.

They had a lovely lunch of mushroom omelette and a green salad followed by slices of what looked and tasted like custard tart with a blob of crème fraîche on top. They limited themselves to one glass of white wine each and then went on to cups of tea while they sat with their dogs in front of the fire. Grace found a music channel on the TV and they listened to what they presumed was the French equivalent of Classic FM. Whatever it was, it sounded peaceful and relaxing and every now and then they would play something that they thought they recognised, along with a scattering of more festive tunes.

Wiggling her toes inside warm socks, Grace also found herself thinking out loud. 'This is perfect, isn't it? It's just how I imagined it would be. I was dithering all the time about coming here by myself and now, it feels like a home from home. I'm so glad I didn't chicken out.'

Grace was gazing into the fire and turned, just in time to catch Max out because he'd been staring at her, making her stomach contract and her heart miss a beat.

'I don't think I put too much thought into what it would be like. I just wanted to be away for Christmas and made the booking after a night of soul-searching which led to me feeling proactive. It could have all gone horribly wrong though. I might have been sitting up there in the gîte with my baguette for one, wondering what the hell I was doing in the middle of a field on my own. But lucky for me, you turned up, and not Miss Trunchbull, so I'm glad I was hasty. Otherwise I wouldn't have had an omelette for my lunch, a buddy for Ginger and someone to stoke the fire for me.' Max raised his eyebrows and smiled at her, just before the cushion made contact with his head.

'Very funny, but can I ask you something? And tell me honestly. Apart from wanting to do something a bit different this year, was there any other reason why you prefer to be alone at Christmas? I'm only asking because you seem such a nice bloke and I'm sure you have loads of friends you could spend it with, and your family of course.' Grace was being quite bold but she wanted to know what made him tick or worse, if he was running away from a dark secret, or even himself.

Max sighed and put his cup on the table, then reclined back onto the sofa, crossing his arms behind his head. When he glanced over and saw Grace's earnest, green eyes, waiting patiently, he sensed she was watching for signs that he was being truthful. At that moment, Max knew he didn't want to fob her off with half a story, or save face either. This was his chance to tell her about Carmel and how rotten she'd made him feel, the mistakes he'd made with women and why he'd been totally celibate ever since. Maybe, in the telling, he could let her know that this time he was serious and ready for a proper, grown-up relationship, as his sister had so bluntly put it.

'It will probably sound a bit weird but one day, it just occurred to me that I'd backed myself into a corner. After enjoying a bit of freedom then meeting a complete nutcase, swiftly followed by a period of self-enforced celibacy, I realised I was turning into a lonely old hermit.' Max folded his arms across his chest and looked at Grace, then continued.

'Shall I leave now or do you want to hear more?' He waited for her reply and tried to gauge her reaction so far.

'No, please go on, I'm intrigued, especially about this nutcase.' Grace tucked her legs underneath her, and once she'd stopped fidgeting and moving cushions, Max got on with his story.

Max was completely truthful, no holds barred and had Grace in stitches when he got to the part about Mad Melissa. The laughter relaxed the mood and was oddly therapeutic because after she'd scared the living daylights out of him and almost given him a nervous breakdown, it was good to finally see the funny side and in doing so, shake Melissa off for good.

'So, even though I faced up to the fact that I'd become the reclusive, grumpy, history teacher, living in splendid isolation on the top floor, I still didn't want to be the fifth wheel at Christmas. You're right, I could've gone to family and friends but it's really just one day that I feel duty bound to endure and can actually live without. I also wanted some time to take stock of my life and work out what I wanted for *my* future. The intention was to return in the New Year with a foolproof master plan and a positive outlook.' Max felt like he'd shed a skin telling Grace all that, even the bit about his foray into the crazy world of dating.

She still looked quite friendly and even though he may have come across as a bit heartless in his brief encounters, Max hoped she would understand that he had been hurt and was subconsciously protecting himself from a repeat performance.

'So, there you have it, warts and all. Come on, tell me what you think. I suppose I've not painted the best picture of myself and you're thinking of ways to shuffle me out the door in the kindest way possible before you turn the key and slide the bolts across.' Max was teasing yet praying he was wrong at the same time.

'Oh, shut up. You just sound like a normal, sane bloke who's had his heart broken and fixed it the way he thought best at the time. I'm sure the women who went on the dating site knew what they were letting themselves in for and it sounds like you were upfront about what you wanted from a relationship, right from the start. So no, I'm not going to shuffle you out the door. In some ways, I know how you feel. I've been on the receiving end of helpful friends trying to set me up, and would you believe, I even had my very own persistent admirer but not on your grand scale, thank God,' Grace replied and then got up and took the cups to the kitchen. 'Right then, shall I make us some coffee, or do you want another cup of tea?'

Max thought Grace looked a bit edgy and suspected she was avoiding divulging truths of her own so tried to lure her back to the sofa.

'Hey, don't think you get away with it that easily. Get back in here and give me the low down on what you've been up to and while we're at it, why you decided to come here for Christmas. I'm sure it would have been much easier to stay at home with your sister, no matter how annoying she is.' Max was watching

Grace as she filled the kettle and decided to tease her into a confession.

'I hope you're not on the run from Europol. Oh my God that's it! You're the real-life Black Widow and you've enticed me into your lair, so I reckon I'm the one who should be scared. Come on, don't be shy, tell me your secrets, I can take it. Mad Melissa toughened me up. Come on, it's your turn on the psychiatrist's couch.' Grinning, Max patted the space next to him on the sofa and raised his eyebrows at Grace who obediently came over and sat down.

Pulling her legs up and tucking them underneath her, she grabbed a cushion and held it close to her chest as if for protection, then while the logs crackled and the dogs snored, Grace told him her side of the story, warts and all.

CHAPTER 13

race's tale was far less amusing and nowhere near as
interesting as Max's, but she told him anyway.

During his confession, it had occurred to Grace that she
wasn't as experienced with the opposite sex as Max was and felt
rather naive in comparison. Perhaps he'd think she was a bit
boring because she'd only ever slept with three people and one of
them was just a blur. Her first (very brief) encounter was with
the most unsuitable, unfaithful boy in college who broke her
heart when he went off with her best mate. Then there was Ben,
and for her sins, the scumbag, Mr Trumpy at the Christmas
party.

To her surprise, Max seemed impressed that she had managed
to remain friends with Ben and that their children had been
mature enough to accept the situation. Grace was also rather
pleased when he said that Janice sounded awful. Despite her
honesty it seemed he still wanted to know more about the relationship between her and Ben.

'I was a bit curious when you bought a "Ben" *santon* from the
Christmas market. I sort of wondered if you still had feelings for
him or secretly hoped that one day you'd be a united family.'

When she heard this, Grace's eyes widened and her voice went up a notch.

'No, not at all! Like I said, he's my oldest friend. And I don't hate him or anything like that. Sometimes he's just too blooming nice and I do end up feeling sorry for him because his good nature gets taken for granted. But apart from that, our ship sailed a long time ago. Even in my lonely moments I know it would be stupid to rekindle the flame because it would go out again and it's not fair on either of us.' Grace hoped she'd made that point clear.

'So, do *you* get lonely then? I know I do, even though I have work and my mates and Jack, now I see him a bit more. But sometimes, late at night or when I come in from work, the empty flat gets me down.'

Max didn't seem to mind telling Grace this, and the truth was, she felt exactly the same. It made her realise it was nothing to be ashamed of.

'I'm so glad you said that because I feel the same way. I try to fill my life up with all sorts of things. I've got a lovely family but recently I've noticed that when I close the door at night and they're all off doing their own thing, it's just me, and Coco, obviously.' Grace stared into the flames and still felt a bit geeky admitting that, but it was the truth.

'Well, we're a right pair aren't we? But I'm sure there are thousands of people out there who feel the same. I read somewhere, I think it was a quote in a magazine article, that the biggest disease known to mankind is loneliness. It got me thinking that perhaps with all the technology we have at our disposal, plus the fact we are communicating less and less with real live people, that it really is like a modern day illness, slowly creeping up on us.'

Max looked so earnest and Grace nodded in agreement as he continued.

'There's no feeling of community because hardly anyone knows their neighbours. We all have a fast pace of life and I suppose sometimes, you can get left behind. I was thinking of setting it as a homework piece, or class discussion. You know, comparing life in say the fifties and sixties to how communities live now.' Max looked at Grace who seemed engrossed in what he was saying.

'Sorry, I'm going on with myself. I need to remember I'm not with year nine who can't wait for the bell to ring... I have that effect on people, just so you know. So, what made you decide to take a leap of faith and come here?'

Grace shook her head and laughed. 'You weren't going on, I find you very interesting, Sir, and I'd be gutted if the bell rang, that's the truth. Cross my heart.' Grace made the sign on her chest then continued. 'Everything you said struck a chord and besides, my reasons for coming were more or less the same as yours. I was sick of feeling like the odd one out. Even at my daughter's Bonfire party, surrounded by family and friends I felt isolated, different, and I'm sick of it. I didn't want the kids feeling sorry for me either, being stuck at home with my extended family. I suppose I wanted to show them that good old Mum had a bit more about herself, and prove to myself that I could do something crazy before it's too late.' Grace turned her whole body to face Max.

'I know they love me and are proud of me, but sometimes, I actually bore myself. So I threw caution to the wind and came here. I don't want to go to a dating agency, that's where Ben met Evil Janice, so let that be a lesson to all of us. I thought this trip would give me my confidence back and when I got home, if someone came along, well, I'd embrace it rather than pushing the notion away.' Grace's cheeks were flushed from her confessional and the crackling fire wasn't helping either.

Max shook his head and smiled at his earnest companion. 'So, we both had the same idea really. A change of scenery, a confidence boost and a new start next year. And then it all went horribly wrong when we bumped into each other.'

Before Grace could panic and take his teasing the wrong way,

Max took her hand from her lap and held it gently in his before continuing.

'I'm kidding! Don't look so worried and for the record, I'm glad I saw you on the ferry and that we ended up here together. If that's not a sign, I don't know what is. But can I be even more honest with you? I need you to know that I really like you, a lot, and now I've said it, I haven't got a clue what to do next. I don't want to do the wrong thing or make a fool of myself so if you've got any ideas, feel free to interrupt before I turn into a gibbering wreck.' Max kept hold of Grace's hand and waited.

When she felt him take her hand as she listened, Grace had realised that someone 'up there' really was on her side. The sheer relief that his touching words brought to her nervous soul prompted a very uncharacteristic, yet spontaneous, reaction.

Before she knew what she was doing, Grace leaned forward and planted a soft, quite lingering kiss on his lips, smiled into his rather surprised eyes and then sat back in her place. Keeping a tight hold of his hand, she spoke and tried to set his mind at rest.

'I think we should carry on just the way we are. I really like being with you, Max, and I don't want anything to spoil our friendship, either. We've got ages left on holiday and plenty of time to get to know each other more.' Grace closed both her hands around his before she continued.

'The last thing I want is to rush into anything and it end up as one huge, cringey mistake. So, if it's alright with you, can we just take it one step at a time? I really do believe in fate so let's not tempt it anymore by acting like a pair of daft teenagers, although I do feel like one at the moment.' Max hadn't moved his hands away so she took it as a good sign.

Max let out an audible sigh. 'I couldn't have put it better myself. You are so wise. But I don't mind a bit of kissing, you know! That one was rather nice and I'm sure it won't do any harm to practice. I'll just have to keep myself under control and protect my angelic reputation.'

At this Grace laughed, and let herself be pulled closer.

'Right. Now we've both bared our souls, there's one more thing I need to tell you. And no, before you ask, I'm not an escaped murderer or Leicester's answer to the Black Widow, but I do have some news that might affect how you feel and put the mockers on most of what we've just said.'

Max looked a bit taken aback so she just blurted it out and told him about Seth.

On hearing the news Max looked totally un-phased by her announcement. Either that or he was a very good actor. Maybe if it hadn't been for the kiss and the heart to heart, he would've felt a whole lot different. But Grace went to great lengths to reassure him that Seth's arrival wouldn't change a thing, well it would, but they could manage. She also made Max swear that he would join them on Christmas Day because otherwise it would ruin it for her knowing he was sitting further up the track, alone. And there was to be no more feeling sorry for themselves either. Self-enforced seclusion or loneliness, was forbidden.

Max then swore on a copy of *Woman's Own* that as long as Seth didn't hate him on sight then he would spend the day with them. This allowed Grace to relax and after a couple of very nice kisses, they decided to go for a walk. Grace wanted to explore some of the lanes and surrounding countryside so once they'd wrapped up against the bitter Atlantic wind, which was blowing across the fields, they set off with the dogs, hand in hand, towards the pine forest.

It was almost dusk when they passed through the iron gate that guarded the entrance to the field and even the dogs looked a bit tired as they headed towards home. Max had taken them on a circular tour of the village and got a bit carried away with his enthusiasm. Grace was beginning to think they were lost until they saw the sign for St Pierre de Fontaine and the peaks of the village houses, jutting through the trees.

Being Sunday, everything was shut but despite that, it looked very picturesque with the large Gothic church in the centre, surrounded by small shops and a bistro. On the way out, towards the hotel, they passed a large shrine with twinkling lights and statues of the Virgin Mary and below her, a crèche, filled with carved *santons* depicting the Nativity. It was so peaceful and quiet in the village and as they passed through, Grace noticed the lights coming on inside the small cottages and houses that lined the route. Spotting the sign for *Les Trois Chênes*, Grace couldn't wait until she was inside too because her poor feet couldn't take much more and her nose was ready to snap off, it was so cold. When they reached Max's gîte she enjoyed being folded in his arms, feeling a mixture of shyness and excitement. She knew he was going to kiss her in full view of the other cottages and decided to divert him from the inevitable, just a moment longer.

'Right, I'm going to get ready for our French Christmas dinner. Do you think everyone will be dressed up because I'm running out of nice things to wear and I don't want to be the odd one out? It's a special night and I bet the other guests will make the effort.' Grace had plenty of very fashionable woolly numbers with her, but nothing remotely festive and now could've kicked herself for wearing her new skirt. She wanted to look nice for Max and it was either that or her black chinos *again* and there was no way she was wearing jeans.

Suddenly, Max took a sharp intake of breath and looked like he'd remembered something, then held up his forefinger and told her to wait there while he ran inside. When he came back out, he was holding a brown paper bag, tied together at the handles with cream ribbon.

'Here. Open this. I was going to give it to you on Christmas Day if we were still friends but I think you need it more now. It might solve your fashion dilemma.'

Grace looked at the bag then quizzically into Max's eager face.

Pulling off her gloves, she untied the ribbon and pulled out something very soft and wrapped in tissue. As she unfolded the layers, she realised it was the azure velvet dress she saw at the Christmas market. Feeling a lump in her throat the size of a gobstopper, Grace was unable to speak so threw her arms round his neck and kissed his cold cheek.

When she'd composed herself, she managed to say thank you.

'Max, I don't know what to say. It's lovely. I can't believe you bought it for me. I didn't see you though. How did you manage that?' Grace was stroking the soft fabric and couldn't wait to try it on.

'I got it when you went to the loo. I knew you liked it and it was a spur of the moment thing. I nearly killed myself running there and back before you reappeared. Anyway, it's made you smile and I'm glad.' Max looked rather pleased with himself.

'Well, I need to get inside and make myself presentable. I'll walk up to yours about seven thirty, shall I?' Grace gave him a quick peck on the lips then began to back away as Max waved and told her he'd be waiting.

The hotel seemed very busy when they arrived and the lounge was fully occupied so they made their way down the corridor to the small bar area. As they passed through, Max pointed to a line of old, faded photographic portraits which were hung along the walls. He asked Grace if she knew who they were but as she reached the final two, it dawned on him. They were the owners of the hotel, past and present. Smiling from one of the frames was André, standing proudly outside the front door, as were all his predecessors and lastly, Rosie, Michel and their two daughters.

When they entered the bar, Grace pulled him towards a dark-haired woman who was waving and trying to attract their attention. After introductions were made – Anna and Daniel were old friends of Rosie and Michel, drinks were brought from the bar, two more chairs found and the next half an hour was spent bringing each other up to speed on where they were from, how long they were staying and so on. The conversation flowed easily over many subjects, such as family (Anna's daughter worked in France) the weather (it was due to turn even colder) and where they lived (Anna, Portsmouth and Daniel, part of the time in Hemel Hempstead) and before they knew it, Rosie came to tell them their tables were ready, and Daniel made a suggestion.

'Look, why don't you join us, unless you'd prefer a romantic dinner together?' Daniel looked from Max to Grace then at Anna. 'Sorry, have I put my foot in it again, Anna's giving me one of her looks?' Daniel appeared very relaxed and seemed to be the type of person who enjoyed the company of others.

'Daniel, these two have only just met and probably don't want to sit listening to your tales of wine tours and Chelsea Football Club. Sorry, Grace, Max, please don't feel obliged and anyway, it might mess up Rosie's seating plan.' Anna was politely attempting to give them a simple get-out clause.

Rosie, ever the perfect hostess assured them it was no trouble and, saw no reason why they couldn't join Anna and Daniel. Realising it would be really awkward to refuse now, Max looked at Grace who nodded and as Rosie ushered them on, the four of them made their way into dinner, together.

Even though it hadn't turned out to be a romantic meal for two, Max enjoyed himself immensely. Daniel was really good fun and had a wicked sense of humour, teasing Anna mercilessly which she seemed used to, although he did get the odd slap on the arm now and then. Daniel was also very knowledgeable where wine was concerned, so they left him to choose the drinks to match the food, which was out of this world.

What added more enjoyment to the evening was having Grace by his side. Not only was she great company and gorgeous to look at in the dress he'd bought her, it all felt so natural, like they fitted together and had known one another for ages. While they all chatted, Max couldn't help but sneak glances at Grace and pay heed to the voice in his head that told him to hold on to the moment, because as soon as her son arrived all this would probably change.

When Grace commented that she hadn't expected a full-on gourmet extravaganza and naively imagined it would be on the lines of the food they served at the work's Christmas party, Max could only agree. Instead of meat and two veg, tarted up a bit and given a fancy name, the menu for the evening really was something else and Michel had pulled out all the stops.

As Rosie took their orders, she ruefully informed them that tonight, her husband was being assisted in the kitchen by André.

'Now I have to warn you that it might look very serene and peaceful out here but if you heard the bickering and huffing and puffing going on back there in the kitchen, you'd think murder was about to be committed. My André and Michel have always had, shall we say, a competitive relationship so it's like walking through a minefield. I thought it would be a good idea to enlist him but he's turning out to be more of a hindrance. So please bear with me...' At that very moment Pascal the waiter passed by carrying two plates and rolled his eyes in the direction of the kitchen, causing Rosie to sigh and head back into the fray.

While battle commenced in the kitchen, the diners started with an assortment of canapés topped with tapenade and smoked salmon along with tiny foie gras and caviar blinis. Then, there was a huge platter of fresh oysters which Max and Grace had never tried.

'You go first... I'm not sure if I like the look of them to be honest.' Max held an oyster in front of his lips and tried not to look at the slimy contents.

Daniel had already eaten two and was spooning dressing on his third and tried to encourage Max. 'Honestly, mate, just go for it, they are something else. Once you've tried one you'll see why.'

Max remained unconvinced so in the end, Grace turned out to be the brave one.

'Oh what the hell, here goes...' Grace closed her eyes and downed hers in one.

When she opened them she looked at Max who was waiting for her verdict. 'The sea. I swear that's what I thought of when I tasted it, like waves and fishing boats. Go on, have a go.'

Unable to wimp out, Max did as he was told and tipped the shell and then its contents into his mouth and hoped for the best. Once his ordeal was over, Max shuddered and prayed it would stay down before he spoke. 'Nope, definitely not for me... you enjoy the sea, I'm staying on land!'

The starters followed, Max avoided anything remotely fishy and stuck to pâté, however, the main course involved a difficult choice between duck and raspberry sauce served with fresh vegetables, or turkey stuffed with chestnuts accompanied by green beans cooked in garlic butter and herbs, and just to confuse even more, roasted goose soaked in brandy.

Max was enjoying the food, the company and also the compliments that Grace and her blue dress were receiving. She really was stunning and so different to anyone he'd met before. Her fair, smooth complexion was complemented by soft pink lips and green, sparkling eyes. Max thought she was one of those women who didn't really need make-up, she was naturally beautiful and he just loved her red hair that was cut short in a cute, very trendy style which made her look individual and stylish. He'd caught her glancing at him now and then and when their eyes met, he hoped she felt the same surge of excitement, not to mention a wildly fluttering heart whenever he thought of their kisses.

The platter of cheese brought him back to his senses and calmed him down a bit and by the time the traditional *Bûche de*

Noël arrived, he was focused and in the zone. Dessert was his favourite part of any meal and the delicious looking sponge log, covered in chocolate and decorated with chestnuts was right up his street. He even ate Grace's because she was just too full. They were savouring the sweet Mont Tauch wine that Daniel had chosen when the chef, Michel, made an appearance and was given a round of applause by all the diners and his very proud wife. Max whispered that André was probably now locked in the cellar or doing the washing up, because he was nowhere to be seen.

After the clapping died down, Michel made his way to each table, greeting the guests and shaking hands. He eventually got to Max's group where Rosie soon appeared to introduce her husband to Grace. The appearance of André carrying a dusty bottle of brandy instigated another round of applause to which Michel laughed, rolled his eyes, and resignedly accepted a glass of amber liquid from his jovial, former boss.

The evening had flashed by and Max's mind wandered frequently to Grace and their talk earlier, and what the rest of the evening would bring. Would she ask him in for coffee, or should he invite her? Max wanted to string the night out as long as possible because this was their last chance to be alone for a while. For now, he just wanted to drink up and head back.

Anna and Daniel had been brilliant company and invited them over to their cottage when they returned from visiting his daughter in Switzerland. Daniel was looking forward to the five hundred mile road trip as it was something he'd wanted to do for ages and expected the scenery to be spectacular. It was an eight hour trip, with dog walking breaks in between, but they hoped to be there by Christmas Eve. They would be back for New Year, so would ring and make arrangements to get together then. Declining coffee or brandy, Max and Grace blamed their departure on the dogs but in his case, Max just wanted some time together, just the two of them.

※

They linked arms as soon as they were outside and chatted all the way down to the gîtes about the lovely food, Anna and Daniel and how very cold it was. Grace was warmed by the closeness of Max and comforted by how natural they were in each other's company. At the same time, she had to steadfastly fend off her growing feelings, which could only be described as red-hot desire. Still, she was going to stick to their plan and take things slowly, so no matter what was going on in her heart, she would just have to obey her head. In the meantime she hoped to string out the evening for a while longer and maybe it was all the wine, but she felt quite bold.

'Do you fancy coming in for a cup of tea, or some coffee? You could watch the dogs while I put the kettle on.' Grace didn't fancy standing outside tonight, it was too cold.

'Coffee please... and how come I get the short straw? What about women's lib and all that?' Max tutted and rolled his eyes with a smile, before agreeing. 'Go on, I suppose I'll let you off this time, but listen out, just in case I get scared or you hear me scream.' Max opened the door for Ginger who was minding Coco, or the other way round.

'Stop whining and get gone. These two are braver than you and one of them is just a baby. See you in a minute.'

Grace marched off to stoke the fire and make some coffee while Max was swallowed by the darkness of the field. This was followed closely by dramatic, blood-curdling screams along with loud choking noises, to which she just laughed and closed the door.

By 2am, they'd used almost all of Grace's logs and she was trying to coax Max into fetching more.

'Go on you big wimp... I'll give you a torch and you can take the boys for back-up.' Grace nudged his arm and woke him from his pretend snooze.

'No way. I am not going to the wood store. Rosie told me that a scary devil-horned dwarf with red eyes and a pointy stick lives in there... we'll be fine here, it just means we have to cuddle up more.'

'Okay, we'll go together. I'll take the sweeping brush and whack the dwarf while you pinch the wood, okay? We'll have to be quiet though. Come on, get your boots on.'

They had been lying on the sofa watching the red embers of the fire and in her case, trying hard to control growing passions. As she playfully pushed Max away and pointed at his boots, her phone pinged. It was 1am in England and she was surprised to get a text at this time of night. Jumping up, she saw it was from Heidi and at first her heart dropped, then she read the words and relaxed a little.

Hi Mum. Worst night ever at the Grim Reapers' residence. Kids miserable, we all are. House is cold, so are the in-laws. Praying tomorrow will be better. Give my love to Seth when u see him. I'm well jel. Might give u a ring tomorrow night. Hope u r having fun. Miss you so much Mum. Love u. Night night x

Poor Heidi. Grace sent her a quick, encouraging reply and told her to ring whenever she wanted and of course, that she missed her, too.

Max was now booted up and waiting by the door for Grace. 'I think it's time we called it a night. I'm supposed to be meeting Dominique at nine, remember? He's taking me on one of his favourite routes so I suppose I'll have to drag myself away and get some sleep. You wait here and I'll run down and get some logs, I don't really want you to come with me, it's too cold for a start.'

He shrugged on his jacket then outstretched his arms, wearing a very forlorn, slightly melodramatic look as Grace walked over and let herself be folded inside.

'You missed your way, you know? You should've been on the stage. I suppose I need an early night too. I don't want to look puffy-eyed when I pick Seth up tomorrow. And don't worry about the logs, I'll manage until tomorrow. So, I guess this is it for a few days, unless I think of some random excuse to run up the track for a quick kiss. I hope I can manage without you for that long.' Grace had her head on his chest as she spoke, then let Max go and watched him open the door, feeling the draught against her legs as the icy wind crept into the room.

'I know. If I get back from my ride in time, why don't you come over for lunch before you go for Seth? I wish I hadn't made plans with Dominique now. Whatever happens, I promise I'll pop over and introduce myself later, and no, before you try to persuade me again, I will be fine by myself and can make my own dinner. I might even start the book I brought with me and then you can have some time with Seth.' Max smiled then whistled for Ginger to follow, before spotting the worried look in Grace's eyes.

'It won't kill us to be apart for a few days, you know. We'll still see each other and I'm very patient, it's one of my good points. Honestly, Seth coming to stay won't ruin anything. I'll be thinking of you all the time, I promise.'

He pulled the door wide open, giving her one last lingering look and stole a kiss before making his way down the steps with Ginger.

'Okay, if you get back in time I'll see you for lunch. Have a good ride and take care on the icy roads.' Grace waved and slowly closed the door.

Turning, she leaned against the wood, taking in the empty room and Coco, who was making his way forlornly back to the rug and the vacant warm patch where Ginger had been. Then a thought struck her, a thunderbolt-epiphany moment. This was how it was at home, just her and her dog and she was bloody tired of it! Without thinking, Grace turned quickly and opened the door, calling up the track to Max. He hadn't got far and ran straight back.

'What's wrong, are you okay? You made me jump, I thought the devil-dwarf was after me!' Max's face, despite his joking, was actually full of concern.

'No, actually, I'm not okay. I'm not patient either and I don't want to be apart, or wait till tomorrow or next week, so can you please come back inside? And I'm freezing to death here so hurry up.' A huge grin soon appeared on Max's face and he didn't need to be asked twice, so calling for Ginger to follow, he ran back up the steps and once he and his faithful dog were inside, Grace closed the door.

CHAPTER 14

Now, in the cold light of day, Grace blushed slightly when she thought of how they'd hurriedly made their way upstairs. Coco and Ginger had seemed just as pleased that they got to cuddle up in front of the fire together, once the humans had sorted themselves out.

It had been nothing like the awful night in the hotel that Christmas, not that she could remember much about it anyway, or even with Ben. Grace placed her hands over her hot cheeks and smiled like an idiot, remembering every detail. She felt like she was starring in a film and it couldn't be happening to her, but it was. This was all so surreal and it was still hard to take in, but last night had been one of the most exciting, intense, loving experiences of her life.

Max made her feel special, sexy (even saying the word left her feeling a bit strange) and for the first time in years, she had actually enjoyed making love. It had been hard to say goodbye when he left that morning but he had to get ready to meet Dominique so they eventually managed to tear themselves apart. Grace had laughed as she watched him run up the track, surrounded by mist, desperate to avoid being spotted by the other inhabitants of the gîtes. Unfortunately, Wilf was bringing wood from the log-store and as Ginger barked and made a huge, noisy fuss, he waved cheerily as Max ran past.

Grace realised it was time she got a move on herself and stopped this girly day dreaming. She needed to tidy up and put the small heater on in the twin bedroom so it would be aired out for when Seth arrived. Grace was looking forward to seeing her son and making sure his arm really was okay. She was going to make him spaghetti for tea and pamper him a bit. Even though she would be thinking of Max, it would be nice to have a night together, just the two of them. They hardly got the chance to sit and talk when they were at home, Seth was always busy or with his mates and sometimes they were like ships that pass in the night so it would be good to have him to herself for a while and catch up.

Rosie's housekeeper popped in with a fresh pile of bedding and checked that they had everything they needed. Ruby was the complete opposite of her tall blonde cousin, very petite with long fair hair and a faint flash of freckles across her nose, but naturally pretty with kind eyes. It must be a family trait, thought Grace as she closed the door, but not before glancing towards Max's gîte to see if he was back.

To take her mind off him, she sent a message to Heidi saying she hoped they were having a happy Monday morning at the in-laws and to ring if she needed to talk. Then, she composed a longer one to Amber, wishing her a safe trip to London and insisting that she let her know the minute she'd met up with Lewis who was down there on business. They were flying to New York that evening from Heathrow and Grace had been receiving daily texts from her overexcited daughter who really was counting the seconds until her holiday. Just to bring her down to earth though, Grace put on her boring 'Mum Hat' and reminded Amber to secure the house and check on Cecil next door before she left.

By midday, she'd given up on seeing Max before she left for the airport and was trying to concentrate on a magazine and enjoy the peace of her surroundings when her phone began to ring. When she saw Elliot's number flash up, Grace's stomach turned over and her heart began to thump. Her first thought was that something must be wrong with Heidi and the baby so nervously, she grabbed the phone and accepted the call.

'Hello, is everything okay, is something wrong with Heidi?' Grace's heart hammered in her chest as a million thoughts raced through her brain and in the seconds before he spoke, Grace silently chastised herself. Heidi had almost lost Finn, so she had been selfish and inconsiderate to come to France and now it would take ages to get back home, to where she was needed, where she should be.

'No, Grace, don't panic, she's fine, we all are, well, sort of. Look, I haven't got long to talk. Heidi and the kids are inside. We're at McDonald's having breakfast. I just nipped outside to ring you.' Elliot was speaking really quickly and sounded stressed.

'Okay, thank God for that. So what's wrong and why aren't you at your parents' house?'

Grace's heart rate had returned to normal but she was still concerned and knew it must be something serious for Elliot to ring.

'Bloody hell, Grace, I've made a right mess of things. Heidi is really upset and I feel like I've let all of them down. I'm fed up and desperate, so seeing as you're an excellent sorter-outer of messes I'm hoping you can get me out of this one. Just let me tell you what happened and then feel free to go mad with me when I've finished. I should've kept my temper and sorted things out sensibly but I just lost it with my dad.'

Once Elliot had given Grace a blow by blow, hurried account of their stay at his parents', she was in no doubt at all who was in the wrong and wanted to throttle Gordon and Vera, season of goodwill or not.

'Elliot, as far as I can see you have done nothing wrong and let's be honest, it's not like they didn't deserve it. He obviously hasn't changed and no matter what his religious views are, or how keen he is on running his own mini-regime, *Gordon*, not you, should've thought about how his words would affect his grandchildren. And while I'm on a roll, it's about time he respected the fact that you are no longer a child and treated you accordingly.' Grace heard Elliot let out a huge sigh of what she presumed was relief, so carried on.

'The kids might be upset now, but they will always remember that you stood up for them and took them away from a horrible place. So stop beating yourself up, okay? I'm proud of you. What are you going to do now, though? I feel awful that I won't be there for Christmas and it's been ruined for you all.'

As she said the words, a crazy thought came into her head but before she could speak, Elliot interrupted.

'Well, that's what I thought but as we were eating our food, I had an idea. Please be honest and tell me if you're not up for it, but I was wondering, is there room there in France for us? I had a quick look at ferries and there's one in the morning. We'd need to nip home and grab our passports first, then head down to Portsmouth and stay there tonight. I even checked out a few motels and we can get a family room if I hurry up. So, what do you think, am I being a bit cheeky and putting you on the spot?'

Elliot sounded like he was almost hyperventilating, and Grace wasn't surprised. All that pent-up anxiety, anger and guilt was probably eating him up inside.

Grace laughed and then almost shouted her answer down the phone. 'Elliot. Shut up and book the ferry. I'd love to have you all here and there's plenty of room. Now, go and cheer your family up and text me with the details. Oh, and Elliot... breathe!'

Grace was smiling from ear to ear as she heard her son-in-law thanking her profusely and the unmistakable happiness in his voice.

When she replaced the receiver, Grace had a huge rush of excitement, then one of panic at the thought of everything she needed to do. Christmas Day was on Thursday, so she only had two full days to arrange a family gathering. She needed to go and see Rosie and ask her *again* if it was okay for them to come, although she knew it wouldn't matter really and then there was Max. It looked like he was going to have a baptism of fire and meet most of her family in one go. But no matter what he said, she would insist he join in and wouldn't take no for an answer, either.

She checked her watch and saw it was time to set off for the airport. Boy, would she have a surprise for Seth when he arrived. They would still have one cosy night in together before they were invaded by the masses. At least Amber was okay, she'd be getting ready to leave for London soon and begin her romantic trip to America with Lewis. Grace picked up her keys and headed outside. First stop, the hotel to speak to Rosie and then the airport. Tomorrow, she had Christmas Day to organise, and she couldn't wait!

Heidi had managed to eat some of her burger but it kept getting stuck in her throat. She knew she had to put on a brave face for her children, and even Elliot who she could tell was punishing himself for what had happened. Despite her assurances in between sobs, that he'd done the right thing and that she was proud of him for standing up to Gordon, he had looked thoroughly fed up as they drove away from his parent's house. Being a grown-up *and* a mother meant you had to be strong, but right now Heidi missed her own mum so much. They were best friends and saw each other most days and if not, spoke on the phone instead. Now, she faced Christmas with the Klingons or maybe it would end up being just the four of them. Heidi told herself to be grateful for that, but in truth, nothing compared to spending it with her mum because she did it the best.

Once Skye and Finn were loaded into the car, Heidi lowered herself onto the passenger seat and glanced over at Elliot who was doing something on his phone. She had assumed that when he left the restaurant he was going outside to ring his father and apologise. It was with mixed feelings that Heidi plucked up the courage to ask if he'd made peace, and worst-case scenario, if they were returning for round two at the House of Horrible People.

'Sorry we took so long, Finn needed the loo, so, did you sort it out with Gordon the Moron? I presume that's who you rang. Did he manage to accept your apology or prefer rubbing your nose in it?' Heidi was tired and getting snappy, and even though she knew it wouldn't help and the kids could hear her spiteful words, right now, she really didn't care.

'No, I didn't apologise because I have no intention of speaking to either of them for the foreseeable future, if ever.' Elliot finished what he was doing and turned in his seat to face Heidi. 'If you must know, I've been arranging a big surprise but before that, I need to tell you that I'm very sorry if I've upset you.' Elliot twisted his body more, so he could speak directly to Skye and Finn. 'The thing is, sometimes grown-ups fall out and lose their temper no matter how hard they try not to.'

Finn (who had tomato sauce on the end of his nose) nodded his agreement while Skye had eyes as wide as saucers, hanging on to his every word.

'Anyway, I want you to try and forget about all that because we've got to get a move on. If it's okay with Mum, we have a long, exciting journey ahead of us and a bit of an adventure to go on. First, we need to pop home and pick something up and then...

we are all going to France to spend Christmas with Grandma Grace! How do you fancy that?'

The screams and cheers that filled the car almost split Heidi's eardrums and attracted a few odd stares in their direction. Their old Volvo rocked about in the car park as the children jumped up and down and Elliot was almost strangled by hugs from Skye and Finn. Once she'd got over the shock, Heidi wasn't sure whether to laugh or cry. So she did both!

'Right, settle down all of you. We need to get our passports and some warmer clothes and then it's off to Portsmouth. We'll stay in a motel tonight because in the morning we are catching a very early ferry to France. We should be at Grandma's by tomorrow afternoon, so… are we all ready?'

Heidi wiped away tears and mouthed 'I love you' to Elliot who she could tell was basking in the role as hero. While Skye and Finn buckled their seat belts and cried YES!! at the top of their voices, Heidi leaned over and kissed Elliot on the cheek as confirmation of his Wonder-husband status. Beaming, Elliot started the engine, put the car in gear and they all headed south.

Grace waited in the short stay zone at Nantes Airport as she watched for Seth amongst the bodies that were piling out of the glass doors. Before long, she spotted him and jumped out of the car and began waving frantically, trying to attract his attention. When he saw her, a huge grin lit up his face and he made his way through the crowds towards her.

Grace's heart went out to her son. He had been so looking forward to going skiing and she knew he would've been disappointed at it all being ruined and then leaving his mates, it was only natural. That's why she was going to do her very best to cheer him up and once he knew that Skye and Finn would be coming too, his spirits would surely lift even further. As soon as he was close enough, Grace gave Seth a huge bear hug, carefully avoiding his arm because she was notoriously clumsy and didn't want to bang into it. Stepping back to take in her tall, muscle-bound son, Grace looked up and noticed his tanned face was erupting in freckles and that his strawberry-blonde hair had lightened slightly in the sun. Apart from his arm, he looked the picture of health and his week in the outdoors had done him good.

'Thanks for coming to get me, Mum. How are you doing with your driving, looks like you've managed to keep the car in one piece?'

Seth was looking at the bonnet of the car, and Grace knew he was being sarcastic and inspecting it for damage and was rewarded with a whack on his good arm.

'You cheeky sod! I've been doing rather well actually and can even cope with roundabouts now, so shut up and get in. And I've got a bit of news for you, we're going to be having some extra guests tomorrow.' Grace got inside and began fastening her seat belt as Seth climbed in and did the same.

'Mum, please tell me it's not Aunty Martha and her lot. I knew she'd wear you down in the end and give you a guilt trip. Well, that's my nice quiet Christmas ruined and I've only just got here.'

'Just shush and listen. It's not Martha, it's Heidi, Elliot and the kids! Happy now?' Grace started the engine and watched Seth's downcast face become awash with smiles.

'No way! That's ace. How come? I love Christmas with the kids. Aww, it's going to be fab. So, go on, tell me what caused the change of plan?'

Seth was too engrossed in the tale to have noticed that Grace was going the wrong way round the car park but she kept cool and somehow managed to find the exit and as the barrier flipped up, she drove on through and told Seth the story.

. . .

It was now late afternoon and they were both settled in front of the fire with Coco, who had been beside himself with tail-wagging joy when he spotted Seth walking through the door. They'd just put their feet up when they received a very giddy phone call from Skye and Finn. They were in Portsmouth and had been along the quayside and seen all the historical sights of the town and the navy ships which were docked in the port. They were now in the supermarket buying a huge turkey and some Christmas crackers and whatever else her overexcited, extremely relieved daughter could get her hands on. The children insisted on speaking to Grace and she could almost feel their exuberant energy transmitting down the line.

Finn went first. 'Grandma, Grandma. We're coming to see you on a huge boat. I just saw one in the sea. We are going over a channel and Dad said he's emailed Father Christmas and told him that we are coming to Franceland. I was a bit scared he'd get muddled up and take my presents to the wrong house. Oh, and Dad called Grandad Gordon a big goat *and* an old git and Mum says they've got tight arses.'

Then Skye snatched away the phone as Grace heard Heidi telling Finn off for swearing and Elliot, laughing loudly in the background.

'Hi, Grandma. Are you pleased we're coming to see you? We can do loads of Christmas stuff now. I'm going to get some glitter from the shop and we can do paintings. Is Uncle Seth there? Tell him I'll bring him some mince pies, will two boxes be enough, or do they already have mince pies in France? Text Mum a list or else she'll forget stuff. She's not stopped crying all day. She can be a bit of a baby sometimes but at the moment she's okay. I've got to go now, love you, see you soon, I'm so excited to see you both.'

Then Heidi came on the phone.

'Hi, Mum, just ignore Skye she's exaggerating, but she's right about the shopping, just text me anything you need and we'll bring it with us. I can't wait to get there. I feel like a kid going on a school trip. Once we've been shopping we're going to go back to the hotel and hopefully get these two to calm down. I spoke to Amber and explained everything, she's on her way to London and should arrive anytime now. She's really pleased we're coming over and sounded more excited than me, if that's possible. Right, got to go, see you tomorrow and give my love to Seth.' Heidi was talking ten to the dozen and sounded overjoyed.

'Okay, love, see you tomorrow and I think you need to calm down too, never mind the kids, I'll text you a list right now and ring you later.'

Grace replaced the receiver and rolled her eyes at Seth and told him to enjoy the peace and quiet because tomorrow, it would all change.

After composing a list and sending it to Heidi, they spent the next hour or so talking and looking at Seth's pre-accident holiday photos. Grace felt slightly melancholy as he swiped each picture on his phone. He looked like he'd been having the time of his life, surrounded by grinning, red-faced friends wearing daft ski hats and green sun block on their lips. Never mind, she told herself, he's safe and will soon be surrounded by his family and he can always go skiing again, if it hasn't put him off forever. She concentrated on the scenery and the chalet maids who were exactly as Seth had described.

It was now completely dark outside and Grace was expecting Max to call in at any time so she would have to explain to Seth who he was before he arrived so taking a deep breath, she began.

'I've not told you about our neighbours, have I? They're all really nice and very friendly. Next door are two Polish couples, let me see if I can get their names right, Jakub and Grazynia, Marek and Karolina. Then on the other side we have Wilf and André, he used to own the hotel and at the end, there's Max. We actually met on the boat which was a coincidence because it turned out he was coming here too.'

Grace watched Seth's face carefully for any signs of suspicion but he seemed unconcerned, so she continued.

'He's really nice and I think he might pop in later to say hello. We went for a day out to Tours together, it saved on petrol and all that. We had a lovely time, as it happens. Rosie, she's the owner I told you about, well she sort of arranged it. Anyway, I hope you don't mind but he's on his own for the whole of Christmas so I thought it would be okay if he called in for a quick drink so he could say hello?'

Grace hoped that she sounded suitably casual and wasn't blushing on the outside, because on the inside she was on fire.

'That's fine, Mum. I'm glad you've met new people. I was worried you'd be lonely and want to go home but as it looks like you've been gadding about and making friends, which is a bit ironic because now, most of home is coming to you and you'll be rushed off your feet as usual. Anyway, have you got any biscuits or a bit of cake? I'm getting hungry.'

And that, it seemed, was that, so Grace jumped up to bring food, relieved that Seth had taken it so well.

As Grace pottered about in the kitchen, slicing cake and choosing biscuits, she couldn't see Seth who was shaking his head and having a quiet chuckle over his mum's waffling and her rubbish attempt at covering up that she fancied this Max bloke. It was a bit obvious, especially as they *all* knew that when their mum was nervous, she unconsciously grasped her neck with her hand. And if that wasn't enough, the rambling on and then the blushes, gave her away instantly. Wait till he told the others.

Despite his amusement, Seth was pleased for his mum. There was something a bit different about her as well, he couldn't put his finger on it but she seemed more confident and assured of herself. Maybe coming here had given her a huge boost and time to recharge her batteries. Whatever it was, it had done her good.

She was still a rubbish driver though and had scared him to death at the roundabouts near the airport, and she hadn't even realised they were going the wrong way in the airport car park. He'd kept quiet because he didn't want to criticise her the second he got in the car but if they went out tomorrow, he was driving, whether she liked it or not. Her car was an automatic and he could easily cope, even with a broken arm!

Max finally plucked up the courage to go down to Grace's so set off purposefully along the track, gift in hand and nervous as hell. He would've ducked out but the thought of her earnest face and the fact that he'd promised, forced him out of his chair and into his coat. He left Ginger behind as an excuse to come back as he knew she would try to persuade him to stay for dinner and he was resolute in the fact that he would spend the evening alone, reading and relaxing, which after last night, he was greatly in need of.

When Max had heard her call his name, he really thought there was something wrong and never imagined she would ask him to go back inside, or that he would spend the night with her. Since his divorce, he hadn't felt in-tune or comfortable with anyone, but with Grace it had all just clicked into place. It was like it was meant to be, from their heart to heart on the sofa where they bared their souls, then the obvious chemistry and building of feelings over dinner to the moments of passion they shared in front of the fire. He really had to force himself to leave, only to be called back again. Their first night together had been perfect though.

Max could also tell Grace was nervous and quite shy when they were in bed, but that made her more endearing, delicate even. They'd lain awake for most of the night, talking, sharing thoughts and the hidden corners of their hearts. They laughed at one another and themselves as they recalled their first meeting in the restaurant and finally confessed to watching out for each other and waiting in vain as they sailed across the choppy sea. The grey, early morning light began to creep slowly into the room before they finally slept, wrapped around each other, the warmth from their bodies mirroring the glow inside Max's heart.

Wow, was he really having these thoughts? Max shook his head at the irony of how his situation had changed, how he had changed, because just thinking about their night together sent Max rather silly, his ticker went mad and his stomach flipped over. Could he really be feeling like this, at his age, after all these years? Previously, in his mid-life crisis stage, meeting a woman would be no big deal. Granted, he would be a bit on edge, borderline nervous but still only mildly excited about going on a date. He never daydreamed about one of his conquests or looked forward to seeing them again and he certainly wouldn't have entertained meeting their family, for whatever reason. All this was completely unknown territory and just a bit scary.

Well, he was here now, quite literally and as he knocked on the door and waited eagerly to see her face (it *had* been almost nine hours after all) Max decided to just go with it. He was happy for the first time in ages and even if her son hated his guts and it was all to end tonight, he had his memories. It was also reassuring to know that he did have a heart after all and even for him, it was still possible to fall in love again.

CHAPTER 15

S eth thought Max was 'a top bloke'. These were the exact words he used to Grace after she'd showed Max out and began to prepare dinner. True to his word, Max steadfastly refused her magnificent spaghetti and insisted on going back to start his novel and cook himself a steak. Even Seth tried to persuade him so stay, which Grace was pleased about. After he'd shared the beer he brought over with Seth and the ice had been successfully broken, Max said his goodbyes and went back to Ginger.

While Grace chopped onions and garlic, she chatted with Seth about her trip to Tours and their neighbours. Grace was brimming with the Christmas spirit as she chattered on about what they needed to buy from the Super U the following day. They were going to get a Christmas tree as well because Skye had sent a text asking if they had one.

Next, they got on to the subject of Amber who should be arriving at St Pancras anytime and would soon be whisked off to New York by Lewis. Grace hoped that her daughter would find contentment with her boyfriend and wouldn't be too disappointed if she didn't get the big proposal she yearned for. Seth said that no matter what advice you gave her, Amber would have the whole trip methodically planned out in her head. Poor old Lewis would be forced to go down on one knee, despite freezing to death in the snow, which would be followed by a yellow taxi ride, straight round to Tiffany's so they could exchange the ring he'd chosen, because it wouldn't be right, nothing ever was for Amber.

Grace chided him gently, saying Amber wasn't really that bad, well, not quite. As long as she was happy and didn't get hurt, that would do. Wasn't that the minimum requirement and what every mother wanted for their child? Anything else was a bonus. The thing was, Amber had such high expectations and had set so much store on this holiday, so while the sauce bubbled and the pasta boiled, Grace crossed her fingers and silently wished her daughter, and Lewis, the very best of luck.

Amber studied her reflection in the window of the train and after much self-scrutiny, was happy with her appearance and confident that she looked like a polished, professional woman who was on her way to the City of London to meet her executive boyfriend. Amber had planned every footstep of this trip. From her outfits to the drinks they would order in the cocktail bar, just around the corner from the bank's headquarters, and the champagne they would share on the plane, her special treat and thank-you to Lewis. Nothing was left to chance.

When the train pulled into the station, Amber smoothed down the skirt of her new wool suit and pulled her case into the aisle. She was very striking and always turned heads, with her slim yet curvaceous figure and long auburn hair. Today, it cascaded down her shoulders in bouncy waves as she strode confidently along the platform, fully aware of the impact she was making in her deep crimson coat, accessorised with black gloves and stilettos.

Even her suitcase was new and jam-packed with warm, uber stylish, touristy clothes that she hoped would impress Lewis and any New Yorker who looked her way. For evenings, she had saved up hard and was going to treat herself to some new outfits from the stores in the Big Apple and then dazzle her boyfriend into submission. As she sashayed along, looking for directions to the taxi rank and trying not to smile like a fool, Amber heard her phone ringing inside her handbag. It was Lewis, probably checking to see if she had arrived, so she stopped and picked up the call.

'Amber, it's me. Listen, I've got some bad news. Where are you now, I can tell you're in the station, look, can you go somewhere quiet? I need to tell you something.' Lewis sounded hyped, not exactly nervous, just very tense.

Amber's heart thudded in her chest because her first thoughts were that someone had died. Doing as she was told, she dragged her case to the wall and waited just by the entrance to the toilets.

'Lewis, what's wrong? Just tell me, you're making me scared.'

Amber turned her back to the other commuters, afraid of what she was about to hear, attempting to protect herself from prying eyes.

Taking a deep breath that was audible at the other end of the phone, Lewis got on with basically ruining Amber's day, and her dreams.

'Please don't freak out because if I could change any of this, I swear I would. Look, there's no easy way to say it, but we can't go to New York.'

There was a long, stunned silence as blood pumped manically around Amber's stricken heart and there was a strange whooshing sound in her ears and then her boyfriend's voice again, saying words that just couldn't be true.

'Guy has come down with the flu, I mean proper flu, not just a cold and he's really sick but was hoping he'd still be able to drag himself in for this big meeting with the Chinese construction company. Anyway, he's just too rough... Amber, are you still there?'

Lewis heard her squeak 'yes' before continuing.

'Well, you're not going to believe it but he's asked me to take over his pitch and has also given me the job of entertaining them for the next two days. He's sent over all his files and is entrusting me with this HUGE deal. If it all goes to plan, and they sign the contracts on Christmas Eve, well, it will be massive for the bank and for me as well. He says he owes me one already for getting him out of this fix, so can you imagine what he could do for my career?'

Amber knew that Lewis would be fizzing with the thrill of his imminent rise to stardom and would be desperate for her to see the benefits, even if it did ruin their plans.

'But, Lewis, why does it have to be you, can't someone else take over? Surely there are other people in your department that could do it, people who weren't going away for Christmas, it just seems so unfair.' Amber was shaking and felt really queasy while doing her level best not to cry.

'He wanted *me*, Amber. Can't you see what an honour this is? And besides, I helped him with the pitch and did most of the leg work so I think I'm the best person for the job and so does he. Look, just get in a taxi and come over to the bank. I'm going to have to work for another couple of hours here but I've booked us into a swanky hotel. Or you can wait for me there if you prefer and enjoy the facilities. Guy said to put it on expenses to compensate for cancelling our holiday. It's really swish, wait till you see it. I promise I will make this up to you, but I have to do it, Amber, please say you understand. Look, I've got tons to do but I wanted to sort things out with you first.' Lewis sounded impatient.

Amber managed to find her voice. 'But what about Christmas,

what are we going to do now? All my family are away, apart from my dad and I'm not going anywhere near Janice. Your mum and dad have gone to Tenerife so we can't go there, either.' Amber had never felt so miserable in all her life.

It had all gone wrong. Crashed and burned. Months of planning and hoping had gone right down the drain, all thanks to stupid Guy who she'd always thought was a bit of a prat, anyway.

'To be honest, Amber, Christmas Day is way down on my list of priorities right at this moment in time. Look, are you coming over because I really need to get on? If you'd rather go straight to the hotel that's fine, we'll talk later. Just make your mind up quickly because I have to go back into a meeting now, they're calling me. Go get a coffee and text me, okay, and I am sorry, Amber, I really am.'

She could hear the impatience in his voice and a hint of annoyance so told him to go into the meeting, saying she'd let him know what she was doing as soon as she'd got her head round it all.

Right up until the moment Amber picked up the phone her world had been lit by every colour of the rainbow and her pot of gold was waiting for her, just on the other side of the City. In a matter of only seconds, it had been cast into darkness. The vibrant station scene in front of her was transformed into monotone, black and grey misty figures merging with the hot, angry tears of disappointment which pumped from her eyes.

After Lewis disconnected, rather too quickly for her liking, Amber walked slowly to the coffee shop and bought herself something in a paper cup then found a table in the corner from where she stared silently into the distance, completely devoid of any emotion. A few moments later she looked down at the empty cup in her hand and couldn't remember buying it, never mind drinking it. Amber's body was numb, along with her mind, which was actually her saving. Anything was better than blubbing in full view of all the other customers and making a complete fool of herself.

Then the 'F' word filtered into her anaesthetised brain. Oh God, she was going to look such a FOOL, especially at work, never mind what her family would say. She hadn't shut up about this trip for months and had revelled in the fact that all the girls in the office were green with envy. Well, pride comes before a fall and now she'd been slapped down in grand style. Amber could never survive the humiliation and would be a complete and utter laughing stock at work.

How could he do this to her? And he didn't even care that it was Christmas and her family were miles away. All Lewis cared about was his stupid job and making money. Hot tears began to well in her eyes. Amber tried to brush them away casually with her hand, clinging on to what remained of her dignity just in case some nosey parker was watching. Well, Lewis could stick his fancy hotel up his big fat bonus, and she wasn't going to trot over to the bank like a good girl and sit around waiting for him to finish his meeting, either.

Apart from being certain of that, Amber didn't know what to do next. She needed to speak to her mum. She always had the answer to any problem, so noticing the cafe had emptied slightly, Amber took out her phone and pressed the call button. When it was obvious her mum wasn't going to answer, Amber felt even more desolate and her bottom lip started to tremble. Everyone was deserting her. Desperate to hear a friendly voice, she looked at her contact list. Her eyes were blurred by dripping tears but just about able to focus on one familiar name. Instinctively, she pressed the call button and like a bubbling kettle, ready to boil over and release vats of pent-up steam, Amber waited for what seemed like ages for Heidi to answer her phone.

Despite thinking and feeling that it was the end of the world and her life sucked, in the end, it was all very simple and so easy to solve. Once Amber managed to get the words out, through angry sobs and a smattering of swear words directed mainly at Guy the Prat, she flung the rest in the direction of Lewis and the male population in general. After the flood gates had opened and the waves of Amber's disappointment eventually subsided, Heidi managed to get a word in edgeways.

'Amber! Just calm down, okay. It's very bad timing I agree and I know how hurt you are right now but you need to put yourself in Lewis's position. He's worked really hard to get this chance and you've seen for yourself how tough the competition is at the bank, so instead of making things difficult for him, why don't you set him free to do his job? He will thank you for it in the end and will be able to focus completely on the deal, rather than worrying how to make things right with you. Give him some space and yourself time to get your head round things and see how you feel about him then. If you do this simple thing, I can guarantee that you will come out on top because Lewis will think you are really mature and selfless, instead of self-centred, unreasonable, and unforgiving.'

At the other end Amber winced but rather than disagree or react to Heidi's comments, she asked instead what she should say to Lewis because she was *so* mad right now and knew it would all come out wrong.

'I suggest you send him a message telling him that you've thought it through and he should just crack on and seal this deal without you distracting him. Wish him well and ask him to let you know how it goes and that even though you are very disappointed, you'll get over it and can understand how important this is to him.'

'But that means he gets his own way and I'm Billy No-Mates at Christmas.' Amber's voice cracked again, just as Heidi interrupted.

'Well it's either that or you'll spend a rubbish few days mooching about London on your own, or worse, singing karaoke with the Chinese businessmen. You'll be feeling sorry for yourself the whole time and I can guarantee it'll culminate in a huge row. If that happens, Christmas really will be ruined, and you could even break-up for good, and you don't want that, do you?'

Amber listened between sniffs to Heidi's words and appreciated that she was only being honest so rather than going on the defensive, Amber just felt defeated and unusually accepting of her sister's wise summing up and sensible verdict.

'Okay, I'll text him now. I suppose you're right. If I stay in London we will only end up rowing and I don't want to lose him, even though I'm still so angry with him. But what about me? Do you think I should ring Dad and ask if I can go to his on Christmas Day?'

Amber was going to cry again, the thought of going all the way home *and* being with Janice was just too much and the sound of Heidi laughing really wasn't helping.

'No, stupid, I don't think you should ring Dad. I think you should get your bum into gear and on a train to Portsmouth. If you pull your finger out you can be here in a few hours and if there are no rooms left in the motel, you can squash in with us. You've got your passport so come to France and see Mum and Seth, then we will all be together for Christmas. What do you think?'

There was a long silence as her words soaked into Amber's brain.

'I think you're brilliant and the best sister in the world. I'm going to the ticket office right now to find out how to get there. Will you tell Mum and then see if they've got a room where you are? I'll let you know when I'm arriving. Thanks, Heidi, for putting me straight. I can't wait to see you all. Big kiss, love you, bye.'

Within seconds Amber had hung up and was marching through the crowds, hair bouncing and the spring in her step fully coiled and ready for action.

Just over seventy miles away, Heidi laughed to herself and went back inside the motel room to inform her family that it might be a bit of a squeeze in the car the next day. Then, she was going to ring her mum and tell her the news. It really was ironic, that even though they'd faced the prospect of Christmas apart and borne the awful guilt they felt at leaving their lovely mum behind, after all the planning, hideous relatives, air miles, train rides and various motorway journeys, in the end, she was getting them all back for Christmas. Whether she liked it or not!

When Grace unplugged her phone from the charger and it came back to life, she received a text message from Heidi telling her to ring ASAP. Grace hadn't realised it was flat and felt instantly guilty that she had been out of touch. Doing as she was told, she tapped Heidi's number and waited for it to connect.

First, she got a telling off for being unavailable, according to Heidi the first law of motherhood is being on radar, 24/7. Then, Seth was in trouble as his phone was on silent, which according to Heidi was just stupid and a really annoying habit, so he got told off as well. Finally, after putting the world to rights, she repeated the tale of Amber and Lewis to a very concerned Grace. The disappointment she felt on behalf of her daughter was soon replaced by jubilation that another one of her brood would be arriving the following afternoon. Beaming from ear to ear, she ran straight downstairs to tell Seth who was oblivious to the drama and by now, tucking into his second bowl of pasta.

Grace had a lovely evening with her son, and Max had been right, it was nice to spend some time with Seth, just the two of them and she made a mental note to try and arrange nights like this every now and then when they got home. She also wondered what Max would think when the last of her chicks turned up tomorrow. He'd taken it well when she mentioned earlier that Heidi and her lot were coming over. Perhaps he thought they were all mad and incapable of going anywhere on their own, but at least he'd get to meet them all in one go. A veritable baptism of fire, or something along those lines.

Later, as they were having a bedtime cup of tea and some biscuits, Seth surprised Grace with a question.

'So, what's going on with you and Dad? He looked really fed up the last time I met him in the pub. I suspect he's not getting on too well with Janice because he actually turned his phone off while we had a drink. She pesters the life out of him, you know? He did mention that he thought he'd upset you but wouldn't go into detail, he said it was up to you to tell me and he didn't want to speak out of turn. So, what has he said?' Seth continued dipping his biscuit in his tea while Grace tried to decide how much to tell him.

'I wasn't going to say anything until the New Year but I suppose I may as well tell you now, it's no big mystery though. The thing is, Dad and Janice are going to get married so he wants a divorce.' Grace thought she'd let that nugget settle before she hit him with the double whammy.

'You're joking! He never said anything to me. Are you sure, Mum, has he gone mad? She's a *total* nutjob that's for sure and deffo not right for Dad. I can't believe it... married... to Janice. Amber's going to implode when she hears about this.'

Seth looked genuinely shocked, so Grace had a feeling what he was going to hear next would do nothing to lift his mood.

'And that's not all. I think the divorce is sort of urgent, however, he also mentioned the house, our house that is. Dad and Janice, or probably just Janice if we're being honest, well they want to move out of the flat and make plans so that means giving him his share of number 32 Market Lane.'

Grace knew Seth was truly shocked, his face had lost all its colour.

'So, you've got to sell our house, just so she can set herself up somewhere with Dad. He's lost the plot. Really, Mum, he's not thinking straight. Just wait till I see him. I'm going to tell him she's bad news and he needs to see a shrink. It's about time I told him what I think instead of trying to keep the peace. Why didn't you say something before? I bet you've been worried sick.'

Seth had now gone a bit red with the shock of Grace's revelations and the last thing she wanted was a huge family row.

'Look, don't go falling out with your dad over this. It's only fair, you know. It's his house too. Not only that, you and Amber are adults and both working, so really, he should get his share. I know you don't like Janice but if you and Dad have a row, she will love it and if you isolate him, she's won and will control him even more. Anyway, let's not talk about it tonight. It's put you in a bad mood and will spoil our evening, and don't say anything to the others, either. After all these disappointments I don't want to add to your woes, let's just have a good time, okay?'

Grace felt like she'd been forced to tell him the truth and was cursing Ben for letting something slip and dropping her in it.

'Well, that's easier said than done, but you're right. We shouldn't let anything ruin this Christmas. It's going to be ace and I'm glad I'm here with you. I just feel bad that you had stuff on your mind and didn't say anything, just to protect our feelings. Like you said, we're all grown up now so in future, spill the beans, we can handle it.'

Seth jumped up and gave Grace a huge hug and a kiss on the head then offered to wash up, which was a Christmas miracle in itself.

Grace yawned. 'Okay, I promise. Let's tidy up and go to bed. We've got lots to do tomorrow before everyone arrives so we should get some sleep. As a reward for washing up I'll let you choose which bunk you sleep on. First up, best dressed and all that.'

Grace hauled herself out of her chair and opened the door to let Coco out for a quick run round and a wee.

The lights in all the other gîtes were off and she imagined Max, under the covers and half wished she was with him but for the next few days, family came first and she was going to pack as much fun and laughter into her time with them as humanly possible. Calling for Coco to come inside, she closed the door on the wintry night then slid the lock across and went to help Seth in the kitchen. Smiling to herself as she pottered about, her heart fluttered with happiness because tomorrow, out of the blue and against ridiculous odds, they would all be here, in France, safe and sound in her lovely Christmas cottage.

Grace and Seth were up bright and early the next day, list in hand and raring to go. The mist hadn't even lifted from the field and the scenery beyond was obscured by the white-grey swirls which hovered just above the frosty grass. After introducing Seth to Rosie, they nipped across the lane to ask Dominique about a Christmas tree. His friend Bruno lived in the next village of Le Pin and on his farm, was, as the name suggested, a forest of pine trees. After a quick phone call it was all arranged and they were to arrive before lunch to pick one out and Bruno would chop it down there and then so they could take it away.

Seth had tried to convince Grace that he could drive one-handed but she was having none of it and he was consigned to the passenger seat for the whole shopping trip. As they drove along the lanes, admiring the small cottages and rolling hills, Seth announced that he'd been having a bit of a think about the divorce situation.

'I know you want to forget all about it for now, but last night,

I was going over what you said about our house and I think I might have a solution to your problem. Just hear me out before you tell me to shut up, and I promise I won't mention it again if you say no.'

Grace was curious so did as she was told and let him carry on.

'Well, as I see it, if you have to sell, then all three of us will end up homeless and have to buy somewhere else or go our separate ways. I like our house and don't particularly want to move, I also like living with you, and on occasions, Amber. So, what if *I* bought Dad out? I reckon I could get a mortgage or a loan and you never know, my lovely sister might pull a few strings at her bank. I've got a good job and savings so hopefully it won't be a problem. That way, we can stay where we are while my deranged dad gets the cash for his love nest.'

It was Grace's turn now to take things in and ponder on her son's wise, generous and heartfelt suggestion. Her brain whirred into action, turning over the pros and cons of his offer and after a short while, she replied.

'Seth, I think that's a brilliant idea and could definitely solve our dilemma. I'm always hearing how hard it is for young people to get on the property ladder so this could be a way for you to take a step up. I bet you thought I'd dismiss it straight away, but you know what, it's something to look into once we get home. I feel tons lighter already, so thanks, son, for even offering, it means a lot.'

Seth looked pleased with himself and Grace wasn't kidding, she felt genuinely relieved.

After a tour around the supermarket buying an array of Christmassy treats for everyone and crusty bread to go with the soup she was going to prepare when they got back, they headed off to the pine forest to pick a tree. Heidi would probably have a fit when she saw the macaroons and bonbons she'd bought for Skye and Finn but Grace thought she could sweeten her up with a box of croissants and pastries for breakfast the next day. They also had an assortment of very fresh vegetables and a large box of satsumas to balance the books, so she might just get away with it. Seth chose the biggest *Bûche de Noël* in the shop and was in charge of the drinks department, so Grace left him to it and went to pick up a box of oysters, she wanted to add a taste of France to her table on the big day.

Bruno was a jolly, friendly man who took them on a mini tour of his forest, enthusiastically pointing out likely candidates for the Shaw Family Christmas Tree. Even though they had to rely on sign language, they eventually found one they all agreed on, which he proceeded to remove with his mini digger, carefully protecting the roots. They thought that this way, rather than chopping it down, Rosie could plant it in the field after they left and give it a second chance at life.

Getting it in Grace's car was a bit of a performance, but in the end Bruno tied it to the roof, telling her to drive very carefully and she would be fine.

Seth wasn't so sure. 'Well it's a good job the gîte is only five minutes away because you, French roads, or any roads really, plus a big dangly pine tree on the roof is a recipe for disaster any day of the week.'

'Oh stop being soft... ooh look, a cyclist.' Grace had to bite her tongue and almost said she'd recognise that bottom anywhere.

'Right, well give him a wide berth, and keep both hands on the wheel... mother!' Seth was looking through his fingers and the branches of a tree that were slipping further down the windscreen.

As they overtook the rather sexy bottom riding a bike, Grace gave Max a toot of her horn and a wave as she passed and from her mirror, watched him waving back. As they bounced along the track, Seth commented that soon the car would be camouflaged and that Bruno obviously wasn't in the scouts because his knot tying skills were abysmal.

When he arrived at the field, Max pedalled straight down to the gîte and helped Seth get the tree off the roof.

'This looks very fresh. Have you been pinching trees from farmer's fields?'

Max was admiring the tree as Seth pulled a very loose rope from the roof.

'No, thank God… after Mum's driving my nerves won't take any more excitement today.'

'I heard that!' Grace popped her head from the boot and began taking the shopping bags inside.

Max winked at Seth then grabbed one end of the tree. 'I'll give you a lift to get it inside. I bet it'll smell very festive in there once you put it up. Have you got some lights?'

Max was holding the heavy root end while Seth carried the pointy front bit up the steps. They leant it against the wall and then Seth got on with bringing more supplies inside.

Grace was admiring her tree. 'Yes, Rosie has a spare set she said I can borrow and a barrel to stand it in. She'll be down just after lunch. Talking of food, would you like to help us eat one of these huge baguettes, I've got some nice cheese and meat to tempt you with.' Grace had missed Max and hoped he'd accept.

Max gave her a quick peck on the cheek and whispered in her ear that she didn't need food to tempt him and yes, he would come for lunch, a split second before Seth bustled in with the last bag of shopping. Grace's eyes widened in mock warning as Max made his way to the door, flashing her a wicked smile and a flirty wink as he left the room. Knowing he would be back soon, she attempted to quell the giddy feelings and lustful thoughts which raced about various parts of her body. While her son enjoyed a pre-lunch snack, Grace busied herself with packing away the shopping and concentrated on making soup, buoyed by the imminent arrival of the others. Soon, everyone she cared about most in the world would be here, and she couldn't wait.

CHAPTER 16

The soup was bubbling on the stove so Max and Seth had taken the dogs for a walk into the village with strict instructions not to go on some mad hike around the Loire Valley. Heidi and her mini coach party would be there in a few hours and Grace was on pins, wanting them all together, safe, in one place. The pine tree looked lovely if a bit bare, however, tomorrow she would make some decorations with Skye and Finn and best of all, she was going to show them the nativity crèche she'd bought from Tours and then let them set it up.

Rosie called by as promised with the fairy lights and a wooden barrel and joined her for a cup of tea. As Grace served her guest, she took the opportunity to ask how Christmas in France compared to ones in England.

'Well for a start, Christmas Eve is the big night here. It's called *le réveillon* and most families sit down to a huge meal that, as you can imagine, goes on and on. Some people go to midnight Mass or *la Messe de Minuit*, but here in our village, they have an earlier one at six. It's better for the children and afterwards we can tuck into our feast. You should bring Skye and Finn up to the church tomorrow, it's a lovely service and it won't matter if you don't understand what's going on, we all know the nativity story and the little ones act it out.'

Grace smiled, thinking that Rosie was always trying to gather people in and make them feel welcome.

'I'll ask their dad, as I mentioned, he's already had one to-do with his own parents over church and religion so I might just steer clear of that subject, which is a bit ironic when you consider why we are all here in the first place.'

Grace thought it would be lovely to attend a Christmas church service in France but she would ask Elliot how he felt about it first, the last thing she wanted was a bad atmosphere.

Rosie sipped her tea then continued. 'We don't go to church regularly but I like Sabine to know what it's all about and not have her growing up thinking Christmas is just for presents. In French schools, religion isn't taught, apart from awareness classes where they explain all faiths so unless you attend a private school, these days, the Nativity isn't promoted at all. It's left up to parents to decide what they tell their kids. Because France is a secular society, they don't mix religion and beliefs with State affairs.'

Rosie was wiping coconut from her fingers after tucking into the macaroons, then went on to describe various French traditions.

'We always put a candle in the window, just in case the Virgin Mary passes by and I have a little crèche and *santons* which Sabine loves. Oh, I almost forgot, on Christmas Eve, you have to bring in a big Yule log and keep it burning until New Year's Day. I think it brings luck for the following harvest – the farmers put the charred log in the fields when they plough and scatter in spring.

'I wish we had traditions like that at home. Maybe English farmers do the same, I might find out when I get back. I've got my crèche though, so that's very French and we can do the Yule log thing, although I can't promise to keep it going. My log burning skills are rubbish and the fire's always going out, but Seth might have more luck.' Grace wanted to give Skye and Finn some new experiences while they were here so they could tell their teacher and friends all about them.

'Why don't you get them to leave their shoes or slippers in front of the fire? French children don't have stockings, they just get shoes full of treats when they wake up and tiny gifts of fruit and sweets hung on the tree. Adults don't go mad with presents for each other either, just token gifts and then exchange bigger ones at New Year. Having said that, I once got two gorgeous puppies on Christmas Day, so you *are* allowed to break the rules now and then, but it's more for the kids really.' Rosie had finished her tea and stood up, ready to go.

'And tell them that Père Noël only gives presents to good children and his friend Père Fouettard has a spanking stick for the naughty ones. It works a treat in my house but unfortunately only the week before Christmas.' Rosie headed for the door and gave Grace a hug.

'Well, I might just need that little gem of information if they get a bit hyper. Thanks for dropping the lights off, Rosie.' Grace's head was buzzing with information and she was eager to get the tree up.

The ringing of Grace's phone signalled it was time for Rosie to leave. After saying goodbye and closing the door on the harsh wind that was whipping across the field, she saw Ben's name on the screen. Her first thought was of impending doom and that Ben wanted a place at the inn, so whispered out loud, 'You have got to be kidding me?'

Even though it was the season of goodwill, she was going to draw the line at inviting her ex-husband over for Christmas. That really would kill off any hopes of romance. Taking a deep breath, she answered her phone to Ben and hoped for cheerful news.

'Hi, Grace. Sorry to disturb you on your holiday but I'm in a bit of a fix. Actually, I'm at my wits' end and I really didn't know who else to ring.'

Grace could hear the strain in his voice and went into panic mode, literally dreading whatever came next.

'It's okay, Ben, don't worry, you're not disturbing me. What's wrong, you sound stressed, are you in some kind of trouble?' The thought zapped through Grace's mind that she might just be on some kind of game show and had been set-up, so scanned the room nervously for hidden cameras, just in case.

'No I'm not in trouble, but I've had a massive row with Janice. She's thrown me out and to be honest, I'm glad, I really am. She's bloody mental! I might be sitting in the car with all my clothes in bin bags, covered in mud and nowhere to go, but I'm sick of her, Grace.' Ben sounded deflated but there was the merest hint of defiance in his voice.

'Oh no! What has she done? Just tell me what happened. I'm sure we can sort something out.' Grace felt sorry for him even before she'd heard the story while at the same time, the words 'déjà vu' and 'no room at the inn' pinged into her head.

'Well, it all started with this bloody wedding business. I came home from work tonight and was just keeping my head down and minding my own business, getting a can out of the fridge and praying to God my dinner contained meat because I'm flaming sick of soya, then out of the blue, she said she had a big surprise for me.'

Ben appeared to be on a roll but stopped and took a breath. Grace chuckled lightly and then stopped herself, hoping he hadn't heard as he carried on with his tale of woe.

'It seems she's been up to the travel agents this morning and only wants to get married in Las flipping Vegas! What's wrong with Leicester Town Hall for crying out loud? And that's not the best of it, she only wants some bloke dressed up as sodding Elvis to perform the ceremony, well not bloody likely!'

Grace had tears rolling down her cheeks now and her hand pressed firmly over her mouth to stop herself from laughing.

'Anyway, I told her straight that it wasn't happening, any of it. She argued the toss for a bit and then when it dawned on her that I meant it, she just went berserk! She's trashed the flat and thrown all my clothes on the communal gardens. It's pouring down here and everything's soaked. After the humiliation of picking my socks and undies off the privets, one of the neighbours came out and gave me some bin bags and helped me bag it all up. Jan was still at it, screaming obscenities from the balcony and not caring who heard the embarrassing things she was saying about my body parts, and then, she only went and chucked my golf clubs out of the window and nearly killed the poor bloke who was helping me out. The bloody psycho! Anyway, I've had it with her. I'm not going back even if she begs. I was on the verge of getting rid of the nutter anyway so I'm glad she chucked me out, but that still leaves me homeless unless I stay in a hotel or go to our Heidi's.'

Ben stalled slightly, hesitating before he went on, which Grace was glad of because it gave her plenty of time to compose herself.

'And that's where I was wondering if you could help. I know yours is empty and it would only be for a few days, until I sort myself out or she clears off. I don't want to go to Kenny's either, they took me in when we split up and I'd feel like I was imposing at Christmas, brother or not.' Ben sounded exhausted, and desperate.

'Ben, I'm so sorry. I hope nothing I said to you the other week has caused you to feel differently about her. I was only trying to help, you know?'

At first, Grace had seen the funny side of the goings on outside Ben's flat but now she felt sorry for him. She was also slightly relieved that he hadn't asked to tag along and come to France with the rest of them.

'It's not your fault at all, Grace, but you did get me thinking about my life and it sort of made me look at things from a different perspective.' Ben sounded weary.

Grace didn't hesitate to help out and thought Ben deserved a break, from Jan especially. 'Look, just go and stay at mine, ours, well you know what I mean. But you'll have to sleep in Seth's room. It's too weird thinking of you in our bed. I changed his sheets when he went skiing so it's nice and fresh. Oh, and there's plenty of food in the freezer so help yourself.'

Grace was actually glad he'd turned to her and that he was finally seeing through Janice as well.

'Thanks, love, I really appreciate it. I've been sitting in Sains-bury's car park for ages wondering what to do. I feel like a right prat.' Ben laughed weakly and sounded utterly defeated.

'She's the prat, not you. Just get yourself over there and settled in. I'll tell the kids what happened and I'll make sure Amber doesn't take it upon herself to ring Janice. You know what she's like and it'll only make things worse. Text me later and let me know how you're getting on. And get your undies in the washer, we can't have you wearing muddy boxers. Oh and Ben, there's nothing wrong with your body parts, remember what we told the kids about sticks and stones?'

Grace was trying to lighten the mood and she did get him to laugh, just a bit. 'And don't let that cow get to you.'

'Right, will do. And I'll nip next door and let Cecil know I'm there. I'll leave you in peace now. Say hello to the kids for me and thanks again, you don't know how glad I am to be gone.' Ben sounded a bit perkier, so saying her goodbyes, Grace disconnected.

Poor Ben. He sounded so... lost. And now she felt guilty. If she hadn't come here, the kids would be at home and he'd have them there to cheer him up and keep him company. But then, she wouldn't have met Max and after all, she didn't start the mass Christmas exodus, they did. Conscience cleared once again, Grace got busy unravelling the tree lights.

By the time she heard footsteps on the decking outside, she'd talked herself round to thinking Ben would be alright. He had a roof over his head, a freezer full of food and most importantly, he was away from that madwoman. He could still go to his brother's for Christmas dinner, or if he was really desperate, Martha's. Anyway, he might have patched things up with his delightful fiancée by then, but deep down, Grace hoped that he wouldn't.

Seth had been to the village bistro with Max and they were both full of Christmas cheer, due mainly to bumping into Wilf and André, which spoke volumes. Seth merrily announced that he was now quite fond of pastis (with a touch of water, the French way) as was Max. Apparently, the latter needed a little lie down after their sortie but would nip along later that evening to say hello. Ignoring the feeling of disappointment that she'd have to wait even longer to see Max, Grace rallied her pink-cheeked son into action. After he'd secured the tree then attached the lights while she put another log in the fire, Grace started to tell Seth all about crazy Janice, Elvis and the killer golf clubs.

Heidi was going to ring Grace's phone twice when they reached the village, then Seth would wait by the entrance to the field with his torch and guide them in. They had directions to the hotel but they thought it was better to have someone show them where the gîtes were. At 5.48pm, the phone chirped into life and they got the two-bell alert. Seth jumped up and pulled on his jacket, grabbed the torch and shot out of the door, then ran to the top of the field followed closely by a giddy Coco.

Grace took one last look around the room. The fire glowed and the tree twinkled. The bunks and the twin bedroom were aired and made-up, the cakes and coffee cups were neatly laid out in the kitchen and the dining table set for their dinner. Grace was beyond excited and ran over to get her jacket and then went to wait on the decking for the car headlights to appear.

The temperature had dropped again and she was sure it must be approaching the minuses. With the cold air pinching her cheeks, Grace scanned the field and could see the light from Seth's torch as he waited at the gate. Suddenly, a white glow broke through the darkness, becoming brighter as it approached and finally lit up the figure of her son and her giddy dog. She saw the yellow beam waving to and fro, then the car entering the field as Seth and Coco led the way, jogging towards the gîte.

Grace felt warm tears sting the corner of her eyes and a huge lump obstructing her throat. She ran down the steps, waving her arms and jumping up and down. It had only been five days since she'd seen them but it felt like a lifetime of incidents and heartache had passed by since then. As the car pulled up, Grace ran over and opened the back door of the battered Volvo estate to see the excited faces of Skye and Finn who looked a little sleepy after their journey. Wedged in the middle was Amber, with a huge turkey on her knee.

'Grandma, Grandma, we're here. France is lovely and your house is beautiful, come on, Finn, get out.' Skye quickly unfastened her seat belt and launched herself into Grace's arms.

Finn ran round from the other side and grabbed her legs and held on tightly, Coco was going a bit potty and didn't know who to greet first so he went round twice and said hello to everyone. Heidi heaved herself out of the car and waited her turn and as Grace breathed in the peachy soap her daughter always used on her hair, she kissed her tenderly on the head, so glad she was there. Elliot was next and gave Grace a hug as the children pulled at her hands for her to take them inside. Then they heard a disgruntled voice from inside the car.

'Err, excuse me all you happy, kissing people out there, but can someone get this blooming turkey off my knees. My legs have gone numb.' Amber was still in the car and must have been stiff as a board from being sandwiched in.

'I suppose we'll have to let her out sometime. Come on then, grumpy knickers, pass it here.' Seth popped his head in the car to relieve his sister of her burden.

Grace waited for Amber to slide out and stretch her creaking limbs and then held out her arms to her crumpled daughter.

'Hello, sweetheart, how're you doing? Come on inside and let's get you all something to drink. You can unpack the car later. Good grief, what have you got in the boot? No wonder the giant turkey wouldn't fit in, I hope you remembered my mince pies in that lot.' Turning back to Skye and Finn, Grace let herself be dragged up the steps and out of the cold.

When they opened the door and went inside, the pungent scent of pine infused with wood smoke and Grace's homemade soup was a sensory accompaniment to the sounds of giddy children. Skye and Finn were squealing with delight as they tore around the gîte, admiring the tree and discovering their bunk beds while Grace smiled ruefully as she watched them all settle in. Seth was showing Elliot the log burner, which Grace knew he loved and had taken sole charge of but might be persuaded to share. Heidi was enjoying the comfort of the sofa while Amber playfully fought with Skye for the top bunk.

If, when she booked her French retreat, Grace had hoped for a quiet Christmas and a chance to unwind, she realised that any hope of that had now vanished and it was business as usual at the temporary Shaw residence. But as she poured the water into the cafetière and sliced the brioche, Grace knew she wouldn't change it, not even for the world.

Christmas Eve had finally arrived, along with a deep mist that covered the field and blanketed the countryside, all combined with freezing temperatures and the threat of snow.

Rosie had told Grace that she and Michel got married just before Christmas amid the worst snow storm the Loire had seen for years. Today's weather forecast had predicted the chance of a light sprinkling over the next forty-eight hours, but that's what they said the night before Rosie's wedding and it didn't stop for days.

It was 7am and Grace was snuggled up in bed, basking in the memories of the previous evening and the happy faces of her family. Once they'd settled down around the table, they ate their soup and got through two giant baguettes while they chatted about Christmas and the ferry journey over, which Skye and Finn loved. Everyone steadfastly avoided any subject or persons that had caused upset, apart from when Grace informed them of their dad's current predicament.

All three children were suitably outraged and defensive of their father, at the same time as being shocked and horrified at the marriage revelation. Grace left out the business about the house because there was a chance, for now, it would no longer be an issue. Just as they began to worry about their dad spending an unhappy Christmas alone, Grace received a rather upbeat phone call from Ben which, when she returned to the room, she related to her worried family.

Rather than sobbing into his cocoa, Ben was having a relaxing night in. He'd ordered a takeaway and was watching a documentary about extreme deep sea fishing. He told them not to worry as he had been invited to his brothers *and* Cecil's daughter's for Christmas dinner. Lauren was next door visiting her dad when Ben popped in earlier to say hello, and after she heard his tale of woe, insisted he accompany Cecil and eat with them. Next, Ben announced that if there were any car dealers open on Boxing Day he was going to swap his red pimp mobile for a nice Range Rover, just like his old one. He'd also put the washer on and taken a pie out of the freezer for his tea tomorrow, so was settled in nicely with some of Seth's beers he'd found in the fridge.

They were a bit worried when he said his car was hidden in the garage because Janice was still going bonkers and had left some very irate, threatening messages on his phone. Ben said she'd never suspect in a million years he was at Grace's but it was better to be safe than sorry. He finished by telling her he was turning his phone off so he could get some peace and quiet. That way, he could enjoy his curry and a celebration can of beer without receiving death threats. He sent his love to them all and told them to enjoy themselves, because he was, and bloody loving being single again.

Once they were assured that Ben would survive the night, everyone tidied up and finally persuaded Finn and Skye to get their pyjamas on and ready for bed, sweetened by the promise of making decorations and a walk through a forest in the morning if they were good. It had been a long day since they boarded the ferry and the excitement of the last two days was catching up with everyone. Grace wanted to sit by the fire and relax and was wondering where Max had got to when they heard a tap at the door. When Coco bounded across the room and gave a woof, and received another in reply, Grace knew who was outside.

Max was waiting on the other side like a nervous teenager, dreading meeting his girlfriend's parents for the first time. He seemed to have passed the test with Seth who he thought was a great lad and a credit to his mum and dad, but now, the whole family were here and it might not be that simple. As usual, he was using Ginger as an excuse to leave, saying he was taking him out for a quick walk before bed and wanted to say hi. That was how he rehearsed it and thought it sounded casual and polite, giving him a plausible reason to make a swift exit if he got a frosty reception.

He needn't have worried because in the end, he actually had a brilliant time, in fact it was all a bit of a revelation, being around a family again. Max was on the same teacher-wavelength as Elliot, and Heidi was very easy-going and welcoming. The children were cute and good-mannered but had fallen asleep in front of the fire so he didn't get much chance to talk to them. Amber resembled her mother the most. She was extremely pretty, very intelligent and friendly enough but more guarded than the others and if anyone was going to give him trouble, he sensed it would be her.

When Elliot carried the children to bed, one by one, Max saw it as a good time to leave and really let Ginger have a quick run. He was awash with tea and chocolates and a sense of having made a good impression, which he suddenly realised mattered. He got the feeling it mattered to Grace too because she'd spent much of the night clasping her neck, watchful and in his opinion a teeny bit on edge. Seth offered to do the honours with Coco, which disappointed Max as he'd hoped to get two minutes alone with Grace. To his barely hidden relief, she announced that she'd take Coco out while Seth and Amber took a turn at washing the pots.

Once they were outside, enveloped in the darkness of the bitter night, Max and Grace shared an illicit kiss. They giggled in the blackness and hoped the stars and the partially hidden moon hadn't given them away. Max assured Grace that he thought her family were lovely and, thankfully, didn't bite and she in return told him she was sure they all liked him, then reminded him of his promise to not be a stranger. Max swore he wouldn't change his mind and confident they'd got away with it the first time, they stole one more kiss and made their separate ways inside.

A few metres away, the three Shaw children were peeping through the little square window, squinting into the night, trying their hardest to see what was going on. As they jostled each other and fought for a space against the glass, they tittered and joked at the expense of their poor, naive, mother.

'I'm telling you, there's deffo something going on. I saw them yesterday having a sneaky snog while I brought the shopping in. And she was doing the nervous-neck-thing before, didn't you see? It's obvious. They're definitely at it. I'm telling you now, Amber, that's your new step daddy out there, so try to be nice.' Seth was sniggering as he knelt down while his sisters leaned on his shoulders and peered outside.

'Aww, don't be mean, Seth. I think it's lovely that Mum has met someone and he seems very nice. It's about time she had some fun, and let's face it, Dad's not exactly been shy with the ladies so now it's Mum's turn for a bit of romance.'

Heidi was genuinely pleased for Grace and sensed that Seth was right in his assumptions. She'd noticed that her mum seemed a bit different, and the way she looked at Max.

'Well, he's very good-looking, I'll give him that. And he seems okay to talk to but it's not like he's going to blow it on the first night, is it? He was obviously trying to impress and on his best behaviour. Anyway, now Dad and Jan are history, maybe there's a chance him and Mum might get back together, it's a possibility, you know?' Amber couldn't see a thing out there and, if she was honest, didn't want to either.

Hopefully, Seth had been imagining things and Heidi was a bit soft in the head anyway and far too easy-going and mumsy for her own good.

When Seth replied to Amber he sounded exasperated. 'Don't start all that again, Amber. Face up to the fact that Mum and Dad are over. They won't be getting back together so don't go being a cow and spoiling things. Shit! She's coming back. Quick, get out of the way.'

Seth ducked down and the three voyeurs scrambled along the floor and back onto the sofa, just in time to see their innocent looking mother walk casually through the door.

'Everything alright out there, Mother Shaw? You look a bit flushed. I hope you've not been up to anything you shouldn't because I'm keeping my beady eyes on you.'

Seth always referred to his mother that way when he was teasing but managed to keep a straight face, despite the titters from behind the two cushions on either side of him.

'Yes, everything's fine thanks. And of course I haven't been up to anything. Honestly, Seth, you do go on. I was just walking the dog. Right, I'm off to bed. Have a good sleep all of you and say goodnight to Elliot for me.' After kissing them all briefly on the head and ignoring Seth's cheeky wink, she walked up the stairs, followed by more titters and shushing from Heidi.

Grace stretched out in bed and decided to get up and check the fire. She had heard the giggling and whispers the night before and was somewhat relieved that the kids had an inkling about Max. It would save having to sit them down and endure a serious talk with them, which no doubt they'd find hilarious. But for now, it was between her and Max and she didn't want to say or do anything that would make the situation awkward, for anyone. Grace was just about to get up when she heard the creak of the stairs and as she looked over, saw the cheeky face and tangled hair of Skye, peeping from the top step.

'Grandma, I couldn't sleep. I'm too excited. I love Christmas

Eve. Can I get in with you and cuddle up?' Skye was making her way over to the bed as Grace pulled back the duvet and welcomed her granddaughter in.

They lay there in the warmth while Grace told Skye about Christmas in France and all the things they had to do that day and before long, they heard more footsteps on the stairs and Finn appeared. By the time she'd gone through it all again for her grandson's benefit, there were signs of life below. They heard the sound of a kettle being filled and soon, Heidi calling them downstairs because they had croissants and hot chocolate waiting. They didn't need to be asked twice and all leapt out of bed before making their way hastily downstairs. The Shaw Family Christmas was about to begin.

CHAPTER 17

The gîte had been transformed into a Christmas
wonderland, thanks to foraging in the forest and Skye's
stash of coloured card, glitter and glue. They'd collected pine
cones, some of which were huge, along with thorny sprigs of
holly from the hedgerows, liberally scattered with deep red
berries and with Bruno's permission, they took some pine
branches from his field. After sprinkling the cones with glitter,
they made sparkly snowballs from cotton wool and little
snowflakes from the card then hung them all on the tree.

Grace had bought some roll-out cookie dough from the
supermarket which they cut into stars; the room filled with a
wonderful aroma while they were baking and, once cooled, they
were placed on the tree. The pine branches were hung around
the room and bound together with Skye's red hair ribbons. She'd
been saving them for Christmas Day but gave them up in the
interests of interior design. Grace had saved her crèche until last
and when she brought the brown box to the table, everyone was
eager to see what was inside. She explained the story of the
santons and how, even when people were very poor, they
managed to make little statues out of bread or twigs, but these

were even more special. They unwrapped the wooden stable first, then placed the straw on the base and spread it out.

'I chose a *santon* for each of us and tried to find ones that look a bit like our family. They are usually the people from a village and represent all the jobs they do or the shops they work in. Next year, when our new baby comes and we know if it's a boy or a girl, we'll get another one and make a special place for a crèche at home. But first we need to unwrap these, because they are the most important people of all in the Christmas story.' Grace passed the smaller box to Skye and Finn and watched as they carefully took out the nativity characters.

She was glad they recognised each one and once the stars of the show were gathered around the crib in a very higgledy-piggledy fashion, Grace passed them the other statues who had called to the stable to welcome Jesus to the world. They cheered in delight as they undid each one and guessed who it was. They knew the teacher (Elliot) and the builder (Seth) and the lady with a pinny was definitely Grandma, then there was a man who wore dirty clothes, so that was Grandad Ben, mending cars, and then Heidi and Amber, which were slightly more obscure, but the hair colour was perfect. Then finally, out came a little brown dog and two small children, a boy and a girl.

Once the innocent bystanders were placed amongst the crowd of angels, shepherds, wise men and an assortment of farm-yard animals who had all gathered to say hello to Baby Jesus, Seth carried the stable to the coffee table and precariously placed it in the centre for everyone to see.

Finn was kneeling in front of the scene and was taking it all very seriously. 'I bet Baby Jesus is pleased we all came to say hello. I'm going near the front though, I can't see from the back because a shepherd is in my way.'

Skye was also unhappy with her position. 'It looks like we are the first ones to visit, but I want to stand right next to the crib and be near the baby.' For the next half hour, while Grace, Amber and Heidi scraped up glitter and glue, the children arranged then rearranged the stable, while poor Mary probably wished everyone would just sod off home so she could get some kip.

Grace's thoughts turned to Max who had gone cycling and wouldn't be back until after lunch. She'd told him to call by anytime and that he was invited for dinner that evening. Skye and Finn wanted to go to the play area in the middle of the field and after pestering everyone to death, Elliot and Seth dragged themselves off the sofa and took them and Coco for a run.

While Grace prepared their lunch and there were no little ears about, Amber decided to broach the subject of Max.

'So, come on then, Mum, it's just us girls now. Spill the beans about what's going on with you and Max. Are you having a sneaky holiday romance that's been ruined because all your kids have turned up to play gooseberry?'

Amber was being playful but Grace knew her daughter well and could hear a hint of accusation in her voice. Before she could reply, Heidi jumped in.

'Amber, leave it alone. It's got nothing to do with us, just ignore her, Mum. But for the record, I think he's lovely and if you fancy him, just go for it. Don't let Miss Nosey Parker here put you off.' Heidi was wiping the table and glared at her sister who appeared unfazed by the death-ray stare.

'It's okay, Heidi, she won't. I'm sure you've all guessed that something is going on but it's early days. We're both free and single and enjoy each other's company, so we'll see how it goes. We've only known each other a few days but we seemed to click. I suppose that's the best way to describe it. But thank you for making him feel welcome last night. I was a bit nervous about him meeting you and I think he felt the same. Anyway, enough about my private life. How did you leave things with Lewis, was he upset about you coming here?' Grace was now deflecting attention away from herself.

'Lewis was fine. I just told him to go for it and that I'd see him after Christmas. He sounded relieved and mega guilty and promised to make it up to me, and he'd better keep *that* promise or he'll be sorry. If the deal comes off he has to finish the paper-work and make sure the Chinese delegation get to the airport, so Heidi was right, I would've been bored and in the way.'

Amber seemed to have accepted the Lewis situation but was far more interested in Grace.

'So, how serious is it then, with you and Max? Have you been sneaking up there to his cabin when all the lights are out for a night of passion or are you just at the flirty look stage?' Amber could be very obtuse and painfully direct sometimes.

'Amber! Just shut up, that is an awful question to ask your own mother. Don't answer her, Mum, she's just being annoying.' Heidi looked shocked and a bit embarrassed by her sister's line of questioning, her cheeks glowed red and mirrored Grace's.

Grace knew there was no point in avoiding it any longer so decided to nip Amber's nosiness in the bud and stopped midway through her preparations to answer.

'Well, I wasn't going to say anything... so cover your ears, Heidi, if you don't want to listen, but between the three of us, we've made very good use of that bouncy mattress up there, and Max is a complete animal in bed. Honestly, he can't keep his hands off me. Talk about rampant! It makes me blush just thinking about it. I was a bit relieved when you lot said you were coming because I could do with a rest but once you're all on your way, we can pick up where we left off, that's if the bed can take the strain.' Grace had been talking directly to Amber who for once, seemed lost for words then glanced over to Heidi and winked.

Walking over to the sink to fill up the kettle, Grace smiled as she turned on the tap before addressing her red-headed, silent daughter. 'Close your mouth, Amber, you look like you've got lockjaw. I can't understand why you're so shocked, we're all adults, and you did ask, after all. Right, anyone for coffee?'

Grace was spooning granules into three cups when Heidi came and stood beside her and opened the cupboard, searching for plates and whispered. 'Nice one, Mum, and good for you. I think that might shut her up for a bit, it's about bloody time someone did.'

'I heard that, Heidi! And, Mum, no more gruesome details, I've had far too much information for one day and I feel slightly queasy now. Hurry up with that coffee, have you got any brandy? I need it to steady my nerves.'

By the time the coffee was ready, the conversation had moved on to other things and Grace began to relax and felt rather liberated. Her account of their first night together was a bit of an over exaggeration but who knew what the future had in store, because it *had* been special and hopefully, things could only get better.

Christmas Eve was turning out to be non-stop. They had just finished lunch and were about to make a start on the preparations for the following day when there was a knock at the door. After calling for her visitor to come inside, Grace saw Zofia appear with a carton of fresh eggs and her two grandchildren, Paula and Orla, in tow.

While Grace put the kettle on, Skye and Finn were eager to show the children the *santons* and get their felt pens and colouring books out.

Zofia took a seat at the kitchen table and after admiring the decorations, talked of her own family's preparations. 'I cannot stay long, like you, I have so much to do today. I have just cleaned my house and Grazynia is doing the same next door. I am so tired, but we have a tradition in Poland that on Christmas Eve, we must clean the home from top to bottom because how your house looks on this day is how it should be all next year.'

Zofia watched the children playing and smiled, then commented to Grace and Heidi. 'See, even though they cannot speak the same language, the kids, they can always communicate somehow.' And as she spoke, just to prove the point, all four jumped up and asked if they could go outside to play.

Once they were gone, Zofia relaxed and drank her tea, her last chance to rest before the cooking began. Later they were having a huge feast called Wigilia because in Poland, Christmas Eve was their special night and to be made the most of. Grace was intrigued and asked Zofia to explain.

'So what do you eat? Is it the same as our Christmas dinner in England? I love hearing about what other people do.' Grace then listened intently as Zofia described a Polish Christmas.

'Apart from the children, it is normal for adults to fast on Christmas Eve so once it starts to go dark, the little ones watch for the first star in the sky because then the feast can begin. We have thirteen dishes, a combination of fish and vegetables. No meat is allowed, I save this for the next day. Anyway, we eat beetroot soup, dumplings, jacket potatoes, ravioli stuffed with mushrooms, herrings in a pickle or a cream sauce. Sometimes, if we can get it, there is carp, baked in the oven and I always have smoked salmon.' Zofia had everyone around the table hooked with her mouth-watering culinary descriptions.

'Yum! It sounds lovely and a bit more interesting than turkey and veg. I think we should make some of those dishes next year,' Heidi commented as Zofia continued.

'We put pieces of straw under the tablecloth or on the floor to remind us of the stable where Christ was born but most important, is that before we sit down, everyone checks that all the things we need are on the table. It is bad luck if once we are seated for somebody to get up and fetch what we have forgotten. At the start of the meal we have a big biscuit called an Oplatek, it has a picture of Joseph, Mary and Jesus painted on it. Each member of the group snaps a piece off and eats it. It shows the love we have for our family and that we wish each other long life, good health, joy and happiness.'

Grace could see the light in Zofia's eyes as she described the scene.

'You must *always* leave one chair free at the table, this is in case a stranger or someone in need or alone passes by. If they knock on your door, you must welcome them in and give them food. It is to symbolise Joseph and Mary knocking on the doors in Bethlehem, looking for someone to take them in. In Poland, even today, many homeless people are invited into homes or offered food on Christmas Eve. It is a good thing to do, I think. It is kind.' Everyone was captivated and waited for Zofia to carry on.

'Once the meal is finished, the youngest member of the family has the job of giving out all the gifts which we open then, not the next day. I love this night so much and remember the days when I was a child in my mother's kitchen and how excited we were. Despite it being the Cold War and not having very much, we were always *so* happy with the simple things in life.' Zofia looked wistful and seemed to be in a world of her own.

'Well, I think we will do the same tomorrow when we eat our Christmas dinner. I've got some straw and we can put it under the tablecloth and we will leave a chair for someone who is on their own, because I know who can fill the space. Thanks for sharing with us, Zofia, it sounds perfect.' Grace was gathering quite a dossier of festive information and where appropriate, decided to use elements of it in their celebrations from now on.

It was soon time for Zofia to go. Grace quietly asked if they would be going to the village church that evening with Rosie, and Zofia confirmed that they would be making the trip, and also suggested she bring her own family, it was apparently a very moving service. They all said their goodbyes and Heidi went outside with Grace to call the children as Orla and Paula waved in unison, following their grandmother up the path. Skye came running back, red-cheeked with a runny nose and watery eyes but looking like she'd had fun. Finn remained behind for a few minutes and eventually, followed his sister, much slower and deep in thought. As she ushered him inside, Grace gave her quiet grandson a hug and a kiss on the cheek.

'Come on, dopey duck, you are always the last one back. Did you have fun in the park?'

'Yes, I had a great time. I like those girls but they talk funny, don't they? And I'm not really a dopey duck, Grandma, I was just saying bye to the old people, they were very nice too.' Finn was unwinding his scarf and pulling off his gloves.

'What old people? I didn't see anyone.' Grace looked back over to the swings but nobody was around, the place was empty.

'They've gone now. They said they were visiting their son. They come every year at Christmastime because they miss him.'

Finn, having imparted his information, then ran inside and sat in front of the fire, bringing the conversation to an abrupt end.

Still, Grace sneaked one more look up the empty path then hung Finn's scarf up and soon forgot all about it. She had a box of vegetables to peel, a turkey to prepare and a favour to ask of her son-in-law.

They had a surprise visit from André and Wilf who called in with a bottle of pastis, which Seth insisted on opening and initiating Elliot into the *apèro* sensation. They were closely followed by Max, carrying a large bag of chestnuts, which Skye and Finn wanted to cook straight away on the log burner. By the time André and Wilf had left, and while Max and Elliot mused about Ofsted, the ladies had peeled a mountain of carrots, swedes, potatoes, and parsnips and even trimmed the green beans.

It was pitch black outside and approaching 6pm by the time everything was deemed to be ready. Skye and Finn were trying to watch a film when Elliot glanced at the clock and gave Grace a wink, then asked everyone a surprising question.

'Who fancies a walk up to the village to see the church and watch the Christmas Mass, I've heard it's very interesting and it'd be a shame to miss it?'

Heidi's eyes very nearly popped out of her head before raising her hand and saying in an excited voice that she'd love to.

Within minutes, Skye and Finn were suited and booted, as were the rest of the Shaw family, including Max who said he'd tag along. Coco and Ginger were left at home, guarding the fire.

The church smelt of incense and pine mingled with the underlying scent of beeswax and musty bibles. The interior was very impressive with huge curved beams stretching upwards, their arches pointing towards the sky. The large stained-glass windows depicted bible scenes and ancient symbols, while the altar dominated the front of the church, embellished with golden candlesticks and glowing candles.

A group of small children were sitting on the floor in front of the first row of pews. Some were dressed in stripy bed-sheets with tea towels on their heads, others wore bright, Wise Men's robes and then she caught a glimpse of a blue dress, Grace knew there was definitely going to be a nativity play.

From behind wooden panels, they could hear quiet, faceless incantations, a soothing sound that washed over the parishioners as they piled into the church and took their seats. Grace and her family sat right at the back so as not to intrude or draw attention but they would still get a good view of the proceedings. A few pews in front, she spotted Rosie and Sabine sitting next to Zofia and a long line of her family members. Now and then, the fair-haired, brown-eyed face of Paula would turn and wave to Skye, instantly copied by her cheeky sister, Orla, who was fidgeting in her seat.

. . .

Earlier that day, after Zofia left, Grace had waited for an opportunity to ask Elliot privately if she could bring the children to the Mass. He said yes almost instantly, reminding her that he had no problem at all with any religion, he just objected to having it forced upon him by his father. He agreed totally that Skye and Finn should know the meaning of Christmas and not just see it as an occasion to receive presents and go to parties, so, as long as Heidi agreed, they could go.

Now, Grace glanced along the row at her brood. Heidi was glowing and seemed to be less tense, she had looked so tired when they arrived after the strain of the visit to the in-laws and the journey over the Channel. Seth was engrossed in his phone and discreetly texting someone from between the pages of a hymn book. Max was sitting to her right, squashed very close. Grace loved having him by her side and had fought the urge to grab his hand, all the way down to the village. Amber looked lovely as usual and stood out in her red suit jacket, tasselled scarf and black jeans. She was never one to miss an opportunity to dress up and make an entrance. Lewis had sent her a message to say that the deal was done and he'd just seen the Chinese delegation off at Heathrow and apart from having a mountain of paperwork to complete, all was well in his world.

The voices from behind the wooden panels gradually became louder as serene looking nuns, singing a madrigal hymn, made their way towards the front of the church. The hairs on Grace's neck stood on end and the congregation fell silent. The early midnight Mass had begun.

They all walked home together, a gaggle of frozen, chattering friends and family, mingling together as they made their way along the lane under a jet-black sky, which was lit up by bright stars and an almost full moon. It had been a lovely Mass. Even though Grace and her family didn't understand what the priest was saying, they all got the gist of things and enjoyed the little play put on by the village children.

There had obviously been some kind of power struggle going on between the archangel Gabriel and the Virgin Mary, which resulted in a tussle over Baby Jesus during one of the songs. To prevent a punch-up, one of the nuns intervened and placed the now, one-armed doll in the crib herself, much to the amusement of the congregation. When it was time for everyone to take communion, Zofia asked Grace if Skye and Finn would like to go up to the alter and be blessed, assuring them that it didn't matter what faith they were, the priest would be happy to do it. Grace watched with great pride as her two grandchildren held hands with Paula and Orla and made their way to the front to receive a blessing. Even Elliot looked a bit watery-eyed as they marched back to their seats, pleased as punch at having joined in.

'I'm glad we came to Baby Jesus's birthday party, aren't you, Dad? I bet he's really pleased that all these people turned up, he's got loads of friends and the singing is ace!' Finn made everyone smile and they all had to agree, that Jesus would be very happy indeed.

As they made their way down the wintry lane, Zofia invited them in to share their Wigilia feast but Grace declined. Zofia's daughter, Kamilla, and son-in-law Robert had made a long car journey from Poland to be with her and it was their special family time, so rather than intruding they all said goodnight and continued on with Rosie and Sabine towards the gîtes.

Just as they began making their way across the field, Seth

shouted 'SNOW' to which they all looked up to see faint wisps of white falling gracefully from the sky. Skye and Finn were whooping and running around with their hands held out, catching the flakes on their gloves, trailed by Sabine who copied their movements and stamped her feet on the glittering grass.

'Don't get your hopes up, kids. The forecast said it would only be light snow so it might not stick or carry on falling,' Rosie said, laughing at the children who were planning snowmen and sledge rides.

After saying her goodbyes, she almost had to drag Sabine away to see her papa who was in the hotel kitchen, cooking their dinner. They too were having family over soon and she needed to check that André wasn't bossing her husband about, or vice versa.

After they all waved goodbye, Skye and Finn were given extra time outside until their dinner was ready, watched by three, not very wise men with frozen feet and rumbling stomachs.

Max was keeping an eye on the dogs and, on seeing the children playing with Seth and Elliot, his thoughts turned to his own son, Jack. He'd had a few texts from him saying he was fine and that he'd been to a couple of parties and was looking forward to Christmas Day. It pained Max's heart that since the divorce he'd not spent one single Christmas morning with his son. Carmel simply refused to share him on the 25th, however, she had no qualms at all when it came to New Year because that's when she jetted off for her fancy hotel break, and Jack became a hindrance.

As the snow continued to fall and his toes went numb, Max made a pact with himself. No matter what he was doing next year, Carmel could damn well share their son – Jack would be spending Christmas with him, he could even stay until the New Year if he wanted. The days when he rolled over and did as he was told were gone. It was supposed to be a fresh start and Max wanted a bit of this for himself and his own child.

He would never have thought it possible, that his whole outlook and life could change in the short space of a few days. He had a different perspective of himself and the future now. Max was deeply grateful to Grace for insisting he joined in with them and was included in their celebrations. It had reminded him what it was like to be with his child, belong to a family, and not necessarily feel like the odd one out. His hardened heart had finally thawed and Max only hoped the rest of his body would follow suit. When they were called in to eat Grace's shepherd's pie, for the first time in ages, he didn't think about making an excuse or wonder if he was in the way or intruding. Instead, Max just stood up, stretched his icy legs, dusted off the snow and went inside.

CHAPTER 18

C hristmas Day began as most do when there are children in the house. It had been a long while since Grace had been woken at some ungodly hour by the shouts and screams of excited, little people. Hearing Skye and Finn downstairs gave her a long-forgotten zing of excitement and took her back to the times when her three were knocking on the bedroom door, insisting that she and Ben got up to 'see if he's been' at 4am. Today was exactly the same and she could hear them downstairs, calling her name and whooping with delight at the pile of gifts under the tree. Smiling, Grace jumped out of bed, looked over the mezzanine and took in the scene below.

'Grandma, Grandma, it's Christmas. Come down and open your presents. Look, Father Christmas has been. The special big log is still burning so it's lovely and warm, come on, hurry up.' Skye said, bouncing up and down on the chair.

Grace put on her slippers and did as she was told.

With Heidi hovering by the door, Grace braved the cold and went outside with the children while they checked if Rudolph had eaten the carrot they'd left on the steps. She marvelled with them that Santa had eaten all of his mince pie *and* finished his

PATRICIA DIXON

milk, but best of all, it had snowed – really snowed. If it hadn't been for the lure of presents under the tree Grace was sure they'd have got straight on with a snowball fight. They were soon back inside and after Finn and Skye emptied all the sweets from their shoes onto the rug, went to get Amber and Seth who were dragged from their bunks, half asleep and still yawning as they took their positions around the tree.

Amber and Seth had stuffed their gifts into their respective luggage before they left home; they had fully intended to open them in New York or the Alps so thankfully, everyone had something under the tree. As the madness began and the coffee brewed in the kitchen, Grace sat back and watched them open their presents. She still couldn't believe they were all here.

Her thoughts were then of Ben. She hoped he'd have a nice Christmas Day and that Janice would leave him alone, for twenty-four hours at least. He was having Christmas dinner with Cecil and his daughter after the two ex-neighbours had rekindled their old friendship.

Grace's mind then wandered to Max who was going to go for his early morning ride and would join them when he got back. He'd seemed a lot more relaxed last night and after waiting patiently for some time alone, in the end, Heidi had tactfully orchestrated a mass exodus from the front room, just before midnight.

After the traditional ritual of leaving a mince pie and milk for Santa along with a handwritten thank-you note from the children and then Rudolph's carrot being placed on the frosty step, Heidi herded Skye and Finn to bed. When they were sure both were fast asleep, Elliot and Seth sneaked outside to bring in the two bin liners from the car that held their gifts. Once Heidi and Amber had arranged the array of packages under the tree, they all sloped off to bed leaving Max and Grace to 'wash up'.

234

'Alone at last,' Grace said as she emptied the sink.

She felt a little self-conscious and on edge now it was just the two of them, listening all the time for a creaky floorboard or a door to open.

'Don't worry. I'm not going to pounce on you, let's just sit by the fire and watch that jumbo log burn. It's almost Christmas and it's the first time in ages I've had someone to share the night with, so let's make the most of it.'

They sat contentedly together on the sofa and talked about Christmas Days gone by, along with Max's resolution for the future and his plans to spend next year's festivities with his son. By the time he said goodnight, there was a crunchy layer of snow outside and the flakes were still falling. Ginger hopped about like a spring lamb, slightly unsure of what the white fluffy stuff was. Max did the honours on Rudolph's behalf and took a few bites out of the carrot, then set off towards his gîte, munching on a mince pie while leaving foot and paw prints in the virgin snow.

Grace's French family Christmas would go down in history as one of the best ever. Skye and Finn were beside themselves when they'd spotted the snow getting deeper and couldn't wait to go outside and make a snowman. When Max turned up later that morning to say Happy Christmas, he told them that it was almost impossible to cycle along the country roads so had given up. Once he had thawed out and was treated to a huge bacon sandwich, Grace whispered to Finn to bring the last present from under the tree and pass it to Max.

'Here, Grandma says Santa left this for you, Max.' Finn and Skye loved the act of giving, just as much as receiving and gathered round to see what it was.

Max looked taken aback while at the same time, was extremely touched that Grace had bought him a gift. As he unwrapped his present, he felt the small shapes beneath his fingers and as the tissue paper fell away, guessed what it was, aided by Skye.

'Oh look. It's *santons*, like what Grandma got for us. You've got a teacher one, just like our dad, and a dog one for Ginger, and there's a boy, have you got a little boy at home, Max?'

Skye was most impressed but Max found himself lost for words and a tiny bit emotional forcing Grace to step in.

'Yes, he's called Jack and he's fourteen, he lives with his mum in Cambridge and is spending Christmas with her.' Grace quickly realised he was in a bit of a predicament so spoke for Max.

Undeterred, Skye continued to fill the gap and unwittingly gave him time to recover.

'Shall we put them with ours for today? You and Ginger and Jack can visit Jesus in the stable, we're all in there. You don't want to miss out on being with the baby on his birthday. Here, Finn and me will do it.'

Max willingly passed the *santons* over and turned to Grace.

'I didn't see you buy those, but thank you, they're great. It was a lovely thought and Jack will love them.' Max smiled at Grace.

'Ha ha. While you were sneaking about buying me a dress, I was doing the same thing, choosing those. Great minds think alike, see.' Grace winked, then watched Skye and Finn rearrange the stable and squash the three extra *santons* inside.

It was time for a tidying-up session because the room was covered in wrapping paper so Max went home to change and the children went outside to make footprints in the snow. The turkey was cooking in the oven and there was a Christmas film on the telly, Amber was texting Lewis, and Seth was eating chocolates from the tin, so Grace decided to go upstairs to change into her blue dress. As she listened to the chatter from below and inhaled the combined scents of Christmas, she closed her eyes and smiled to herself, committing the day to her file of very happy memories.

. . .

Dinner was *almost* a disaster when Grace realised the turkey was taking ages in the small oven and needed extra time and then, horror of horrors, there would be no room for the roast potatoes. In the end, the crisis was averted because they cooked them at Max's and just before they served up, he had to sprint down the track with a hot tray of sizzling roasties.

Grace had explained to Finn and Skye about the Polish tradition of leaving a spare chair at the table, they were wide-eyed and took the whole tale in. So when Max knocked at the door (as previously arranged) and asked if there was room for one more for dinner, both grandchildren shouted enthusiastically that he should sit in the space they'd saved. The day was further livened up around teatime by Wilf and André who called in with *meilleurs voeux* and to share a glass of Christmas cheer. They were followed shortly afterwards by their Polish neighbours on their way up to Zofia and Dominique's. Grace thought it was a good job Heidi had gone mad at the supermarket in Portsmouth as the mince pies and Christmas cake went down a storm, along with turkey and stuffing sandwiches and a rather large jar of pickles.

The rest of the day crept on, in much of the same way as it did in England and by evening everyone was too full to move and were flat out in front of the fire or playing board games. Amber had point-blank refused to play Monopoly saying it was the most boring game ever invented so Max bravely stepped into the breach. As a punishment for not joining in, Grace made Amber dry the dishes and at the same time took the opportunity to have a few words with her daughter about Lewis.

'So, how is he doing? I hope he's not too fed up, stuck in the middle of London on his own in a hotel on Christmas Day.' Grace felt a bit sorry for Lewis and hoped he'd at least had something nice to eat for his lunch.

'He's okay. He said he's working through a pile of documents and should have them done by morning. His boss was really pleased and the Chinese businessmen promised to put in a good word for him. I think he's a bit shattered because he says they really know how to party and as well as loving whisky and night-clubs, they wanted a tour of the sights of London. He's not stopped since I left so I'm really glad I came here.' Amber sounded proud of Lewis but Grace sensed she was still hurt that her plans went to pot.

'Maybe all this has taught you a bit of a lesson, Amber. I know you'd set your sights on Lewis proposing, and don't look at me like that, I know that's what you were hoping for, I'm your mother, I can see right through you! But even if you had gone to New York, he might not have asked and then you'd have come home deflated and in a foul mood, thinking your trip was a waste of time.'

Grace was stacking the plates in the cupboard, waiting for Amber to take the huff.

'Okay, so you're right. I know you all think I'm pushy, but we've been together for ages now and I want our relationship to move on, or at least have a sign that we are on the same track and he feels the way I do. I've dropped enough hints, so surely he knows how I feel by now?'

Amber put the cutlery in the drawer, pushed it shut with her bottom then leaned against the worktop looking thoroughly downhearted.

'Can I give you a bit of advice, love? Men are notoriously oblivious to hints, no matter how hard you drop them and if I'm honest, it's better that a proposal comes from the heart and not because you're forced into it. Look at your poor old dad. He was almost bossed into marrying Janice and there's no pride in knowing your boyfriend feels backed into a corner and is doing something just for a quiet life. You've proved to Lewis you love him by letting him be free and he *will* respect you for that, I know he will.'

Amber looked a bit tearful and Grace felt bad for being so blunt so she tried to soften the blow.

'Just take things one step at a time. You are still young and take it from me that time flashes by so fast and before you know it, you've got wobbly bits and the flaming menopause is looming on the horizon. Try to enjoy life and make sure that you lay solid foundations before you take the plunge, and sod what the girls in the office say. Stop trying to compete with them. You're gorgeous and you've still got Lewis, the new Star of the Bank, so you're already a winner. Now come here and give me a hug. And I'm so glad Guy got the flu because I've had you here with me, how's that for being selfish?'

Amber smiled and did as she was told. 'Mum hugs always make me feel better and you know what? I'm sort of glad that Guy got the flu, too.'

Boxing Day was a lazy affair and even Skye and Finn did everyone a favour and slept until after nine. They had one more rampage in the snow but were becoming tired of soggy socks and stinging fingers, and therefore weren't too bothered when the white blanket began to thaw.

According to the weather report on the telly, translated by Elliot, it seemed the Loire got off lightly because the southern half of France was still being battered by heavy snowstorms and plummeting temperatures, with impassable roads and some, more remote villages became cut off from the rest of civilisation.

It was late afternoon and while some of the family nodded off, the others played games or read until the peace and quiet was interrupted by the unexpected sound of a car outside, then tapping on the door. Everyone looked at each other in surprise before Skye, who was the most inquisitive out of all of them, jumped up to see who it was.

'Oh, hi, Lewis. How did you find us here in France? Amber, it's Lewis!' Everyone in the room looked at each other, all of them as shocked as the next. Apart, that was, from Heidi.

'Skye! Don't just stand there, let him in,' said Amber as she leapt from the chair and at the door in seconds.

After giving Lewis a huge, somewhat bemused hug and a kiss, she pulled him in from the cold and closed the door. It was fair to say the poor man looked exhausted but at the same time, incredibly relieved that so far he'd had such an enthusiastic welcome. As everyone looked on, Lewis explained wearily that he would've been there earlier but the smaller country roads were a nightmare and in some places, hazardous. He'd managed a bit of sleep after he boarded the first ferry he could find which was leaving for France that morning and, even though he knew that Amber hated surprises, didn't ring to say he was on his way in case she worried about the journey and the weather.

Lewis was well aware of Amber's perfectionist nature and that she liked to be totally prepared, so being caught on the hop might not go down too well, but it was a chance he was willing to take, especially as she might have told him not to bother. When he drove into the field he'd been praying she wouldn't still be in her pyjamas or make-up free with greasy hair, not that he cared, but Amber would. As it happened, she was wearing what looked like Seth's sweatpants and a thick woolly jumper, her hair was tied back in a bobble and there wasn't a hint of anything remotely fake on her face and Lewis thought she looked totally gorgeous. Remembering his manners, he addressed Grace who thankfully, also looked pleased to see him.

'I hope you don't mind me just turning up like this, Grace. I just needed to see Amber, and Heidi secretly gave me your address. It was a spur of the moment decision really and I wanted it to be a surprise.' Lewis looked a bit anxious about crashing a family holiday, but now, the focus had moved from him to Heidi, who had gone decidedly pink.

Ignoring Heidi's sheepish expression and glowing cheeks, Grace set about reassuring Lewis. 'Don't be daft! It's lovely to see you and the more the merrier. Now sit yourself down and let me get you a drink. Have you eaten? I can make you a sandwich. Come on, Seth, budge up, make room and move that tin of chocolates.' Grace shot off to the kitchen followed closely by Heidi.

'Fancy Lewis just turning up like that. Why didn't you say something to me? And she'll kill you for not warning her. Look, she's got Seth's baggy pants on and no make-up.' Grace said nodding nervously in the direction of Amber.

'I didn't tell you because you would've got all edgy and given it away by encouraging her to get changed or something. Anyway, I wanted her to be herself for once so Lewis could see the real Amber, not some preened, prickly princess. She tries too hard to impress everyone and needs to let him see who's underneath. See, she's glowing and looks so natural. And it's not like Lewis was sick all over his shirt when he saw her so I think she'll be fine.' Heidi was filling cups with teabags as she spoke.

'You're right, love. I probably *would've* given it away and I'm glad I didn't know. You are very wise. You must get that from me.' Grace bumped her hip gently against Heidi's and winked.

Amber and Lewis walked hand in hand up the lane and past Zofia's on their way back to the gîte. He'd quietly suggested they go for a walk while Grace and Heidi prepared their Boxing Day tea, which, as always, was to be a buffet style feast of whatever they had left over from the day before.

Rosie had told them that as far as the French were concerned, after the 25th, it was all over until the New Year's Eve celebrations began. Spotting an opportunity to share a bit of England amongst her French acquaintances, her mum had invited their neighbours from the gîtes, Dominique and Zofia's gang, along with Rosie and her family, for Boxing Day tea.

Amber stopped at the swings on the little park which was lit up by the lanterns on the front of the four dwellings. She could never resist them, gliding through the air made her feel like she did as a child, when she was young and carefree. After reliving her youth, the pace slowed and the momentum was replaced by a gentle creaking as the swings moved back and forth, side by side, and it was then she noticed that Lewis had fallen silent.

He'd already told Amber all about the events in London and how the Chinese businessmen had run him ragged and then the triumphant moment he sealed the deal and they signed on the dotted line. It was also very likely that Lewis would be going over to China in the New Year as the businessmen had many associates and contacts they wanted to introduce him to. No wonder he was flavour of the month at the bank! Amber couldn't help but feel proud of him and thought he deserved to reap the rewards because he'd worked so hard for this chance. But now, she felt he was nervous and very thoughtful, perhaps he was going to tell her he was moving to London, it was necessary for work and they'd see less of each other in the future. When he finally spoke, she wasn't sure what to expect.

'Listen, Amber. There's something I wanted to say, well ask you really. It's been on my mind for ages now but there never seems to be the right time. I'd planned to talk to you about it in New York but we all know what happened there.'

On hearing these words Amber's wary heart changed pace and nearly bounced out of her chest, then began beating away rather erratically.

'I hope you know how I feel about you, even if it means being a mind reader. I'm not very romantic, as you know, and I don't find it easy to put things into words but you really do mean the world to me and I think it's about time we took the next step. I know you've been disappointed before so I wasn't sure if it was a good idea or not, or if you'd turn me down. Anyway… bear with me while I make my speech, I rehearsed it on the way over and I'm a bit nervous, so here goes.'

She saw Lewis steal a glance at her and she remained unusually silent while he carried on.

'When we get back to Leicester, I was wondering if you'd like us to move in together, you know, find a place of our own. I'm sick of coming back to my empty apartment and even though I realise I'm going to be travelling more, it would mean a lot to know you'd be waiting for me when I got back. My lease is almost up so I thought we could look for somewhere new, to buy together. I'm going to get a huge bonus and a pay rise so we can choose a really nice place, whatever you fancy. There, that's it, I've said it. What do you think?' Lewis stared into Amber's eyes as he waited for her to speak.

It only took a second of thought before Amber leapt off the moving swing. Maybe Lewis thought she was going to run straight back to her mum's place, horrified by the idea but instead, she pounced on top of him, hugging him in a vice-like a grip that would make a sumo wrestler proud.

'Of course I'll move in with you, you fool. It will be perfect, I'll make sure it is. And I will be there waiting for you every time you come home, I promise. I love you so much, Lewis, I really do.' Amber kissed the life out of him until he begged for air.

'Oh, and there's one more thing. Guy felt awful for spoiling our trip, especially because I've got *no chance* of getting my money back on the travel insurance, so he's arranged some amazing compensation. If you're up for it, how do you fancy a week in Paris, no expense spared? Guy even booked us on a champagne cruise up the Seine to see in the New Year. So, Madamoiselle, will you accept my second offer of the night and come with me to Paris?'

When Amber burst into tears, she hoped he knew it meant yes.

'And by the way, just for the record, I love you too and I love you *even more* in your baggy pants and with no make-up on. I don't want a girlfriend who isn't real, Amber, I know you like to look your best for work, but with me, you can be yourself. When you were so cool about not going to New York, I fell in love with you even more and when you came to the door today, just the sight of you took my breath away and it sealed the deal.' Lewis held out his hand which Amber took.

'Come on, it's freezing out here. Let's get inside before we both get hyperthermia and from now on, I'm going to practice being me. I've enjoyed embracing my country girl look, but just for you mind.' Amber pulled Lewis in the direction of the gîte.

As they made their way back, she couldn't wait to share her news and thought she might die from sheer happiness before she made it up the steps. When Amber spotted the silhouettes of her family inside the cottage, she realised that she was blessed, with all of them, but most of all, felt so grateful because she had the wisest mum *and* sister, in the whole wide world.

CHAPTER 19

S aturday morning was a bit of a contradiction in terms where weather conditions were concerned. The pale blue sky that stretched endlessly across the hills was almost cloudless, and the valiant winter sun battled against other elements to warm the stiff earth and melt the last of the snow. It was still bitterly cold and a sharp easterly wind blew across the fields in sweeping gusts, as if to remind you that it was still December.

Everyone was outside to wave off Amber and Lewis, who were ready to start the three hour drive up to Paris. The previous evening, when they announced their plans, the whole family were overjoyed at the news. Seth had punched the air and mouthed a silent 'YES' when he heard that Amber would be moving out (again), which was followed by a warning look from Grace.

By the time Max turned up for his tea, Amber had whipped herself into a complete frenzy with plans for new dresses, sightseeing in Paris and house-hunting the second they got back to Leicester. Heidi said she was like an overexcited five-year-old and if she didn't chillax, Amber would need a lie down with a cold flannel on her forehead and then an early night.

'Right, you two. Let me know when you've arrived and Lewis, please drive carefully. And don't forget to send us some photos of the fireworks on the Seine at New Year and just... have a lovely time.' Grace was firing off last minute instructions and driving everyone mad with her fussing.

'Mum! We will be fine, stop stressing. Thank you for a fantastic Christmas, it's been the best. I'll ring you later on and let you know what the hotel is like. Go inside now, it's freezing.' Amber kissed Grace and got into the car as Lewis started the engine.

Lewis looked refreshed and raring to go after a good night's sleep on the sofa. He'd been so tired the previous evening that even amidst the noise of multi-lingual conversations, Wilf's impromptu yodelling demonstration and André's Abba CD, he'd still managed to fall asleep, so they covered him with a blanket and left him where he was. It did curtail any ideas of togetherness that Max and Grace might have harboured but they had only one more night to go, and then they could be alone.

Heidi had to be back in England for her antenatal appointment on Monday, and Seth would have to go into work and show his boss his injuries. There wasn't much call for a one-armed builder but he was hoping they'd find him something to do in the stores rather than go on the sick. They would all be leaving together the following morning, taking a ferry from Caen and as much as Grace wanted time with her handsome neighbour, she would be sorry to see them all go. With a pip on the horn for Max as they passed him on their way up the track, Grace watched Lewis and Amber set off on their journey, to begin a brand new chapter in their lives.

Elliot, Heidi, Seth and Grace were sitting on the decking, keeping an eye on Skye and Finn, drinking hot chocolate and making plans for the summer.

Earlier that morning, before Amber and Lewis left for Paris, during breakfast they had been discussing the events that led them to France and all agreed that no matter what, they would never consider spending Christmas apart again. It was too blooming stressful for a start and each of them realised now, just how much they appreciated one special, traditional day together and they would never jeopardise that in the future. Seth had suggested they return to France next Christmas but after talking it through, everyone came to the conclusion that a return visit might not live up to their high expectations and fall a bit flat as a result. Grace was just about to agree when Elliot had an idea.

'Well, Christmas might not be on the cards but what about the summer holidays? The camping sites in England are getting a bit pricey and it's becoming a lottery with the weather. Look what happened last year, it chucked it down for a whole week and the kids were bored to tears. Apart from coming here and Amsterdam for my cousin's wedding, they've never been abroad and I'd like to broaden their horizons, so, what if we all came here? We could ask Rosie if this gîte was available and split the cost between us. There's loads to see in the area. I was looking through the file that she left in the drawer. It's packed with places to go and we can do something a bit different with Skye and Finn. What do you think, Heidi?' Elliot had already sold the idea to himself and hoped his wife would agree.

'I think it's a fab idea. The baby will only be a few months old by the summer and I don't fancy camping with a little one, but if we came here it would be like a home from home. Do you fancy it, Mum? And will you come too, Seth, or is it a bit sad going on holiday with your big sister?'

'Can't see why not. I'm going on a lad's holiday to Crete in July so I might need another one, just to recover from that. As long as it doesn't clash, count me in.' Seth gave them all the thumbs up.

'You can count me in as well. I love it here and it will be nice to explore France in the summer. I'll go up and ask Rosie later, so that just leaves you, Amber, and Lewis of course.' Grace was thrilled at the prospect of returning, especially with her family in tow.

'I'd love to come too but we'll have to see what Lewis is doing. If we can make it over together and his work commitments allow it, then we will be here, won't we, Lewis?' She turned to get approval from her weary boyfriend who nodded in agreement. 'Or if he's away, maybe I could fly over for a few days, just as long as I'm there to look after him when he gets back.' Amber smiled sweetly at Lewis and grabbed his hand.

She never failed to surprise any member of her family and in less than twenty-four hours, Amber had transformed herself into supportive girlfriend and cosy homemaker. While she passed Lewis another croissant and poured him more coffee, the others flashed amused glances around the table. Seth on the other hand made sick noises and in return, received a swift slap from his mother.

When they'd finished their hot chocolate, Grace and Heidi collected the children from the park and continued up the path towards the hotel. They wanted to ask Rosie if the gîte was free next August. Even though Grace was thrilled that they would hopefully be returning in the summer, thoughts of Max and the future threatened to take the edge off her happiness.

She had no idea how things would pan out for them. Was this just a holiday romance for two lonely forty-somethings and doomed to end the minute their cars rolled off the ferry? Or, could they make it work when they got home? Grace tried to give herself some sensible advice. What would she say to one of her children? All she could come up with as they walked up to the hotel in search of Rosie was to take it one step at a time and not include Max in any plans for the future. She should focus on the here and now and let destiny take its course, because to be fair, it hadn't done a bad job so far.

Grace and Heidi were welcomed inside by a young girl who introduced herself as Océane, who then sent them in the direction of the restaurant where they found Rosie, setting tables. Her daughter, Sabine, was sitting in the corner, colouring and chattering with her cousin Lily and waved happily when she spotted the arrival of the children. Skye went straight over to join in, leaving studious Finn to look at the various paintings and photographs on the walls.

After they'd discussed Amber's departure and the weather, Grace broached the subject of summer, which sent Rosie shooting off to get her diary so she could check the bookings. When she returned and began flicking through the pages, both Heidi and Grace crossed their fingers and watched intently as Rosie's gaze fell on the month of August before seeing her smile, then telling them they were in luck. The last two weeks were free and the gîte was theirs if they wanted it. Rosie pencilled them in and said she would send them a confirmation email for when they got home.

Calling for Skye to say goodbye to the girls, they all began walking back along the corridor towards the lounge when Finn stopped abruptly as he reached the bar area. He'd spotted the photos of Rosie and all the previous owners of the hotel and pointed towards the grainy, black and white image next to the one of André. It showed a middle-aged couple, the man leaning on a walking cane and the woman, all dressed up in her best

PATRICIA DIXON

clothes and a jaunty hat so when Finn spoke, his words surprised them all.

'There's the old people I was talking to at the park. Look, Grandma, that's the old man and the nice lady I told you about. He's got a new stick now and she had a different hat on, it was woolly because of the cold.' Finn sounded pleased and then waited for a response from the three dumbstruck adults standing before him.

Seeing as Hugo and Clémence had long since departed this world, it was impossible for Finn to have seen them, yet he seemed so adamant, so sure. Rosie found her voice first.

'They are called Clémence and Hugo. What did they say to you, Finn, can you remember?' Rosie's voice quavered slightly.

'Yes, I can easy remember. They said they were visiting their son and come every Christmas to make sure he is okay because they miss him. Oh, and the man said he is very proud of him and everything looks nice and tidy.'

Finn looked back at the photograph and then at the teary eyed lady who had gone a bit quiet.

'Well, thank you for passing that message on, Finn. I know their son very well and I'll go and tell him straight away. Your message will make André very, very happy.'

Rosie spoke softly, barely able to hide her emotions and Grace could tell that she believed Finn's words completely and got the feeling they meant a lot to her, as well.

'Right, come on, Finn, and you too, Skye, we've kept Rosie long enough. Your mum wants to go to the supermarket so we need to get a move on. Chop chop.' Grace said and shepherded the children outside while Heidi lingered in the doorway.

Once the children were out of earshot, Grace quietly explained to Rosie Finn's apparent ability to see things nobody else could and hoped that he hadn't freaked her out. Rosie had no such qualms and couldn't wait to tell André, assuring her that

Finn had inadvertently given them all a very special Christmas gift.

As they walked back towards the gîtes, Heidi whispered to Grace that sometimes her son's imaginary friends gave her the creeps and she hoped that as he got older he would grow out of it. She also let Grace into what she called a 'spooky secret'.

It seemed that during Skye's end of term Christmas play, Heidi got chatting to the elderly lady sitting next to her. After talking about this and that, it turned out that Eliza (the lady's name) grew up on the street where Heidi now lived, in the house directly opposite. Not only that, she knew the people who lived there long before the Lambes moved in.

'This is really going to freak you out, Mum, but you know how Finn says that Mr Grumpy sits on the stairs or the bloody chair on the landing? Well, he also told me that the old man is always in a bad mood because his wife has gone to the shops and he's waiting for her to get back. I never thought anything of it until Eliza told me that when she was a teenager there had been a bit of a to-do at our house. It turns out that the man who lived there was a real miserable old sod and nobody liked him, especially his wife.' Heidi paused to check that Finn and Skye couldn't hear before continuing. 'Anyway, one day, she put on her coat, picked up her bag and told him she was going down to the shops. But, get this, she never came back! She ran off with the man who collected the pools money and was never seen again. Honestly, I didn't sleep a wink for days. It scared me to death. I was going to arrange for an exorcism in the New Year, but Elliot told me I was being daft because Mr Grumpy wasn't doing any harm. I forget about it most of the time but now and then it gives me the willies and let's face it, if the story is true, his wife isn't coming back and he's not going anywhere soon, is he?'

Heidi was making Grace laugh with her wide eyes and dramatic telling of the ghostly tale.

'I agree with Elliot. The old man is just sitting there waiting

PATRICIA DIXON

for his runaway wife. You can't see him and it's not like he's making a nuisance of himself. It's all a bit sad really. Just try to forget about it and hope he doesn't take to sitting on the end of your bed so he can tell you his problems. After all you are the sensible one in the family.'

Grace winked then watched the look of horror form on her daughter's face, just as Finn ran back to show them a huge pine cone he'd found and the subject was quickly closed.

As he plodded along in front of them, examining his find, Grace spoke to Heidi.

'I wonder if my mum and dad come and see me now and then. I've never given it much thought until now but seeing as André gets regular visits, it's made me wonder.'

It was Finn, not Heidi that replied to her question. He'd been earwigging, as usual.

'Of course they come and see you, Grandma! They always like to be there on your birthday. Your mum puts her best flowery dress on and some big coloured beads and they watch you blow out your candles. They even sing the happy birthday song.'

Finn looked at Grace as though she was slightly stupid and then ran off to catch up with Skye, leaving her and Heidi staring at each other in the melting snow.

Heidi shook her head. 'Well, you did ask. And it serves you right for saying that about Mr Grumpy and the bed. And don't come crying to me if you have nightmares when you get home. Flowery dress and beads, what is he going on about? In fact, don't tell me, I'd rather not know,' Heidi said, then held up her palms before waddling off towards the gîte, muttering as she went.

Grace respected her daughter's wishes but had to flick away a lone tear that had escaped her eye, smiling as she remembered her mum's favourite summer dress. They'd bought it from M&S in the sale and it was covered in giant orange and yellow flowers. Then, she chose a string of big wooden, multi-coloured beads that didn't even match her frock, but Winnie thought they were

252

fabulous and wore them anyway; in fact, she took the opportunity to put them on whenever she could. Grace inhaled the winter air and looked up to the bright blue sky, squinting at the sun, then gave both her parents a silent wave, blew them a kiss and carried on home.

Grace was a bit tearful when she saw them all off the next morning and felt like a part of her was being driven away. Seth had bagged the front seat because of his broken arm so Heidi was cuddled up in the back with Skye and Finn, and would probably spend the whole journey reading stories and colouring in. At least she didn't have a giant turkey on her knee like poor Amber on the way down. After she'd told Seth where the clean bedding was kept so he could change his sheets when he got in, Grace had let them all go but remained convinced that her son thought magic fairies went into his room to vacuum and make his bed.

Ben had rang to say he'd reclaimed his flat after receiving a terse, non-violent message from Janice saying that she'd gone back to her mother's. He was still a bit wary so had taken his brother with him for back-up, just in case she was waiting in the bath with a meat cleaver like the nutter in *Fatal Attraction*. Apart from a rather vulgar message she'd left on the bedroom wall, written in red lipstick, it seemed as though mad Janice really had left the building.

There was even more good news on the horizon for Ben who had also managed to part-ex his pimp mobile for a nice black Range Rover, which he would be picking up any day. And, while he was at Lauren's (Cyril's daughter) on Christmas Day, he was unexpectedly introduced to someone rather nice. Her friend Rona was divorced and had two teenage daughters who were spending the day with their dad, so she had been invited along for dinner too. Ben and Rona got on like a house on fire and they were going to watch a show in Birmingham the following week-end. The mention of the word 'divorce' prompted Grace to bring up their own impending proceedings.

'Look, Ben. Now that you and Janice aren't together you might not be too bothered about getting a divorce but perhaps it is time we made things final and sorted our finances out. It'll just save any messing about in the future, that's all.'

Grace hated talking about stuff like this but it needed to be done so they may as well get it over with.

'Your right, Grace. There's no rush but if you want to make things formal, we should go ahead. Let's talk about it when you get back though. There's been enough upset lately.'

'Okay, but there's one more thing. It's about the house. I had a nice chat with Seth while he was here and he wants to buy your half. It's only right that you should have the funds, just in case you need them. Speak to Seth when you see him and we'll get the ball rolling. And I hope you've had the locks changed at the flat in case the loony decides to sneak back in.' Grace was actually joking, but you never knew with Janice.

Ben assured her he had already made himself secure, then had the last word on the subject of their marriage. 'Grace, before you go, I've been having a good think over Christmas, you know, putting a few things right in my head. Anyway, I just want to say thank you for being a good friend and most of all, for giving me the kids. I know we ended up going our separate ways but I wouldn't change being married to you for the world. Whatever happens in the future I will always be here for you, and you will always be a big part of my life and one of my best friends, that's a promise.'

Ben sounded too choked to continue, still, Grace managed to squeak a few words out.

'Me too, Ben. I'll always be here for you and I have no regrets, you've been one of the best parts of my life. Take care, speak to you soon.' Grace spoke quickly then ended the call, wiping away her tears.

Max had walked down to say goodbye and was standing beside her as Elliot drove them all through the gate and then disappeared out of sight.

'Are you sure you're okay, you look a bit crestfallen?' Max folded her in his arms and was relishing being able to hold her close, whenever he wanted.

'I'm okay, just overemotional I suppose. It's been a whirlwind few days and even though I never expected it to turn out the way it did, I think we had the perfect Christmas and it's made me a bit weepy. Does that sound daft?' Grace looked up and met his eyes.

'No, it's not daft. You're a great mum and you think the world of your kids and they all love you to bits in return. There is nothing wrong with feeling the way you do. It's a pity my ex-wife doesn't have the same moral fibre. Which brings me nicely on to the subject of the New Year. Shall we go inside, it's a bit windy out here and I need to ask you something.'

Max placed his arm around Grace's shoulder and they went indoors.

Once they'd settled on the sofa, Max explained that he'd been thinking about staying on a bit longer and was going to ask Rosie if it was possible to extend his booking. He was supposed to be back in Cambridge on New Year's Eve, which meant he would only have two days with Grace before setting off for home. Max was sick and tired of dancing to his ex-wife's tune and was only going back so he could babysit Jack while she flounced off for her mini-break. Now he'd decided to stand up to Carmel, he was also wondering did Grace fancy stopping on for a bit longer too, unless she had plans for the New Year. If Rosie said they could stay, they would have at least five days together and could travel home at the weekend, on the same ferry if possible.

Grace looked worried as she spoke. 'I would love to stay longer and I'm chuffed to bits you've asked but it's not just about us. Won't Jack be disappointed if he can't stay at yours? You said that you missed him over Christmas so don't you think you should spend New Year with him, and what about Carmel? She's going away and won't be too pleased about a change of plan at the last minute.'

Max had it all worked out

'Look, Jack's almost fifteen and has plenty to keep him occupied, other than his boring old dad. He's already dropped the hint that his best friend wants him to sleep over on New Year's Eve but I know he wouldn't dump me for his mate, so now he can! Jack will be off into town the next day, spending his Christmas money at the sales, so I probably wouldn't see him that much. And why should I be at Carmel's beck and call whenever it suits her? It's always been like this and I'm sick of it. If Jack can't stay at his mates then she will have to cancel her fancy hotel. I'll be back by the weekend so he can stay at mine then, or go to my parents', or Carmel's, there are lots of options. So... have I convinced you yet, or am I still packing my bags on Tuesday night?' Max made a sad face and waited for Grace to answer.

'Okay, let's do it. I'm not that keen on New Year anyway and usually end up on my own watching Jools Holland. I am *such* a saddo. My lot all do their own thing so I won't be missed. I was supposed to leave on Tuesday morning, but it all depends on Rosie now. What if she's got new people booked in?'

'Well, if that's the case, we'll just have to find somewhere else that's dog friendly and go there. Shall I nip up to the hotel now and ask her?' Max was halfway off the sofa when Grace pulled him back down.

'Not so fast, Mr. I think there's something you've forgotten in your haste to get away. I've been waiting to get you alone for days so you're not escaping, just yet.' Grace pulled him closer as the penny dropped.

'Ah, so you want your wicked way with me right now, do you? Here's me being polite and bashful and all the time you've been dying to lead me astray. Okay then, I surrender. Do with me what you will.'

With all thoughts of being polite or bashful banished from his mind, Max gave in to wickedness and quite happily allowed himself to be led astray.

CHAPTER 20

Their five days together flew by in a haze as they tried to pack as much as they could into their final week in France. In the mornings, Max cycled and even managed to persuade Grace to join him on a bicycle he'd borrowed from Dominique. Even though he kept his promise and they didn't go very far, too fast, or up steep hills, any hope Max had of gaining a cycling partner was doomed because the next day, Grace was in agony. Her bottom felt like someone had hit it with a hammer and it was so bruised she could barely sit down.

Knowing when he was beaten, they stuck to a combination of shopping and sightseeing and in an attempt to make amends for her bruises, Max decided to wine and dine her instead. They thoroughly enjoyed their French Big Mac and chips and Grace said she couldn't understand why they didn't have pomme frites sauce in England, it was delicious. Max continued his foodie theme on the way back from visiting *Château de Brissac* with a visit to the Buffalo Grill where they tucked into spicy chicken wings and juicy steaks. As they munched on nachos and potato wedges Max swore Grace to secrecy, saying that Michel would have a coronary if he knew they were eating fast food in favour of his fine-dining experience.

They also fell, by accident, upon an outlet shop called *Noz*, where they spent over an hour rummaging through catalogue seconds and end of lines. Here, they had tittered like children when they spotted silver, zip-up, wedge-heeled boots for two Euros amongst a wide variety of bizarre household knick-knacks and bottles of fish soup. Grace had seemed happy after leaving with a new set of psychedelic cushion covers, five bottles of face cream, two jazzy scarves and some fluffy slippers for Skye and Finn, all for less than 20 Euros!

In between eating and laughing, they would relax and watch a film or read in comfortable silence in front of the fire. Rosie had already booked a couple of hikers into Max's gîte so he willingly moved his stuff, and Ginger, into Grace's. Not wanting to push his luck and having enjoyed all the meals Grace cooked for him, Max gallantly returned the compliment with egg, beans and the worst frozen chips they had ever tasted.

True to their word, Anna and Daniel got in touch and invited them over for dinner when they finally made it back from Switzerland. They were natural hosts and while Daniel was eager to share photos of the Alpine roads and never ending tunnels they'd negotiated, Anna was as warm and welcoming in her own home as she had been when they ate in the restaurant. After a simple meal of pâté, French sausages and creamy mashed potato, Daniel took Max off to see his wine collection which was stored in one of the outbuildings.

While Grace helped Anna wash up, she asked how they both managed to keep their relationship alive, with Daniel living miles away in Hemel Hempstead and her being in Portsmouth.

'It works well for us really, although at first we didn't see each other for weeks but once we got into a routine it seemed to fall into place. Daniel more or less lives with me now. He kept his house because his brother Josh still lives there with one of his friends. They're both nurses at a retirement home. Daniel stays over now and then on his way back from a trip, just to keep an eye on things. The rest of the time we are here or visiting Louise in Switzerland.' Anna picked up the gateau and signalled for Grace to follow her back to the dining table.

'If you ask me, the easy part will be the relationship between you and Max, the hard part comes when you involve children, or grown-ups who act like spoiled toddlers, to be precise.' Anna began slicing the cake, her forehead furrowed.

'Have you had problems with your children? I'm worried it will be awkward with mine, especially my daughter Amber who is the most outspoken and sometimes a bit trying, to say the least.' Grace didn't really want to know, just in case Anna's reply burst her bubble.

'My three are fine now, although if I'm honest, the eldest, Joe, was a bit of a pain at first. I suppose he did have an excuse because my husband had passed away before I met Daniel and it took a while for Joe to get his head around it all. He's over it now and they get on really well. I'd go so far as to say they're good friends but Louise really did cause trouble which thankfully, is all sorted now. It wasn't easy though.' She passed Grace a slice of cake and continued.

'All I'm saying is just enjoy the time you have when you are together, and don't stand for any messing about where the kids, on either side, are concerned, because there comes a time when you have to put yourself first. You might only get one shot at this romance lark, especially when you find someone you really like.' Anna glanced across to the window, then continued.

'I didn't realise it at first but Louise was very jealous of me and she played silly mind games. Daniel and I had our first real argument because of her and then she turned up during our big family holiday and threatened to ruin it. Seriously, she was hard work and I'd had enough of everyone pussyfooting around her so we had a huge row. Ironically it cleared the air and we got to the bottom of it all and now, it's like she's a different person and we all get on well. My best advice to you and Max is that at the first hint of trouble or sulky faces, give the kids a chance to say what's on their minds and sort it out like adults. Otherwise it will rumble on and affect your relationship. And let's face it, men are useless and bury their heads so *we* have to sort it out.' Hearing the door knob rattle and the voices of Max and Daniel, Anna swiftly changed the subject, smiled sweetly, and sliced more cake.

On the way home Grace was subdued and in a world of her own and later, when they were lying in bed, trying to work out which star formations they could see and patiently waiting for a comet to shoot past, Max asked her to spill the beans.

'I can tell you've got things on your mind, so come on, out with it. Have I done something wrong? Please don't tell me you are sick of me already and I need to sleep outside in my car, in the scary dark.'

Grace whacked him and told him not to be so stupid before explaining where her troubled mind had been all evening.

'It's just something that Anna said, about how they manage and the problems they've had with family, stuff like that. It's made me a bit worried and let's face it, neither of us have been brave enough to discuss what happens after Saturday.'

Grace turned on her side and faced Max, who did the same and as she stared into his earnest eyes, continued. 'I may as well say it because you are a first-class cowardy custard at the best of times. Once we leave here, do you want to see me again? Even if you do, we live quite a way from each other so would we be able to make a long-distance relationship work, no matter how casual? I know I sound matter-of-fact and probably a bit pushy but one of us has to be honest.' There, she'd said it. No going back now.

Max leant forward and kissed her softly on the head. 'Of course I want to see you. There is no way I'm letting you go now. We would be struck down by angry gods, enraged that we'd wasted all their time and effort getting us together. Sorry, my dear Grace, but you are well and truly stuck with me. And I'm glad you are the fearless one because while I've been pretending to read my book these past few days, I've thought of nothing else. I have got a plan though.' Max was smiling in the moonlight.

Pulling her close, he gently wrapped his arms around her and then explained his 'brilliant plan to conquer Grace's heart and vanquish whatever evil foes or obstacles that lay ahead'.

Once she'd reminded him that he wasn't teaching history to year eight, Max shared his thoughts and theories with Grace, who hadn't been rejected or humiliated and was now, deliriously happy.

The way Max saw it, there were loads of people who met on holiday and they all took their chances when they got home. It happened to teenagers who'd fallen in love during a mad holiday to Ibiza, or families who got on well as they lazed by the pool in Majorca, and then swapped numbers on the coach to the airport. Some stay friends and keep in touch, the rest just consign their meeting to 'holiday memories' and move on. It just depended on how much both parties wanted it to work and, as far as he was concerned, he would do everything in his power to see her as often as possible. They didn't actually live that far away, an hour and a half at the most, so when he finished his lessons at 3pm on a Friday, Max reckoned he could be at Grace's by five, just in time for her to get his dinner ready and watch the evening news.

He actually received a playful slap for that remark but soldiered on, determined to reassure her.

They both worked during the week which meant spending four nights apart, which wasn't too bad. He could easily drive back to Cambridge on a Sunday night or Monday morning. If she fancied spending the weekend at his, then Grace could do the same, whatever was best. Then there were the school holidays, he still had to go into work for training days and all that but it opened up even more scope for spending time together.

There were loads of couples who only saw each other at weekends, take his cousin Ash. He was in the RAF and based at Marham in Norfolk. He stayed on camp during the week then drove home to Hull every weekend to see his fiancée. And what about people who worked on oil rigs? Pilots and air crews could be away for days on end and long-distance lorry drivers slept in their cab and drove all over Europe. One of his mates at the rugby club worked shifts and so did his wife and *they* managed to make it work, despite passing each other in the hallway every morning.

After hearing all this, Grace conceded defeat and said she would love to come down to Cambridge and stay with him. Adding that her three certainly didn't need her at the weekend so she was free as a bird, but what about Jack? Max had already met her family and passed the test with flying colours. What if Jack resented her? Again, Max had it all worked out.

'He's growing up and soon, he will want to see me less and less. Don't forget, I teach teenagers and from what I overhear, even though sometimes I wish I didn't, their minds are on many things, but least of all their parents. I see Jack during the week and we go cycling on Sundays, weather and his social commitments permitting. The second he gets a girlfriend, which won't be long now, I will be right at the bottom of his list. Anyway, Jack is house-trained and polite so if you are okay with it there's no reason why he can't come with me to Leicester. If he can accept that chinless wonder that Carmel married without batting an eyelid, *you* won't have a problem.' Max thought he should've been a barrister after that speech.

Despite his positive spin on his own family situation, Max also admitted to being a bit nervous about seeing Heidi, Seth and Amber again. Maybe they were just keeping the peace and being polite because it was Christmas. It was now Grace's turn to placate Max and she was adamant that none of them would be a problem. Amber would still be on cloud nine and focused on moving out. Seth was very mature, open-minded and honest, as was Heidi.

'See, it looks like we can work it out, in fact I know we can. So please stop fretting and think positive. I'll be down to see you the first weekend after we get back, that's a promise, and as long as we are honest and a hundred percent committed, we will be fine.' Max pulled the duvet around them and watched the stars, desperate for one to shoot past so he could make a wish.

They talked it through some more, going over the fine details and making plans for visits to both Cambridge and Leicester. Knowing that there were thousands of other long-distance lovers out there had soothed Grace's mind. While she listened to the soft sound of Max breathing and the hoot of an owl somewhere in the forest outside, Grace yawned and was just about to close her eyes when a star shot across the sky. Without hesitating, Grace made her very special wish and then drifted off into a deep dreamless sleep.

The announcement on the ship's public address system told all car passengers to make their way to the vehicle decks and Grace's heart lurched as she grabbed Max's hand and they headed towards the steep stairs and basically, the end of their holiday. In a few moments, they would have to say goodbye and after a morning of saying *au revoir* and *à bientôt* to their French and Polish neighbours, Grace was slightly overwrought.

Once they were loaded up, Max and Grace had been waved off by Rosie and André, who had teased that the magic of *Les Trois Chênes* had worked again. Grace followed Max all the way up to the ferry port. On arrival at the docks they had been split up when the marshals placed them in different lanes before boarding the ship so now, Max insisted he walked Grace to her car and stole a quick kiss before the area filled up with other passengers. Coco was waiting patiently on the back seat and Max gave him a quick stroke before going to his own car.

'Right, Madame, no tears allowed because I'll be seeing you next Friday. Ring me the second you get home, or else! Come here, give me a hug, I don't care if anyone sees us.' Max gave Grace another kiss and waited for her to get inside. 'Promise to text me when you get in, too, otherwise I'll worry. And please take care driving. See you soon.' Max closed the car door and watched as she wound the window down.

Grace merely nodded despite wanting to hug him right until the last second. They could hear the sound of the loading bay doors opening so Max gave her a last peck on the lips and sprinted off towards his car, soon lost amongst a sea of vehicles.

Within minutes, the vehicles ahead of her started up their engines and began to move forward so Grace followed suit. She spotted Max ahead but concentrated on driving down the bumpy metal ramp before emerging from the bowels of the ship into the dark Portsmouth night. To her left, she spotted a long line of cars and vans waiting to board the ferry for the start of their own voyage to France. Seeing them made Grace envious and she wished that she was amongst them, back at the beginning of her holiday and she could do it all over again.

How could she have imagined, while she waited in the queue, she would soon meet the most wonderful, gorgeous man in the cafeteria and end up falling in love? Yes, she said it. The *L* word. She was in love, albeit the early, exciting, thrill-filled days of longing and desire. While Grace remained in control of her brain, just enough to advise caution and engage common sense; her heart had recently developed a strong will of its own and took no notice whatsoever.

As she waited at passport control, Grace scanned the vehicles in front but realised that Max could have passed through already and was probably zooming along the motorway, heading for home. The border officer checked her passport, and Coco's, and then she was given the nod and drove on through. While she waited for the traffic lights at the port exit, Grace chanced one final look but Max was nowhere to be seen and as the signals changed from red to green, she put her car in gear and joined the motorway.

Max sped along the dark M27, forcing himself to keep his eye on the road ahead, frequently giving in to the temptation of looking in his rear-view mirror for Grace's car. It would be impossible to spot it although he knew she was somewhere amongst the bright headlights behind him. Saying goodbye had been bittersweet. He'd wanted their holiday to go on forever but knew they had to go home and face reality at some point, whether he liked it or not. The up-side was that now he had someone in his life to focus on. During those deadly quiet moments in the exam hall when the clock ticked slowly or when he was in his apartment at night, he could think of Grace. They had formed a bond and he was going to make sure it was stronger than superglue. Max knew he was falling in love and as he smiled to himself like a fool, he joined the M3 and headed home, driving on into the night and towards his bright new future, which he knew included Grace.

The trail of red lights streamed endlessly into the distance and somewhere, up ahead, was Max. Grace told herself to trust him and be patient. She had to put her faith in the words they had spoken, the promises they made and those perfect, precious moments they had shared. They had made so many memories, laughed until it hurt and despite any worries she may have, they had a bond. Grace could feel it stretching back from his car to hers, an invisible link that would hold them together until next weekend, when they could rekindle the flame.

Then Grace remembered her wish and smiled. As she lay under the dark winter sky and spotted the shooting star, she had asked for something simple, nothing impossible, or far-fetched. When she closed her eyes she asked the comet to bring her back to the gîte in August, but this time with Max by her side. Grace's wish was just to be together again, with him and her family, under the same sky and the same roof and even though it would be the middle of summer and the frost and snow a distant memory, deep in her heart and mind, it would remain always and forever, her little Christmas cottage.

The End

ACKNOWLEDGMENTS

I hope you enjoyed reading about Grace and she has put you in the mood for your own Noël, wherever and however you are spending it.

My inspiration for this novel came from some of the tales told by my French and Polish friends. I must thank first my dear Zofia, who is exactly as I portray her in the books. Not only is she warm, kind and giving, she is an inspirational woman. We have spent many hours together around her kitchen table, not only laughing and eating her wonderful food, but reminiscing. She has told me tales of Cold War Poland and the life she led with her parents and sisters, but they are for another day and another book, so I will leave it there for now.

As you may have picked up from the storyline, I touch on the subject of loneliness, especially as we approach Christmas when this time of year can be particularly hard for those on their own. I appreciate that this is a complex issue and I have only scratched the surface. It has far reaching consequences and many different catalysts but it prompted me to mention the essence of showing compassion, even if it is just for one day, to someone in need.

I would like to say a very big thank you to all of my readers and the lovely people who take the time to write to me, passing on their enjoyment of my work. The reason I spend hours glued to a chair, absorbed in my story and ignoring the rest of the world is because hearing feedback and reading those letters and reviews, makes it all worthwhile.

To my fantastic team of ARC readers who never let me down and cheer me on, thank you. This writing lark wouldn't be the same without you.

The team at Bloodhound / Bombshell Books, Betsy, Fred, Heather, Sumaira, Tara and Alexina, who work tirelessly behind the scenes and make my job so much easier and the best fun.

Very special thanks go to Heather who has edited all this series of books and made the process one I shall remember always.

Finally, to my family. I'm sure they know but I just want to tell them one more time how much I love them. Brian, Amy, Mark, Harry, Owen and Jess – you are my pride and joy.

Before I go I'd like to wish you all a joyous and peaceful Christmas and the happiest New Year.

With love,
Patricia Dixon

Printed in Great Britain
by Amazon

36613498R00158